OUTLAW MUSE

ALEXA ASTON

OLIVER
HEBER
BOOKS

Created with Vellum

PROLOGUE
ORPHAN TRAIN BOUND WEST—1859

Serena awoke, the scream on her lips. She still felt the rats running over her head, paws tangling in her long, dark hair. While the train rumbled on, she forced the nightmare from her. She wasn't in New York anymore. The rats were far behind them. Her body slowly relaxed in the wooden seat that she had occupied for three days.

She glanced at Bill. Her ten-year-old twin slept peacefully, a mischievous grin on his thin face, black hair spilling across his forehead. She brushed it back, wondering if he dreamed of another successful pick-pocketing exploit.

Serena looked around the railcar. Close to a hundred street urchins had been packed into this portion of the train, headed to Missouri and a new life. She had asked why this particular state and Miss Tinney had told her that Missouri was the central location of many rail lines, with hundreds of farming communities nearby.

Serena stretched her cramped legs, pushing against the small cardboard suitcase that contained her gifts from The Children's Aid Society, a clean if slightly worn blue pinafore and matching gingham dress, along with a free Bible.

Miss Tinney entered the compartment, clapping her hands. She began walking up and down the aisle, shaking children awake.

"We've arrived, boys and girls," she called out in a singsong manner that grated on Serena's nerves. It's Friday, your Day of Reckoning."

Sleepy children rubbed their eyes and yawned. The chaperone continued with instructions.

"Let us wash our faces and change into our clean clothes. We must brush our hair and look lively." Miss Tinney sighed dramatically. "Oh, you are such lucky boys and girls. Some of you will soon be among the chosen. You'll have new, loving, Christian families with all you could ever want to eat."

The woman patted a small girl on the shoulder. "Why, I'll bet they'll even provide you with shoes!"

She clapped her hands rapidly again and smiled, urging the children to a washbasin in the next car. "Hop to it, my little angels. We must rinse our faces to look our best."

Serena turned to whisper a snide remark to Bill but stifled a laugh instead. Bill had snoozed through Miss Tinney's entire talk. She envied him this talent. Her brother had also slept through many of Papa's drunken spells, while he blubbered nonsense for hours at a time. Bill even slumbered during the frequent arguments that occurred between their parents over the lack of money before Papa's death a year ago.

How Bill had slept through Mama's labored wheezing astounded Serena. The sound still gave her chills as she remembered the way Mama had struggled to breathe.

She nudged Bill awake. His eyes immediately went

to his feet to see if he still wore his shoes. It was the first thing those who possessed a pair did. Shoes were a valuable commodity. She and Bill were among the few on the orphan train who owned shoes that actually fit, thanks to Bill's enterprising nature and ability to lift items when needed.

"We need to wash and dress in our spare set of clothes. Miss Tinney wants us looking our best."

Bill snorted. "I'd rather be hawking newspapers or in a coffee cellar drinking, smoking, and gambling, Sis."

"Hush!" Serena hissed. "No one will take you if they hear you talking that way. That means they won't take me, either. Remember, we want a home together."

She haughtily stuck her nose in the air, hoping her angry tone did not betray the hope she had of their being chosen at this first stop. Serena longed for a true home, one that was clean and peaceful, even filled with books. Not the hovel they had always known, where a dirty mattress on the floor served as the bed they shared.

She hoped their new foster family would be as nice as Miss Tinney promised. Serena had grown tired of Mama's brother, Ralph, smacking them when Mama wasn't looking. It didn't surprise her when Uncle Ralph vanished once Mama became seriously ill. Serena doubted that they'd ever see him again.

Serena continued with her instructions to her brother. "No talk of gangs, either."

"But they're how we avoided street violence," Bill protested earnestly. "The gangs are our family, Sis."

"Not anymore. These farmers won't understand the life we come from. It's as foreign to them as living in China would be to us. Let's just make the best of it."

Her twin sniffed. "Without Mama, you mean."

His mournful tone made Serena realize that her brother thought Mama already dead.

She slipped a hand into her pocket and fingered the slip of paper signed by Mama. Serena had read it so often she knew its contents by heart.

THIS IS to certify that I am the mother and sole legal guardian of Serena and Bill Sullivan. I hereby of my own free will agree for The Children's Aid Society to provide a home until they are both of age. I hereby promise not to interfere in any arrangements the Society makes but request they remain together if the chance for adoption arises.

A TEAR SLIPPED from Serena's eye. She, too, knew in her heart that Mama was dead by now. The Children's Aid Society lady had written out the pledge, while Mama lay in bed. Serena had helped Mama sit up and after a horrible coughing fit, she guided her mother's hand in signing the document. Mama then collapsed onto the bloodstained pillow as the woman took the paper from her hands.

Serena reached into her other pocket for the envelope with Mama's name on it. Mama had addressed it herself and told Serena to send news once they'd been chosen by their new family.

But her pocket was empty.

She shot to her feet, panic racing through her. It had to be here. She couldn't have lost it. She turned to Bill, suspicious he was keeping his pickpocket skills in practice. Her brother innocently combed his hair, trying to make his dark cowlick lie flat.

Suddenly, Miss Tinney appeared in the aisle next to her. Serena saw sympathy in the thin woman's watery blue eyes and realized who had taken the envelope.

Very softly, the sponsor said, "You won't need it where you're going, Serena."

"But Mama—"

"—cannot care for you now. She will never get back on her feet. You don't want a life of selling matches or rags or sweeping crosswalks, do you?" Miss Tinney shook her head sadly. "I've seen some girls beg for money on the streets or . . . even worse."

The woman shuddered and Serena knew exactly what worse meant. It was selling the only thing left.

Yourself.

She was street smart enough to understand this final, desperate act. In fact, it was one of the chief reasons she had agreed with Mama to go on the orphan train. Serena had seen children as young as five arrested as vagrants. She knew they were thrown into cells with hardened adult criminals. She'd listened on the streets and heard the stories. She couldn't live that way. Neither could Bill.

Miss Tinney interrupted her thoughts. "Hurry, child. You, too, Bill Sullivan. You must be presentable." She smiled at Serena. "Remember, your mother loves you very much. She surrendered custody to ensure your survival and future happiness."

Serena nodded. She tidied her hair and changed clothes in her seat, turning her back to the car's occupants as she peeled off her wrinkled dress and quickly replaced it with the one in her cheap valise. Poverty led to a loss of modesty. After she layered the pinafore on top of her dress, she looked over at Bill buttoning his fresh shirt. He brushed back the hair from his eyes.

"Do I look ready?" he asked, his voice small.

She grinned at him. "You look wonderful. I know someone kind will want us."

"Maybe," he whispered hopefully, "they'll even have a dog."

The train began to slow and within half a minute, it came to a complete stop. Serena reached for Bill's hand and gripped it, grabbing her suitcase in the other. They followed the procession of children from the train out onto the platform.

Mr. Addison was at the front, his prominent Adam's apple protruding from his white dress shirt and tie. Serena was glad Mr. Addison wasn't up for adoption. She was sure no one would want the bony, horse-faced man.

Still, he had been kind to them on the trip out west, always making sure each child had something to eat at the various stops. Serena listened carefully as he gathered the group of orphans around him, his voice carrying through the crowd.

"We are about to begin the distribution. Remember that we have many stops ahead. If you are not chosen here, you will find a good home later down the road. There are many, many families who seek to share their love and their homes with those less fortunate."

He looked across the sea of hopeful faces. "Chins up. Shoulders down. Single file, please. And no tomfoolery."

Serena thought that they marched off as soldiers going to war. Bill released her hand to walk behind her. She knew he'd have trouble keeping pace with his clubfoot so she stepped from the line and pulled him aside.

"We're in no rush, are we?" She winked at him.

Bill relaxed. "Guess not."

They began walking beside the line, which slowly passed them, until they fell in at the rear. Bill hesitated a moment.

"You don't have to wait for me, Sis." He swallowed, a look of hurt in his eyes. "If you find a family that wants you and not me, I'll understand."

His eyes fell to his misshapen right foot, cloaked in a boot two sizes larger than the one on his left.

"No!" Serena said fiercely. "We stick together. We are twins. They can't separate us. They wouldn't dream of it." She gripped her brother's shoulders. "I won't let them. Do you hear me?" She took his hand again and squeezed it encouragingly.

Bill beamed, her words reassuring him. "You're right. Sullivans stay together. Let's catch up."

They hurried to rejoin the line, which now filed past the train depot and onto a main thoroughfare. Serena glanced around, used to tall buildings and streets teeming with people all crowded together, jostling one another as they passed. Here it was different—all wide and open. The blue sky above them was clear, with clouds of cotton scattered across it.

What surprised her most was the quiet. She was used to the sounds of heavy industry, the cries of newsies hawking their papers, the smells of the food wafting from pushcarts. Instead, these streets were lined with people along both sides. Some whispered, while others merely gawked at the line of orphans who followed Mr. Addison, their Pied Piper, to the town hall.

As they passed, Serena caught snippets in the air.

"I took a boy that lasted three months. He didn't suit so I gave him up."

"I heard they drift from farm to farm. Even go back to New York, some do."

"Bad blood's in 'em, I say. They're nothing but trouble."

"Street urchins. Criminals. Every one of them. I wouldn't have one in my home."

"I won't let my Lola Mae talk to them. Told her teacher that, too."

Serena's stomach twisted into tight knots. As the line paraded before the inhabitants of this nameless town, she realized this idea had been a mistake. At ten, she knew all about mistakes.

"Come along, boys and girls," Miss Tinney chirped, urging the stragglers to increase their pace. "Hurry now."

The children entered the town hall, which was packed with people. Serena caught a glimpse of the crowd. They proved a more favorable impression than the people gathered outside. Those present looked eagerly at the new arrivals, even smiling and nodding at them.

She began to relax. These were the families who really wanted them, not the gossips on the street. She followed the others onto the raised platform at the front of the room. Scanning the sea of faces, she wondered if a new home awaited her and Bill in this town. She looked at her fellow travelers, weary yet eager.

A portly man in a dark suit rose to address the crowd. "As you know, Reverend Alben, Mayor Moore, and I were appointed to check on the qualifications of all families petitioning for a child." He smiled at the group. "You all passed."

A ripple ran across the room, murmuring approval.

"Even Mallory, Doc?"

Laughter sprinkled among those gathered.

The doctor replied, "Especially Mallory. Now you, Mr. Griffin, barely made it by the skin of your teeth."

Good-natured laughter erupted. It gave Serena a sense of calm. She took Bill's hand and squeezed it.

"Please remember to be sensitive to these children's needs. Many have faced parental death through disease, industrial accidents, even starvation. Some have been neglected or abused. But all need your love. Each child, if a parent or guardian is living, has a signed release for placement. You will have a chance to speak to them shortly. They will accompany you home on a trial basis. Legal adoption is not required. Any child may choose to leave if he or she so desires."

A ripple of whispers broke out among the orphans. No one had told them this.

"See, Bill, if we don't like it, we can leave," she told her twin.

Mr. Addison waved a hand to quiet the children.

The physician continued. "The children are expected to work and contribute to the household in which they are placed. You, in turn, promise to house, clothe, feed, and educate them as your own. We shall begin the process."

Mr. Addison rose and introduced each orphaned by name, giving an account of every child as he or she stepped forward for approval. Serena heard her name called and, as if in a dream, moved up and turned in place as she'd been instructed to do.

Bill's turn arrived. He limped forward but stood proudly. She sensed a change in the atmosphere of the room. Gritting her teeth, she went to stand beside her brother, her arm going around his thin shoulders.

"We are twins and we go together," she announced defiantly. Her voice sounded much stronger than she thought possible. Her shaking knees threatened to give out from under her.

"Thank you, Serena," Mr. Addison said and motioned them back. Thankfully, he didn't dispute her words. He finished his introductions and then proclaimed, "You are free to visit with the children at this point."

A sudden rush descended upon them. Serena repeated her name and age over and over, smiling politely, sick to her stomach. She turned and saw muscles being squeezed and teeth being inspected, much as she'd read happened at slave auctions.

A man walked up to Bill and barked, "Open your mouth."

Bill complied and the man thrust filthy fingers inside, rubbing them along Bills gums. Her brother gagged and then bit the man.

"Incorrigible," the dirty farmer announced and stepped over to another boy.

She smoothed her pinafore and stood tall, hoping her new outfit and good posture would attract the attention of a nice couple. She spied a tall, sober man staring at her from across the room. Serena smiled brightly, knowing Mama always told her she looked pretty when she did so. The man gazed at her with longing and she wondered if he only had boys and had always wanted a little girl of his own. It made her wish even harder that she and Bill might be chosen at this very first stop by his family.

He looked at the plain woman next to him and gave her a slight nod. Serena hoped that meant the woman, who must be his wife, would come over and talk with her. She glanced to Bill to tell him but had to wait since a rotund farmer spoke to her twin and she didn't want to interrupt.

Someone tapped her shoulder. She turned her head and smiled. It was the homely woman with huge jowls that stood before her. She glanced and saw the man watching again. She smiled widely at him and the corners of his mouth turned up. Her heart skipped a beat, knowing she'd gotten the solemn man to smile.

"Hands," the woman commanded.

Serena held out her hands, turning the palms up, then back over for inspection. The woman studied her from head to toe before motioning over her husband. He crossed the room accompanied by a gangly boy of perhaps fifteen or sixteen.

Serena hadn't noticed the boy. Excitement ran through her as she looked at the young man as a po-tential brother-to-be. He eyed her as well, his eyes running up and down her. She swallowed nervously, hoping he approved of her as a younger sister. She wondered if the couple would give their own child any say in the matter and then worried the boy might re-sent having a new brother and sister.

Her thoughts raced as her heart pounded. Would they take her and Bill? Should she tell them what a hard worker they both could be? Miss Tinney had made clear to all children on the orphan train that working on the farms would be a large part of why they were chosen. Fertile land in Missouri had brought many farmers to the state. While she and Bill had never seen a farm, much less done chores on one, they were all too familiar with hard work.

She wanted to explain all this to the family before her but her mouth went dry. The words wouldn't come. She realized nerves were getting the best of her and hoped she hadn't ruined their chance for going home with this—or any other—family today.

The man studied her wordlessly, his brow creasing. His face was burned brown from years in the sun, lines etched deeply into his skin. Brown stained his mouth, as well. Serena experienced a pang of jealousy. She loved chocolate candy and wished the man would offer her a piece.

Then he turned his head slightly and spit a stream of soggy tobacco. Serena realized in horror the stains were from chewing tobacco. She focused on the wet spot shining on the wooden planks, dark in color, and knew she could never live with a man who had such for little regard for his own town hall.

"She'll do," the man said to his wife and turned to go.

Panic seized Serena as the woman thrust out her hand. "Give me your papers. You'll learn to speak German."

"No," Serena said softly.

The man turned back and stared at her, his black eyes cold. "You won't sass your mother." He jammed a hand into her pockets, pulling out the custody document and handing it to his wife.

"B-but," Serena stammered, "my brother. Bill. We are twins. We're to be adopted together. Mama said so. It's all in the agreement. We aren't to be separated."

The farmer gave her a steely gaze. "No one's adopting you, Missy. You'll simply come and work for us. We'll only provide what's required by the law."

He glanced over at Bill's clubfoot, a sneer on his face. "But no cripples. And no runts. They're no good for farming."

Miss Tinney and Mr. Addison were already rounding up those unfortunates not chosen at the first stop, Bill among them. She heard the adults promising there'd be more families down the line and not to worry, for every child would eventually be chosen in the long run.

As he was led away, Bill gave her a sad look and shook his head. He mouth to Serena to go. By his dejected posture, she knew he had given up. They'd had several discussions about how difficult it might be for them to be adopted because of his deformed foot but she had always assured Bill it wouldn't be a problem. He had learned to compensate since birth for the malady. True, he walked with a limp and more slowly than others, but that didn't matter.

She tried again. "His clubfoot has never gotten in the way. It doesn't make him tired. Bill is smart. We're both strong and good workers. Bill might even be small for his age but he's got plenty of stamina."

Her pleas fell on deaf ears. Serena found herself being dragged away. She clawed at the gnarled hands of the tall farmer, trying to win her release.

"I don't want to come with you," she pleaded. "Let me stay with my brother. Please. I can't leave him. I can't leave my twin."

The man turned, glanced around, and then slapped her, clutching her arm tightly as Serena crumpled to the floor. The woman and boy had blocked the blow from the bustling crowd.

Or so they thought.

"Serena!"

She saw her twin rushing back toward her, his quick hobbling as fast as any other boy's run. A smile broke out as she watched him race to her rescue.

Bill reached her and fell to the ground, wrapping his thin arms around her, clinging tightly. Then he sprang up without notice and began pummeling the man who'd slapped her, fists flying.

The farmer's son lifted Bill off his feet and pinned

his arms so Bill began kicking, landing a hard blow in the farmer's groin. The man doubled over in pain but his murderous eyes never left Bill. Serena was afraid the man might kill her brother as he straightened and took a menacing step toward Bill.

Leaping to her feet, she blocked the farmer's path. "Please. Don't hurt him. I'll go with you. I'll go quietly. No trouble. I promise."

She faced Bill. "You need to go. Now. I'll be fine. Just . . . go."

Her twin gave her a final look. "If that's what you want."

Yes. That's what I want," she lied, knowing it was the last time she would be able to protect him.

Her throat grew raw, swelling with emotion. Bill limped away from her without further protest. Tears formed in Serena's eyes as she saw the remaining orphans marched back down the aisle and out the door. Bill joined them, hobbling along. He turned and met her gaze, tears streaming down his own cheeks.

"Be glad I want you, Missy," the farmer said through gritted teeth. "It's certain your own mother didn't."

Serena went numb inside, wanting to protest. Somehow, she knew in this world of adults it would do no good. She was led out to a buggy and thrust up into a seat. She sat mutely as the rest of the family climbed in and her new master took hold of the reins.

She no longer had her parents, her brother, or a single friend. She was alone. With total strangers. But she would escape them one day.

Serena vowed she would never give up on reuniting with Bill.

1

L ondon—*1874*

DAMAN REACHED for Daphne out of habit, only to find her not there. Why after a year apart did he continue to do so?

His head might split in two this time. He lay quietly, taking shallow breaths, and then remembered why he ached so. It wasn't his usual drunken hangover, though they'd become too numerous to count. Ever since Daphne left him, so had his muse. He was a playwright without an original thought. He hadn't scribbled a decent line since his lover had announced she was marrying that rotund, obscenely rich, Italian count.

The only thing Daman excelled at these days was drinking. He could go head to head with anyone, choice of liquor be damned. At the end of the night— or early the next morning—he would be the only one left standing. Until he fell into bed and awoke with a thundering headache and a lack of self-respect.

No, this little spree had become far worse than the

usual fare. Worse because his sweet Daphne was now gone.

Dead.

He remembered the excitement her letter contained when she had written him that she was with child. Good old Daph, the most beautiful and rising talent on the London stage—and all she wanted to be was a wife and mother to a brood of brats. Daman had denied her that pleasure. He had showered her with gifts, cast her in two of his three plays, and made sweetest love to her—but he wouldn't marry her and give her the children she'd longed for.

He had tried to explain it to her. That it wasn't the done thing. People in Polite Society did not marry actresses. They simply made them their mistresses, which was a far better option in his opinion. Mistresses were full of romance and sensuality, champagne and moonlight—not the drudgery of responsibility and the decaying relationship that followed the marriage vows.

But Daphne had called his hand, up and walked out on him, refusing to understand his needs. The count was much older than she but he had money and was willing to give her his name and a title, two things Daman didn't have. Daphne said no one in Italy would know she had been on the stage. She had married the man the next day and lived in a glorious villa outside Rome. She wrote Daman often, describing how happy she was. She loved the swelling of her belly and ankles, the softening of her face, even the constant trips to a chamber pot.

Her letters amused him but they didn't inspire him. Nothing had. Daman sensed his talent drying up. An indulgent older brother, feeling guilty, had bankrolled his first two plays. The third had been a real success and Daphne and his own star rose together in the romantic comedy, so unlike the numerous melodramas of the day.

Now, Daman wish to rip the hair from his head, so great was his frustration in looking at a blank page that always stared back, taunting him. He guessed he would never literally tear out his hair since he would hate being bald and was a coward where pain was concerned.

Unlike Thomas, the military man. Look at what his half-brother had lived with for years—the pain of a wife loss to pneumonia—and no legs, those having been sliced away in a freak carriage accident on the way to said wife's burial.

So, Daman did what he excelled at. He drank. And last night, upon receiving the news of Daphne's death, his intake was far greater than previous episodes. He hated that she never got the life she richly deserved. He had denied her what she'd most desired and now, she'd died in childbirth.

He cursed under his breath, swearing off spirits and women. Especially the alcohol. It had been the ruin of his father, and above all else, Daman refused to be like that monster. No, no more liquor, no more women, and especially no brats. He didn't like them and had nothing to give them at any rate. As a third son, his inheritance had been a pittance. He had spent it years ago. And now, though a gentleman in name, he was having trouble making a living.

Daman sat up but the pounding in his head caused him to whimper. He eased back into his pillows, promising himself he'd never get in such a mess ever again. He licked dry lips and decided that if he were to live, he had better sit up and investigate where a glass of water could be found. Before he died of dehydration.

A loud banging at the door to his rooms cause a moan to escape. Daman fell back onto his bed. It was all too much. He'd get up tomorrow when he felt better. Drawing the covers up, he turned on his side. The throbbing was only slightly better in this position but he actually thought he might live to see another sunrise. That is, if he ever got up in time for one.

The rapping continued steadily and Daman drew enough strength to yell, "Go away."

It was the wrong thing to say. Suddenly, the door burst open, slamming against the wall. Staccato footsteps echoed along the floor until they stopped at his bed.

Daman opened his eyes and faced the intruder, the bedcovers ripped away. He saw his much older half-brother standing there, a stormy look on his face. Suddenly, Edward's features softened.

"I heard about Daphne. I'm sorry, Daman."

Fury ran through his veins. "I don't need your pity, Edward. Dissolute rakes don't want it. You're a saint. Thomas is a martyr. But I don't need anyone's sympathy. Hell, I'm a bloody third son who refused to answer the call to the Church. No one should feel sorry for me."

Daman rolled away, turning his back on his only family member. "Leave me alone. I'll die poor and drunk in a garret if I choose to do so."

Edward sighed. Daman was all too familiar with that particular sigh. He had heard it enough times after frustrating the sibling old enough to be his father.

"Quit wallowing in self-pity, Daman. You must shave and bathe. I need you at home." Edward's voice dropped as his eyes burned into diamonds. "Thomas has died."

Instantly, Daman sobered. He sat up, tossing the covers from him, swinging his feet to the floor. "He's dead?"

Edward nodded. Daman felt all the distance between them, the eighteen years hovering more heavily than usual. There'd been twelve years between him and Thomas, who had done his best with his young half-brother, teaching Daman to hunt and ride.

Grief overwhelmed him. Daphne dead. His sister, Cynthia, too. Now, the once robust Thomas, who had wasted away these last few years, saying he had nothing to live for, was also gone. It was too much for Daman to bear.

"We need each other now, Daman. Now more than ever. We're all the family that's left. *I* need you, Brother. For the funeral and the days beyond that.

"In fact, I want you to go to Texas for me, Daman. It's time you took an interest in the family business."

2

K ansas—1874

DAMAN WONDERED if anyone had ever died of a sore arse. He decided it wouldn't be him. God wouldn't be that merciful. The Almighty had already made him suffer through the eight longest weeks in his life, all in the saddle atop a cow pony sporting the grand name of American Quarter Horse. Riding all day, every day, was something Daman had avoided like the plague in his twenty-eight years. He probably aged another twenty-eight all the way from Texas to Kansas.

The trail boss called it the long drive. More like the long way to Hell. Thinking about it, Daman believed Hell might be more pleasant as he looked around the flat plains of Kansas and inhaled the scent of stinking cattle.

He might never put another bite of beef in his mouth ever again. Or beans. Especially beans. Cookie fed the cowboys beans at every meal up the trail from Texas. Had even shoveled pie made from beans down their throats. Daman ate his fill at every stop, sucking up the bean juice with sourdough bread, slurping down the thick sludge Cookie proudly called coffee. Daman had no choice. Long days in the saddle amounted to a cross between starvation and boredom. Bad meals became the highlight of his day.

No, actually, untroubled sleep was what he had learned to enjoy most, something that deserted him when Daphne did. First and foremost, he'd come to appreciate sleep simply because he was out of that bloody saddle for a few hours. Second, the stars shone brightly out on the prairie, twinkling in the night's sky with a rare beauty as he studied them before dropping off into oblivion. Each night on the trail Daman slept soundly, no alcohol coursing through his system for the first time in months. He slept the magical sleep of the bone-weary.

Maybe this trip had been worth it, saddle sores and all.

Daman looked ahead at the dusty line on the horizon. His pulse quickened when he spied something that looked like civilization. Knowing it would hurt like Hades, he still spurred on his horse. The horse responded by trotting along until he reached Mose, one of the swing riders.

Daman eased back on the reins as he stepped the horse next to Mose's painted one.

"Are we finally here?" he asked, not bothering to hide his grumpiness.

The cowboy's smile shone like ivory next to his sleek, ebony skin. "We 'bout there, Mr. Daman."

"It's about bloody time."

Mose laughed softly. "I guess Sappy done lost ten dollars to me."

Daman's brows arched. "I sense a bet?"

"You done sense right Mr. Daman. Sappy's sure you wasn't gonna make it. I's sure you was."

Daman grinned. "I'm glad you had the confidence in me, Mose. I must say I didn't."

Mose shook his head. "When push comes to shove, I knows you gots it in you." The big man touched his chest. "You got some big heart, Mr. Daman. I think if 'n you want, you can do whatever you make your mind up to do."

The grizzled cowboy's words touched Daman. "Thank you, Mose."

Mose squinted and looked to the head of the herd. "Looks like you be needed at the front. Mr. Jackson will be wanting you to go with him and work the deal."

"What does that mean?"

Mose adjusted his hat, pulling it lower onto his brow. "We be staying with the herd just outside Abilene. Lot of cattle coming in this time of year. Town'll be jumping. You and Mr. Jackson'll ride in and hook up with a buyer, that's all."

"And Mr. Jackson is skilled at this business, I'll assume?"

Mose nodded. "He'll get your brother a good price."

The cowboy looked around. "We be coming in with over thousand head, I imagine. Ain't lost too many along the way. Your brother's gonna make a nice profit."

"Then I'm off to negotiate."

Daman tipped his hat to Mose and went bobbing along to where the trail boss rode at the head of the herd. Jackson nodded at him and then looked back at the prairie in front of them.

"We've almost arrived in Abilene, Mr. Rutledge.

The railhead is our final destination. I expect you'll want to come along while I negotiate a fair price for the earl."

"Thank you, Mr. Jackson. My brother wanted me to observe each step of the process and report directly back to him."

Daman kept to himself that Edward also wanted him to use the profit made on this herd to look into purchasing land further west. Rumors already abounded in England that Lord Dunraven was buying up half of Colorado territory by having out of work cowboys file on homestead land. They would then transfer the land to Dunraven's control.

Edward didn't want to fleece any Americans but he had heard land was cheap and plentiful in the American West. He had explained to Daman that as fast as the country was growing and as many natural resources as had been discovered, it was an investment opportunity worth looking into. Thus, he dispatched Daman to see the same scheme through.

Edward had said it might help Daman get over his depression, which had only grown blacker with Daphne's and Thomas' deaths back-to-back. Daman went to Texas out of respect for his older brother, who had already added to the family coffers by investing in this Texas cattle business. It suddenly became the overnight rage with the nobility in both England and Scotland. Besides, what else did Daman have to do? It wasn't as if he'd been turning out any new plays.

The past two months certainly took his mind off his troubles and his lack of creative output. Scorching days of dust followed by drenching rainstorms and hail obliterated rational thought from any sane man's mind. Couple that with rattlesnakes, the fear of attacking savages, and the occasional stampede, and

Daman just felt happy to be alive, sore arse and all. Especially since two cowboys had lost their lives along the trail during this cattle drive, one in a stampede and another to snake bite.

With Abilene now in his sights, all he could think about was a real bath and a shave. And he'd burn the godawful clothes he'd lived in on the trail. He never wanted to get on a horse again. Ever. He had hated riding since he was a child and he knew his arse might never be the same again after all these weeks in the saddle. Even the insides of his thighs were raw and bloody where they rubbed against the horse and his stiff denim pants hour after hour on the trail. Mose gave him a salve to use which provided some relief but Daman knew the best cure was to keep his two feet on the ground, not swaying in a bloody saddle, choking on dust as he rode drag.

He continued beside the trail boss, not wanting to seem too eager when they found a buyer for the herd. Jackson led him to a large saloon on the main thoroughfare of Abilene. After watering their horses, they hitched them to the rail in front of the saloon.

Daman gritted his teeth as he moved toward the door. Blisters throbbed inside his cowboy boots, which had never seemed to break in properly. He locked his jaw against the pain and strode confidently into the saloon after Jackson, glad to hear someone banging out a recognizable tune such as *Beautiful Dreamer* on a piano. He was tired of the harmonica from the trail, especially since one of the cowboys who played it only had three songs in his repertoire. Daman longed for chamber music and a good Wagner opera but he'd settle for the out of tune piano at the moment.

As he walked a few steps into the bar, a long stream of tobacco juice sailed just in front of his chest, landing in a brass bowl with a funnel top. Daman glanced down to see the wooden floor below stained badly with near misses. In fact, the floor looked dangerously slippery. Never one blessed with great balance, Daman carefully picked his way to the bar.

"Two tarantulas," Jackson barked to the barkeep, who slipped a couple of shot glasses onto the bar and filled them with whisky. Jackson locked his hand around the small glass and knocked back the amber liquid with satisfaction.

Placing a bill on the bar, Daman motion to the bartender and said, "Leave the bottle."

Daman wrapped one hand around the bottle and the other around the shot glass that he didn't plan to sip from anytime soon. He had been away from spirits long enough to realize how they clouded his judgment. He'd allow the trail boss to drink the whisky instead. Jackson led them to an empty table in the crowded room. They sat and Daman's eyes skimmed the place.

Even at ten-thirty in the morning, the saloon did booming business. A long, scarred bar ran along one side of the main room, a good dozen men leaning against it, sipping their brews. Countless rickety chairs gathered around small, round tables scattered throughout the bar. Large pictures covered the walls, all showing women in some state of undress.

Jackson murmured, "We'll probably do business with Sampson." He indicated a large man with a silver mane of hair and bushy mustache to match. Jackson downed another whisky and said, "I'm going to work the room."

Daman sat back and watched the lean trail boss go from table to table for close to two hours, indulging in a little gossip, dickering over prices, and drinking a beer or two before he worked his way over to Sampson. Sampson's table of cronies cleared as Jackson sat. Soon, the two men hovered with heads close for over half an hour before Jackson stood and they shook hands.

Daman's curiosity at the interplay ended when Jackson and Sampson came across the room to join him. They seated themselves at his table and shared the price Sampson was willing to part with. It exceeded the amount per head that Edward had hoped for. Although he had nothing to gain from this transaction, Daman couldn't help but be pleased for his older brother.

"Will you care to inspect the herd?" Daman inquired. He didn't know much about business but he supposed a person spending a great deal of money should see what he purchased.

Samsung guffawed. "Already sent my boy to do it while Jackson and I were jawing. We done business before. He's a Texan I can trust."

"Let's head over to the bank, Mr. Rutledge," Jackson announced. "Mr. Sampson will meet us there and close the deal."

The two men strolled at a leisurely pace to the bank, Jackson stopping numerous times to chat with fellow cowboys along the street. They met up with this Sampson, who'd arrived just before they did, and thanks to the bank manager, conducted their business with haste in his private office.

Jackson took enough in cash to pay himself and the men on the drive. As trail boss, Jackson rode ahead scouting for water, pasture, and campsites. He also checked constantly on provisions, kept meticulous records, assigned duties to the men, and settled any problems among them. Daman had soon realized that the trail boss' word was law on their journey. Accordingly, Daman thought Jackson more than earned the two hundred and fifty dollars for two months' work. The man was a professional in every sense of the word.

The cowboys would receive thirty dollars for each month on the trail, while Cookie's pay exceeded that by another twenty per month. The bank manager gave Jackson enough envelopes for each employee. The trail boss doled out the correct amount to each man accordingly after placing his name on the front of the envelope.

Once he finished counting out the money, Jackson passed the sealed envelopes to Daman. "I thought you might like to distribute these, Mr. Rutledge. I'll cable Lord Stanhope that we've arrived and notify him of the profit he's made."

Daman shook his head. "Go ahead and hit the baths, Mr. Jackson. I'll see the men get their wages and that Edward receives your news. I have a few other details to telegraph him about."

Jackson nodded. "Will you be riding back to Texas with us? I run a tight ship so after giving the boys tonight in Abilene, we'll hit the road tomorrow morning. Always plenty of work back on the ranch and if I leave the boys here, they'll spend all their pay in a couple of days and be left with nothing."

Daman suppressed a smile. "I have business in Denver. I believe the rail will take me there." He held out his hand. "Thank you for your company, Mr. Jackson. I will relay nothing but the best of compliments to my brother."

Jackson smiled. "My pleasure, Mr. Rutledge." He shook Daman's hand. "And that bath sounds awfully tempting."

They left the bank and parted ways. Daman stopped to send Edward a cable before he headed back to the saloon to retrieve his horse, dreading this one last time he'd be on the beast's back. He took a deep breath and swung into the saddle, ignoring the aches, chafing, and pain in general.

Daman rode back to the town's outskirts, joining the herd. He gathered the men from his long drive and thanked them for their hard work. He distributed their pay, saving Mose's envelope for last. He slipped an extra twenty dollars into the cowboy's hand as they shook. Mose frowned deeply.

"Just a little extra for when you hit the saloon and store," Daman said. "I value all the advice you gave me and the friendship you offered."

"You don't need to pay me for that," Mose said flatly, anger sparking in his dark eyes.

Daman was disappointed. "I'm not trying to buy your friendship, Mose. That goes without saying. I'm just showing my appreciation for all you taught me along the trail. Besides, you told me about that special lady back in San Antone. If you'd like, use it to buy her something pretty."

His friend nodded sagely. "Now that's good advice, Mr. Daman. I believe I can do that." The cowboy grinned and slapped Daman on the back as he offered him his hand. "Go back to England and find yourself a pretty gal, too."

"I will do my best, Mose."

They parted and Daman rode beside the herd as the cowhands drove the cattle forward for the last time. He followed along, watching as they yarded the herd. The hands placed them into pens alongside the rail tracks, where the animals would be shipped out on the next cattle car to Chicago.

Duty finally over, Daman checked on his departure time the next day. Then he made his way along the streets of Abilene, looking for the local post office. He found it easily and smiled with relief when the postmaster handed over his valise, which he'd shipped from Galveston to Abilene. He couldn't wait to get back into his own clothes.

Next, he decided to find a hotel and a bathhouse. His dismay grew when he found the first place he spied booked up. The hotel's manager directed him to another establishment but he found it also filled to capacity.

And everywhere he turned, drunk cowboys littered the streets. They spilled out from the bathhouses, the saloons, the general store, and beyond. They rode at breakneck speed down the streets of Abilene, hurrahing at the top of their lungs, celebrating the end of their long drives.

Daman thought maybe he could bunk that evening with a local whore at a saloon but he quickly gave up that idea as he entered one. A riot broke out as he stepped inside, with chairs sailing and fists flying and shots ringing out. Daman literally dropped to his knees and crawled from the building, grateful he was in one piece, albeit even grimier than before.

He was dirty, hungry, and tired to the bone. Where could he go? Abilene had become an insane asylum in the space of an hour with hundreds of restless cowboys on the loose, money burning a hole in their pockets. No rest for the weary would be found here.

Daman came up with an idea and trotted his horse down to the local blacksmith's shed. He slipped from the saddle and found a man with bulging muscles and a thick neck.

"Good day, sir. Might I ask if there is a town nearby

where I might find a bath and a room to rent for the night? Somewhere outside this madhouse?"

The smithy finished nailing the shoe onto the horse's hoof he held and then spoke.

"About six miles west of here is a little farming community. Crombar Creek. The Widow Choate rents out a spare room when it's needed and fries up a nice chicken. Don't know about a bath."

The thought of chicken after beef and beans sounded like a dream. "Do you have a cart I might rent overnight to reach this place? I would return it tomorrow."

Daman couldn't stand the thought of bouncing along in his saddle another six miles and back.

The smithy scratched his behind thoughtfully. Daman refrained from visibly grimacing, maintaining a cheery smile.

"Guess I could loan you my buckboard. Here, let's get her hitched up to it and I'll give you directions."

Within ten minutes, they'd settled up, with Daman giving the blacksmith a rental fee and promising to return the wagon the next day by two, in plenty of time to make his train. He headed out of the madness that was Abilene toward Crombar Creek.

He couldn't wait to find some peace and quiet.

3

Serena wondered if this was how Anne Boleyn felt as she was led to her execution. She remembered the queen had ridden to Tower Hill standing in a cart instead of walking as Serena now did. In a last romantic gesture for a wife he once loved, King Henry imported a French swordsman to lop off his innocent wife's head in one swift blow instead of a common executioner hacking again and again until the deed was done.

Unfortunately, no romantic hero would be riding to her rescue. Nobody would make the noose more comfortable as it was slipped around her neck. Serena had heard if done right, her neck should snap immediately. With her run of bad luck, she would probably swing for agonizing minutes until she slowly suffocated.

She trudged along the dusty main street of Crombar Creek, no breeze stirring the dirt of the road. She looked up at the cloudless sky, the last one she would ever see. The July sun baked into her pores, causing a trail of sweat to gather at her nape and slowly trickled down her back.

At the end of her life, all she could think about was her brother. She had never found Bill. Not in the fifteen years since their separation during the orphan train selection. That was the only thing that truly saddened her as she walked to the gallows on the edge of town. She always wondered what happened to her lively twin, with his mischievous smile and talent for sleight of hand. He had been quite the pickpocket before they left New York on the orphan train.

As she shuffled along the dusty road, she moved to touch the gold locket he had once given her. Having her hands bound tightly behind her prevented the familiar gesture. She only hoped Bill was alive and well and prayed that he would never learn how she met her end.

When Serena reached the wooden platform, she stopped. Her eyes rose to the single noose swaying in the slight breeze. A shudder ran through her. For the first time, she became aware of the gathered crowd, their hushed voices murmuring opinions of her guilt as every eye focused in her direction.

In the tiny jail cell last night, when sleep refused to come, she determined she wouldn't cry. In the harsh light of the strong noon sun, her resolve began to melt.

No, a voice screamed inside her head. *Show no emenr* haunted her even at the hour of her death. She had learned the German farmer's lessons, though, and never displayed her feelings. No matter what he did to her. Or how many times.

Sheriff Parker took her elbow and led her up the series of wooden stairs. Serena stumbled, tripping on her long skirts, and smacked her cheek hard against the edge of a step. The crowd tittered and the lawmen yanked her to her feet again. She managed to make it to the landing. A deputy she didn't recognize bound her ankles together and then pulled the looped rope over her head. The rope rested against her dark, high-necked blouse and pressed into her throat. Serena stood proudly before the crowd, knowing she had nothing done nothing wrong.

"Reverend?" Sheriff Parker prompted.

The minister, dressed in black from head to toe, mounted the platform and began to speak. Serena ignored his monotone and focused on not fainting in the heat. He finished the lengthy prayer and touched her elbow, bringing her back to reality before he limped down the stairs.

"Any last words?" the sheriff called out, playing to the crowd.

Serena knew little about him since he had no children at the school but she realized Bud Parker was in his element now. She supposed it was his due. Crombar Creek was a small, sleepy, tired town and not much ever happened. All the excitement occurred a few miles down the road in Abilene, especially when the cowboys brought in their herds from Texas and beyond. The last murder in the Creek occurred in 1842. No woman had ever stood trial here, much less been convicted of murder.

Serena was the first.

She shook her head, not trusting her voice. What could she say that would be believed? She was an unmarried schoolmarm who drifted from post to post with no family to her name. Charles Rayburn—banker, husband, father, church deacon—was a Creek native and had been buried a month earlier. She had spoken briefly at her trial but the truth had made no difference. And with no witnesses, the judge came to a swift decision, telling her she'd be an example to keep others on the straight and narrow when she hanged.

Serena stared out across the townsfolk, blinking back unshed tears, grateful that the Creek was family-oriented enough not to have parents bring their children to her execution. It would have undone her to see the faces of the pupils she loved in the moments before her death. She held her head high, waiting for the sheriff to drape the black hood over her head.

And then her eyes connected with one woman in the crowd. Her thin lips moved, though no sound came from them. Serena wondered if the woman prayed for her. At least someone did, she hoped.

"He did the same to me."

The woman stepped forward when she found her voice, her eyes never leaving Serena's.

"He . . . propositioned me." The woman's face flushed with color as she wrapped her arms tightly around her tiny frame.

Parker froze next to Serena, the black hood he had raised to his shoulders falling to his side.

"What are you saying, Maudie?" the lawman asked.

The woman's lips trembled. "He tried it with me, Sheriff. Charles Rayburn. Don't hang her, Sheriff. Please. Rayburn . . . was a bad sort."

The crowd began murmuring. A second woman moved forward and put her arm around Maudie's bony shoulders. Serena thought the newcomer meant to shush Maudie so it surprised her when she, too, spoke, her voice ringing loudly with confidence.

"Same here, Sheriff," the second woman said. "I went to get a loan when my husband died. I needed a little something to tide me over before the fall harvest came due." She spat angrily onto the ground. "I got my loan—but it was at a price."

Those gathered began openly talking, their tones hushed no more.

"Shut your trap, Winnie Sue Baker!" shouted the local newspaper editor, his voice carrying over the others. He shook a finger at her. "You're slandering the dead. You should be ashamed of yourself. Trying to sully Charles' reputation."

"And all of you should be ashamed of what Charles Rayburn did to me. To Maudie. And to Miss Sullivan here," she responded harshly.

Serena could feel the woman's anger even from a great distance.

Winnie Sue gazed up at Serena. "At least Miss Sullivan didn't put up with his nonsense and found the courage to fight back."

The women in the crowd gasped audibly and the men began to stir, muttering under their breath. Serena's eyes fell upon Charles Rayburn's widow, standing just a few feet from these accusers, her mouth drawn in a tight line. The matron now wearing black mourning clothes had been kind to Serena when she boarded with their family, but Serena always sensed fear in the woman. Mrs. Rayburn seemed to walk up on eggshells around her pretentious banker husband.

"Silence." A strong voice took command of the crowd.

Serena saw it was Mrs. Tuttle who spoke. She was the widow to the general store owner. Mrs. Tuttle knew everyone in the Creek by name since she had done business with those standing here for years. An uneasy quiet filled the hot summer morning.

"These women speak the truth."

A voice from the rear challenged her. "How do you know? Ain't you a bit old to get propositioned?" The sneer was evident even if Serena couldn't see the face of the man who spoke.

Mrs. Tuttle stood tall, all five feet of her. "I know because that's how I've kept my store running the last two years. Somehow, Mr. Tuttle owed Mr. Rayburn's bank a great deal of money. Mr. Rayburn persuaded me that it was in my best interest—and this town's—if the store didn't go under.

"And there was only one way that could be managed."

Serena felt the wave of unrest as if it were physically washing over her. The crowd's voices began to rise, the noise as great as that when the Tower of Babel fell into disarray. She knew Mrs. Tuttle could be the deciding factor here. Generous to a fault, the woman was well respected throughout the community. The widow had no reason to lie. No reason to speak on Serena's behalf.

Maybe the noose would be removed. She might live. These brave women's voices might make a difference and end this nightmare.

"The circuit judge found her guilty. She should hang," one farmer bellowed. Part of those gathered voiced their support at his statement.

"Besides, look at those eyes of hers," another man cried. "It's like she's a witch. She bewitched Charles Rayburn. He was out of his mind with lust. Carry out the sentence. She asked for it. That kind always does."

Half of the crowd roared their approval. And then someone threw a punch. Serena watched as a fight broke out and spread through what rapidly became a mob. Fists flew, connecting with jaws and guts and ears. Ladies shrilly screamed. Parker shouted for his lone deputy to get in and control the crowd.

And in the midst of the melee, the lawmen turned

to her, his tone ominous. "Don't think you're getting out of this, you little harlot. Today, I win justice for Charles."

With that, he yanked the hood over her head. All went black. Her breath caught in her throat. Serena waited for the trap door to fall out from under her.

4

Daman lingered over his breakfast as the Widow Choate bustled about the room.

"You just take your time, Lord Rutledge. Plenty of coffee still to be had. There's more biscuits, too. And the honey—"

"—is right here on the table, Mrs. Choate. You've taken quite good care of me. Please, run along to your engagement. I wouldn't wish you to be late. It sounds quite important."

Daman buttered another of the flaky biscuits and drizzled honey over it. He gave Mrs. Choate his most charming smile and watched the crone nearly melt into a puddle in the middle of her kitchen floor.

"Well, if you're sure, Lord Rutledge."

Daman beamed at his hostess. "Yes, ma'am. Quite sure. I'll simply finish up here and get my things. I have plenty of time to get back to Abilene and make my train. My best to you and yours, ma'am. And thank you for such gracious hospitality."

"Oh, thank you, my lord."

Mrs. Choate bobbed quickly and Daman realized the motion passed for a curtsy in her book. He stood and bowed to her and seated himself again as she backed out of the kitchen, all giggles and smiles.

Lord Rutledge. He almost liked the sound of it. He had never held any sort of title. By being the firstborn, Edward immediately became Viscount Marstairs upon birth and inherited the earldom upon their father's death.

Daman tried to explain to the Choate woman that he wasn't a true nobleman with a title but once she heard his accent, she would have nothing of it. She picked and poked until she got out of him that his brother was an earl. For her American ears, that was enough. An upper crust English accent—plus a brother who sat in the House of Lords—made him a lord to her.

So, he had let her call him Lord Rutledge. After all, what was the harm? Maybe he would write a play about a penniless Englishman coming to America and hoodwinking society into thinking him a duke or marquess. Of course, he could never set the play in New York. Supposedly, New Yorkers were much too savvy and would catch on to the scheme right away. Boston, too. He had heard it a bit snooty but had experienced neither city since he came to the States via Galveston.

Daman finished the last golden biscuit, shaking his head. Why did he think this incident might spark him to write again? He could no more write a play these days than stand on his head before Queen Victoria. No, his playwright days were behind him. He would learn to be a businessman and function in Edward's best interest. He could act sober and terribly interested in stock prices and politics and the weather.

In other words, he would be the opposite of a libertine.

He went to the spare bedroom and gathered his

things quickly, his hand smoothing the feather pillow once more, swearing he'd never take such a small luxury for granted. Two months as a cowboy out on the prairie had taught him well.

At least now he knew how to saddle a horse and build a fire. Those activities and others had been learned on the trail. Daman hoped he never need use those skills again as he hitched his horse to the borrowed buckboard and climbed onto the bench seat. Though it jostled him somewhat, it was nothing like being tossed about in the saddle. He had never understood why so many people were mad over riding. Horses smelled. Especially when their coats became wet.

No, give him a nice carriage with a driver and footmen or even a borrowed phaeton in Hyde Park when in London. He was more than grateful that these American trains went to the far west nowadays. No, no more saddles for him. He would conduct Edward's business with his feet planted on the ground and be the better for it.

Daman flicked his wrists and started the wagon. He would have to drive down what passed for the main street of this little hamlet before turning and heading back toward Abilene. Vaguely, he wondered where Mrs. Choate was off to in such a hurry. Possibly a luncheon date? Her explanation was veiled. He doubted with her girth and age that she went to a secret rendezvous with a lover. Maybe new fabric was arriving at the Crombar Creek general store today. Fabric and hats always seemed to get women moving with particular speed.

As Daman drew closer to the main boulevard, he could see a crowd gathered on the outskirts. It repelled him when he realized it was a western hanging.

He had no stomach for such things. It was simply another tradition passed down from merry olde England, as had been dueling. He couldn't believe these colonials continued to carry on such barbaric customs in this modern day and age.

Yet as he passed in the distance, he drew up on the reins without thinking. A woman stood on the platform, bound hand and foot, a rope around her slender neck. Daman watched in morbid fascination, unable to look away. He climbed from the cart and made his way over to those gathered at the execution site.

A chill ran through him as woman after woman bravely spoke out. He looked at the accused, only known as Miss Sullivan, and swallowed hard. Her tawny eyes haunted him as she stood apart from the restless crowd. He still remembered Cynthia's haunted eyes all these years later and how he had been powerless to act. Although his sister was long dead, she lived on in his heart as the mother he'd never known. He hadn't been able to save her.

This time he would act.

Daman didn't know exactly what he would do but he had to do something. Fast.

And then the melee broke out. Was fighting all these Americans ever did? Daman skirted the mob as he headed quickly toward the platform. He watched a man with a star pinned to his chest move close and say something to the woman before he pulled a black hood over her head.

The lawmen moved away, placing his hand upon a lever. Daman feared he was too late. He raced up the wooden steps as the man pulled the lever. Daman slammed into the sheriff, knocking him off the platform and into the crowd.

Quickly, he yanked the control back. The lever

jammed. Daman turned and saw the woman squirming. Her feet jerked as they swung above a small gap in the platform directly beneath her. She tried to move them to balance on solid wood. He ran to her and wrapped his arms around her hips, lifting her slightly to ease the tension on the rope.

"Don't move!" he shouted.

She stilled immediately. Daman hoisted up his leg to reach for the knife Mose gave him on the trail. The cowboy laughed heartily when he found out Daman didn't carry any sort of weapon and made the blade a gift to him. Over the last few weeks, slipping it into his boot became second nature to him.

As he tried to balance the woman while on one foot, Daman reverted to his usual clumsily self, dropping the knife.

"Bloody hell."

He tried to stretch out his leg and slide the knife over with the tip of his boot but it was just out of his toes' reach.

"Hang on," he shouted, hoping she could hear over the mob's noise. "I've got to let you go just for a moment."

She stiffened in his arms. A whimper escaped her lips. He couldn't think about that now. Time meant everything. He eased her down and lunged for the knife. He grabbed it and immediately slipped back under her again.

Quickly, Daman sawed through the rope above her head and ripped the hood away. She sucked in a breath of air while she coughed and sputtered. He knew that he might have already been spotted. Tossing her over his shoulder, he ran like hell.

He reached the buckboard and threw her into the back. He didn't dare slow down and ask politely about her state of being. Jumping into the cart, he took off, racing past the few storefronts in Crombar Creek. As he passed a wagon parked outside the general store, he stopped and leaped out. Daman grabbed a few of the empty feed bags he saw in it and flung them strategically on top of the woman.

Glancing over his shoulder, he saw no one followed him although the brawl now poured further out into the street. He returned to the seat of the buckboard, took a deep breath, and then started the cart again at a more leisurely pace. He didn't want to look like he was fleeing the scene.

The woman must have figured out his plan since he didn't hear her make a sound as the horse trotted along the street and away from the town. Daman shook his head.

What had he just done?

And what would he do with the woman?

She probably didn't have a dime to her name, but she could easily have made a living on her back. She was a radiant beauty, with a long mane of raven hair and large amber eyes. In Europe, she would have made a choice mistress to the king of any country and retired before she turned thirty.

He waited until a good three miles passed and slowed the cart. Daman decided it would look decidedly suspicious to pull up in Abilene and uncover this woman on a public street. Glancing in both directions and seeing no one out on the road in either direction, he stopped the buckboard and got out.

Still marveling at how he had gotten himself into such a situation, he lifted the empty bags from the woman. It was then he realized her awkward position.

"I'm sorry. I'd forgotten your hands and feet were bound."

He took his blade and sliced through the tightly drawn ropes. Then more gingerly, he pulled the bunched cord away from her neck and cut through it, casting it aside. An angry ring encircled her neck. Her wrists were red and raw. Daman stomach roiled. He looked away. He had never been one blessed with a strong stomach.

The woman sat up and winced as she rubbed her wrists. "I seem to have lost the feeling in them."

Ever the gentleman, he took a slender wrist in his hands and tried to restore the circulation, rubbing her skin. She cried out, startling him, and he back a step away from her.

"Am I being too rough?"

"No. I don't think so. It's just burning. Stings like the dickens. It must be the blood starting to move again."

"I see."

Daman stood there awkwardly. He watched her shake her wrists and grimace. It was then he noticed the welt on her face. Without thinking, he brought his fingers to her cheek and touched it.

She flinched.

"I'm sorry," he apologized. "It's a fresh bruise. Looks awfully nasty."

She rolled her eyes. "I stumbled mounting the stairs and wasn't able to catch myself." She ran a hand through the temple of dark waves. "I must be a sight."

Despite the bruise, her beauty struck Daman. And struck him dumb, as well. He couldn't think of a single thing to say.

And so he laughed.

She looked at him warily but then she, too, began laughing. She shook her head. "I'm sorry. I've just been snatched from the jaws of death and I haven't even properly thanked you, much less introduced my-self." She held out a hand to him. "My name is Serena Sullivan."

He took it gently and raised it to his lips for a kiss. He saw her eyes widened, the amber going fiery for a moment.

"I am Daman Rutledge, recently visiting my broth-er's cattle ranch, and hoping to return one day soon to London."

He released her hand reluctantly, finding he liked holding it more than he should. He thought of the first excuse that would allow him to hold it briefly again.

"Might I assist you into the cart and let us be on our way?"

She nodded. "That would be nice, Mr. Rutledge, but I fear you shouldn't be seen with me much longer. Foreigner or not, you would be in a lot of trouble. I don't think you could plead ignorance for your ac-tions." She gazed upon him in sympathy. "Where are you headed?"

"Abilene."

She thought a moment. "I could get a train out." A frown creased her lovely brow. "If I had money for a ticket, that is."

Daman smiled at her. "I think I could provide pas-sage from a dangerous situation for a lady in distress."

Serena's eyes lit up. "I would pay you back, Mr. Rutledge. As soon as I find a new post, that is." She sighed. "I don't think I'll be using Crombar Creek as a reference this time."

He laughed and climbed onto the bench seat, holding out his hand to her. She took it and he pulled her up, glad that the small bench would force her to sit close to him. Daman took up the reins and started the horse toward Abilene again, pleased that her thigh rested next to his.

As they rode, he asked, "What kind of post will you look for, Miss Sullivan?"

"I'm a schoolmarm."

Daman forced himself to keep his eyes on the road. A powerful mistress. An actress. Even a socialite, perhaps. But a teacher? It was the last occupation he would have chosen for such a beauty.

5

S erena sat ramrod straight next to the best-looking
man she had ever seen. Daman Rutledge was a
few inches over six feet, with dark brown hair that
gleamed with russet highlights in the hot Kansas sun.
His penetrating blue eyes had danced with mischief as
they'd briefly spoken.

She wondered why a well-dressed Englishman
would want to be in Kansas. Of course, he did mention cattle. He must be here checking on his family's
investment as the herds came in from Texas. Yet his
face and hands were burnished to deep brown, as if he
had been outside with the cattle himself for a long pe-
riod of time.

"I realize I'm not your responsibility," Serena
blurted out. "I am so grateful for what you did and I
do promise to repay you in time. Will you be in
America long?"

Daman turned to look at her. Lord, but that stare
made it seem he could see right down to her very soul.
Serena lowered her eyes to her hands lying in her lap.
It didn't seem particularly polite to stare at such an
upper crust Adonis. And he was beautifully made,

with broad shoulders and classically chiseled features that some famous sculptor might have created.

But looking away from him only made her conscious of his nearness. Her shoulder rubbing against his. Her hip practically joined to his. She moistened her lips and dared to look back up. He still studied her.

"I'm here on business for a short while. My brother, the Earl of Stanhope, invested in some Texas livestock. Mainly cattle. I'm simply here on his behalf, seeing to his interests."

Serena found herself disappointed. "Oh, business."

Daman looked back at the road. "You sound a bit disillusioned with my mission, Miss Sullivan."

Serena shrugged, reluctant to share her thoughts. Then she decided she had nothing to lose at this point.

"Frankly, I am. You dashed to my rescue like some knight of old. I suppose I pictured you more as an adventurer. Or a painter. Maybe even a romantic poet." She sensed her cheeks heating and glanced away.

"Well, I am a playwright."

Her eyes snapped eyes back to her rescuer.

"No, truly, I am," he assured her. "I may not be Will Shakespeare but I can claim three of my plays were produced on the London stage."

Excitement flooded Serena. "I've never met an actual writer before. You must live a terribly exciting life, dreaming up all kinds of wondrous things to entertain people. I would love to hear about your previous work. Might I be so bold as to inquire what your next project is?"

Daman shook his head. "New material," he said

with a trace of bitterness. "I'm afraid there isn't any. It's sad, but my muse left me, and writer's block has set in."

He turned to look at her, the playful light dying in his eyes. "It's more than a figure of speech. My lover and leading lady ran off to be an Italian countess. My well of imagination simply dried up after that. I can't seem to put a coherent thought on paper, much less one that would amuse people. I can't talk an investor into bankrolling something that I haven't even created.

"I'm stuck here for the time being on this godforsaken windy prairie, where the dust has settled even into my ears and the only smell that registers anymore is cow dung."

Serena sensed how deeply the hurt ran through this man. She didn't know him but somehow she wanted to protect him. He drew her in some inexplicable way, unlike any man had ever done. She knew she should be shocked by him openly discussing his lover in front of her but she also realized that writers were a more bohemian sort of society unto themselves.

"Find a new inspiration," she advised him, her logical sense believing if he found a new muse, he could write successfully once more.

Daman gave her a grim look. She noticed his hands tightening on the reins. "No. No more writing. I've already decided. That part of my life is over."

Serena had spent a long month in jail before her trial and then execution date arrived. She thought about what else she might have done with her life. She believed she might be able to help this unlikely savior who had helped her cheat death.

"Teaching is performing," she told her companion. "I must keep my sometimes rowdy audience informed and entertained, always guessing what is to come next. I must say I'm rather good at holding their interest." She hesitated. "I always thought if my circumstances changed, I might like to be an actress. Maybe . . . maybe you could write a play for me?"

He looked intrigued for a moment before he shrugged his broad shoulders. "No, you would never step foot on a stage. You think you would but you wouldn't. It isn't respectable, you know."

Serena took a deep breath. So much for trying to inspire her rescuer to write again. "It will be back to chalk dust and McGuffey's readers for me then, I suppose. Of course, a long way from Crombar Creek and Kansas. They'll be looking for me. Sheriff Parker has a reputation for being ornery. He won't let an escaped criminal off so easily."

She crossed her arms and stared out across the flat land, wishing she did have the opportunity to start a whole new life. For just a moment, she pictured herself on a stage, performing, the audience entranced with her words.

As the horse plodded along for the next mile, Daman sensed her disappointment in him. He also recognized how desperate her situation truly was. She had spoken lightly of returning to teaching, coupled with the fact that she would be the object of what could be an intense search. She had no money, nowhere to go, and he had no idea how good the prospect was of her being detained.

The thought of Serena Sullivan swinging lifelessly from the hangman's noose tore at his gut.

Without thinking, he said, "You'll need to come with me."

Serena's head whipped up. She stared at him in obvious disbelief. "I couldn't possibly do that! An unchaperoned woman in a man's company? You must be mad."

"I owe it to you. It's something the Chinese believe. If you save someone's life, then you are responsible for that person for the rest of your life."

Daman grinned. "I did save that pretty neck of yours."

Serena blushed and looked down again. A protective wave swept over Daman as he looked at her profile. He began thinking aloud.

"Now, how can we pull it off?" He looked her over. "My sister? No, we're nothing alike, though we could say you favor Mother's side of the family."

Serena gazed at him in shock, her lovely mouth open, nothing coming from it.

"How about my ward? Yes, the American cousin and poor relation who has lost her parents, I think."

She narrowed her eyes. "I am twenty-five, you know. A little long in the tooth for being anyone's ward."

"Hmm." Daman's imagination began to soar, constructing the storyline as he spoke. "Still, a cousin could work. Maybe your parents died and a loving but stern aunt raised you. She died and left you a nice inheritance—but you were taken advantage of by a man that wanted your money and not you."

Serena gasped at his words. Daman amended the story he spun.

"No, you look too much too intelligent for that storyline to occur. Shall we say train robbers killed your fiancé? Or wait. A bank robber. Who's that James character I've heard of?"

Daman smiled as the wheels and his mind turned

rapidly. "Never mind that now. We can iron out the details later. We'll make you heartbroken. Practically a widow. Robert could have died a week before the wedding."

"Robert?"

"You know, Robert, your dead fiancé. If we—"

Serena interrupted him. "For having given up writing, you have quite a fertile imagination, Mr. Rutledge."

Excitement overcame Daman. It had been a long time since the creative juices flowed through him. In the space of a few minutes, he seemed almost his old self again. Creating seemed natural once more.

"Back to our storyline. I came to represent your British branch of cousins at the wedding. Now, I'm your greatest comfort. We can say you'll accompany me back to London when my business is completed here."

Daman thought a moment. "You'll need props. The proper clothes. Sorry, but you'll have to be in mourning. Unless the tragic event happened six months ago."

"Westerners don't typically conform to such conventions as lengthy mourning," Serena informed him. "Of course, I have no clothes, mourning or otherwise."

Daman wave that got away. "The earl has scads of money. That won't be a problem. What else needs to be done?"

His excitement built. He knew a large part of it was weaving the fantasy once again, playing God with people's lives, bringing into existence what he wished to be and then making it so.

Yet another hidden part of him knew that spending time with the lovely Serena Sullivan also encouraged him to continue fabricating a history for her.

He hadn't been attracted to a woman in ages. Not since Daphne left. Of course, he had physically satisfied himself with a string of women, but none captured his fancy.

Serena Sullivan did.

6

The buckboard continued toward Abilene in the burning afternoon sun, dust clouding the road behind them. Serena looks nervously over her shoulder. Had Sheriff Parker managed to calm his ugly temper and the free-for-all brawl yet? Had he formed a posse to pursue her?

Daman continued with his plans, distracting her momentarily. "I have a train ticket to Denver that leaves in two hours' time. I mentioned the business I am managing for my brother. If you are to accompany me to Colorado, we can't let them think you've gotten on that particular train, else they'll wire ahead and be looking for you either on the train itself or one of its stops."

He paused, a devilish look lighting his clear blue eyes. "We need to have them believe you're headed elsewhere. Most lawmen would suppose you would be on some kind of train if they managed to believe you got as far as Abilene. Might you know of other destinations that leave from the Abilene depot?"

Serena realized her fascination with trains and schedules would finally come in handy. "What time is it?" she asked.

Daman consulted his pocket watch and turned it toward her. "You have something brewing, Miss Sullivan?"

"The next train is scheduled to pull out in forty minutes. It's headed for Cheyenne," she informed him. "Then the Chicago half an hour later. Then Denver. That's the last train going west today. The next Chicago train leaves at four-thirty today and another one at six, which continues on to New York. No more trains will leave until tomorrow morning."

Daman stared at her, obviously impressed. "You memorized the train schedule because you found no other entertainment in Crombar Creek?"

Serena shrugged. She also knew the stagecoach routes and departure times, as well. Any time she arrived in a new community, she stored away that information like a squirrel hiding away its nuts. In case she received a tip on Bill's whereabouts, she wanted to be able to leave at a minute's notice. In fact, she would have already headed to Denver if she hadn't been jailed back in Crombar Creek. She had been packing, on the very brink of leaving at the end of the school's term, when Charles Rayburn stormed in and demanded a tryst with her.

Serena kept all this to herself. Daman Rutledge might have rescued her from an impossible situation but she never shared her past with anyone. She never revealed why she moved about as much as she did although many in her profession did the same. No one knew she had a brother or anything about her past— New York, the orphan train, or her life with the von Wormers.

Daman continued. "Then Cheyenne, it is. That is the train we need to have Sheriff Parker think you took." He flicked the reins lightly and the horse picked up its pace. "We ourselves best not go by train—at least for a few days—so we shall take tomorrow's stage and head west on it for the time being. We can switch to the train after a few days if we decide to do so."

"The stage leaves at seven-thirty, from in front of the Alamar Hotel."

"My, aren't you a fountain of knowledge as far as travel is concerned?" his eyes twinkled with amusement.

"Very well. It will be Denver by way of stagecoach. In the meantime, the authorities must feel absolutely certain you are on the Cheyenne train unless we're running behind. Then it will be the one bound for Chicago. I'll give you money to purchase a one-way ticket inside the train station. The ticket agent will need to remember you so flirt a little bit for good measure."

Serena grimaced at that thought. "Just because I purchase a ticket doesn't mean I set foot on that train. Sheriff Parker maybe muleheaded, Mr. Rutledge, but he's not stupid. He would find out I'm not on it."

Daman's sly smile gave Serena pause. "Oh, you'll get on the train, Miss Sullivan. You'll just get off it before it goes very far."

"And I suppose I would simply jump off?" Serena said it in an offhand manner but the look in Daman's eyes took her aback. "You can't be serious! You actually want me to jump? Off a moving train?"

He shrugged. "In essence, yes." He waved away her apprehension. "I have ridden on many a train and they simply don't get moving quickly for a few miles. They have a lot to transport and they must build their speed slowly. It takes a while for that to occur.

"You, my dear, will very obviously board the Cheyenne train heading west. The train depot is right on the edge of town. I visited it yesterday when I purchased my own ticket to Denver. The train will still be huffing and puffing for a good three to five minutes before it ever works up any speed."

"What will I be doing while these minutes pass?" Serena eyed her rescuer warily, not bothering to mask her sarcastic tone.

"You will calmly make your way to the last car and step out for a smoke." Daman's eyes danced with glee. "We'll let you be really scandalous and even show your cigarette before you open the door and step out onto the rear platform. That'll get the audience talking."

"Mr. Rutledge, may I kindly remind you that we're not in one of your melodramas? This is *my life* we're talking about." Her mouth set in disapproval of such a harebrained scheme.

"My dear Miss Sullivan, of course I remember what's at stake. I do want to be absolutely clear, however. I never author melodramas. Too mundane for my tastes."

Serena rolled her eyes but it didn't stop the Englishman's enthusiasm.

"At any rate, you shall step out onto the outside of the rear car. You should do this in the first two minutes. The train will have barely picked up any speed, yet it will have left the station and Abilene behind. No one will be watching you."

"As I leap."

Daman frowned and shook his head. "Leap might be too strong a word. If you'll simply ease over the gate and step down, obviously letting go of the railing, you'll be right as rain. I've seen fellows run along and jump onto a train. Getting off one shouldn't be nearly as difficult."

"Have you ever done so yourself?" Serena demanded.

"Not yet." Daman tried to hide a smile. "Besides, if you do fall and skin a knee, well . . ." His voice trailed off as mischief blanketed his features. "You are a little worse for the wear now. I shouldn't think a little tumble would hurt your appearance."

Serena tried to ignore his comment about her appearance. She decided to play along and see how far he would spin this outlandish idea.

"Once I'm off the train, a scant mile or so out of town—with my knees possibly scraped—what then?"

Daman nodded at her reassuringly. "Why, I'll be there, Miss Sullivan. I am going to meet you when it grows dark. You will need to hide in some bushes or bramble or prairie grass until then. I'm certain there's something of that nature available. Just keep yourself out of sight."

"What on God's green earth will you be doing until nightfall, Mr. Rutledge? Buying ointment for my knees?"

Daman took a deep breath. "I will have a lot to accomplish in the time allotted. I'll book us two seats on the morning coach out of Abilene. I'll reserve rooms for myself and my lovely cousin at the nicest hotel I can find. I will go to the biggest general store and try to find a few items you will need to keep our charade from falling flat."

He shuddered. "Store bought clothes are certainly not of the quality we'll put you in later, but I should be able to pick up a nice hat. Bonnets, I think you Yanks call them. Can't have you freckling out in this hot Kansas sun. A clean dress or perhaps a lovely blouse and skirt such as you are wearing now will suffice."

Daman glanced down. "Your boots seem serviceable so I shan't worry about that." He grinned again, like a naughty boy. "And if they have a few undergarments, I'll try to latch onto them, too, as well as gloves." He lifted one of Serena's hands in his, inspecting it carefully. "You have lovely hands, Miss Sullivan. We must protect them at all cost."

Serena's stomach did flip-flops at his touch. What was happening to her? She had avoided the notice of men for a decade. She tried her best to keep attention from being drawn to her. She knew oftentimes attention brought nothing but harm. Franz von Wormer and Charles Rayburn both taught her that expensive life lesson.

Now, this very charming Englishman barreled his way into her life, albeit in a very good way, and had her pulse quickening and an army of butterflies swirling around her insides. She couldn't afford to have these kinds of feelings for any man. She needed to escape Sheriff Parker and resume her search for Bill.

If she could ever gather a coherent thought again, that is.

With more calm than she thought possible, Serena asked, "You will rendezvous with me after all this is done, under cover of darkness?"

Daman agreed. "See, you're warming to the plan nicely. Everyone—that is, if anyone comes looking for you—will think you have left town. Meanwhile, we shall sneak you up some back entrance at the hotel so no one will get a glimpse of you."

He broke off and gave her a steady look. "Not that you appear all that bad for having almost hanged. You seem remarkably fit, I'd say. Still, I'd rather install you in a room and send for a bath. You can scrub yourself clean and then dress in the new items I shall purchase for you. I'll have dinner brought up, we will get ourselves a good night's rest, and then be off at first light on the western stage.

"Well, Mr. Rutledge, you seem to have thought of everything," she said, barely able to hide her sarcasm. "I'd guess it must be your quick writer's mind that invents such outlandish details on the spot."

Daman puffed up a bit. "I'm glad you recognized the brilliance of my plan, Miss Sullivan."

His last comment blew the lid off her contained calmness and Serena exploded. "You, sir, are a dreamer whose schemes will never work in this practical world. Are you mad? I'm to spring off a moving train. What if I break my ankle? Or worse? I could dislocate my kneecap. Snap my neck more quickly than if I'd gone ahead and hanged. What if someone sees me leap from a moving train, and they would, Mr. Rutledge. Abilene is as flat as a child's slate."

Serena crossed her arms. She remembered the sassy street child she'd been all those long years ago in New York. Sullivans took care of themselves no matter what the circumstances. Sullivans didn't need anyone. Sullivans weren't afraid of anything.

Except possibly one devastatingly handsome English playwright.

Serena took a deep breath to compose herself. "You're enjoying this adventure, aren't you, Mr. Rutledge? At my expense. Well, no more, sir. Stop this wagon at once. I shall walk the remaining way to Abilene. I spy the buildings ahead as it is. I will formulate my own escape plan. Thank you for all your help."

She turned away from him, ready to jump down once the cart stopped. When Serena realized the buckboard wasn't slowing, she decided to leap instead. After all, he had expected her to do the same from a moving train, hadn't he?

But as she got ready to push off, Daman Rutledge locked his hand around her elbow and kept her on the seat even as he pulled back on the reins, halting the horse's progress.

"Why, Miss Sullivan." The corners of his mouth turned up slightly. "I'm very sorry that you didn't like my scheme. I suppose it wasn't very considerate, having you throw yourself from a moving train. I did think the rest of it quite good, however."

Serena looked into his crystal blue eyes and saw the hurt and disappointment there, despite his light tone. Well, he had rescued her from death. She supposed she could stroke his ego a tiny bit.

"The rest seemed quite nice, Mr. Rutledge. I'm sorry if I sounded ungracious and unappreciative. You saved my life. I will never forget that."

"I shall continue to do so." He thought a moment. "I shall drop you at the rail yard. Stay out of sight until you see me purchase my ticket. I'll signal you whether it's Cheyenne or Chicago. In fact, I'll pull on my right ear if it's Cheyenne. No ear pull means Chicago. Then do the same, just as we planned. I shall find us those rooms in the meantime. Then we'll have a place to hide until morning when the stage leaves."

"But—"

"No buts, my dear. I realize we're pressed for time as it is. You shall do exactly as we planned. Buy your ticket, being memorable, of course. Get on the train and look for me. We'll both get off somehow. Before it leaves the station. I promise you that."

Within five minutes, they arrived in Abilene and moved down the crowded main thoroughfare. Mass confusion reigned. Serena doubted the sheriff's posse would find anyone sober, much less a witness that would tie her to Daman Rutledge. She would do as he asked and remain out of sight until she spied him purchasing his ticket. Then she would saunter over to buy her own ticket at the last minute.

DAMAN STOPPED the cart in front of the train depot. He stepped down and reached up for Serena, his hands encircling her waist as he lifted her to the ground. He handed her some money to purchase her ticket, which she slipped into her skirt's pocket, having brought no reticule to her noon appointment with the hangman's noose.

He bent and brushed a quick kiss on her cheek. "Goodbye. Cousin Serena." His eyes glinted with amusement. "I shall see you shortly. Remember to lie low."

Serena looked at him as haughtily as any duchess would. "Believe it or not, Mr. Rutledge, I have vast amounts of experience in areas you could never begin to imagine. I know how to turn myself invisible. I will meet you as planned, on the train of your choice."

Daman watched Serena enter the train station. She had assured him she knew how to remain anonymous yet what man wouldn't notice the sweet sway of those hips? Or the beautiful bow of her mouth? Or the lustrous black waves?

Of course, she twisted her hair up as they'd ridden and had somehow managed to knot it together with nary a hairpin. In his opinion, that was a talented woman.

Daman opened his valise and pawed through until he found a light gray frock coat. He exchanged it for the dark blue he wore. If anyone remembered seeing him free Serena, they would put him in a dark coat, whether blue or black. The dove gray might help throw them off the trail.

Daman then went back to Abilene's Main Street. He needed to find a hotel quickly and get back in time to make their train. He looked both right and left and spied a large sign advertising the Alamar Hotel, wondering how he'd missed it yesterday. Of course, he had walked to the right, back toward the bank and all the confusion and had never glanced left. It looked to be a decent establishment. Serena did mention the stage departed from this point.

Daman pulled up the wagon, parking in front of the hotel. He hitched the horse to the rail before he lifted out his portmanteau easily. Carrying it, he stepped inside the large lobby. He was glad to get away from the hordes of cowboys and roughnecks still spilling out into the streets from every establishment along its way.

Glancing about, he saw that the Alamar was a hotel of quality, at least compared to where most of the rowdy chaps would spend the night. He walked across a gleaming hardwood floor and up to the service desk. No one sat behind it so he rang the small bell as indicated by the sign on the desk.

A middle-aged man with gold pince-nez and an air of wanting to please about him step from a rear room.

"Good day, sir. How may I be of service to you?"

"My name is Daman Rutledge. I'd like to book a room for myself and one for my cousin. We leave on tomorrow morning's early stage."

The desk clerk frowned slightly. "Two rooms, you say?" He flipped through a register sitting on the desk, tsk-tsking to himself, his nose working like a small rabbit's.

"Mr. Rutledge, I am so terribly sorry. With several of the herds coming in this week, I have many buyers staying here. The Alamar is convenient to the trains, you see. I do have one suite remaining, though. It's a bedroom and sitting room. The sofa is quite large and will accommodate one of you, allowing the other to have the bedroom. Would that be to your satisfaction?"

The man leaned over the desk slightly as if to include Daman in on some secret. "Might I say, sir, for someone of your station, this would be the most suitable arrangement. You will find the other local hotels . . . lacking in high standards. I also fear the class of people staying in them would keep you up most of the night with their carryings-on."

Daman didn't hesitate. "Book the suite, please. Would it be possible to have dinner sent up tonight? I'd rather not be exposed to the elements you mentioned before we leave tomorrow."

"I quite understand, Mr. Rutledge. That will be simple to arrange. If you'll sign the register here, please."

The man rotated the turntable the book sat upon and lifted the ink pen from its well. Daman scrawled his name across the line as the clerk turned his back for a moment to reach for a room key.

"May I carry up your luggage?"

"Yes, please. Where is the room?"

"Second floor, at the very back, sir. In fact, there's a back staircase if you would find that more convenient."

Daman knew good fortune smiled upon him as he pocketed the room key. "I'll have some packages sent over from the general store, as well, if you could see them up to the room."

"Of course, Mr. Rutledge. You might try Chaney's. It's on the same side of the street, about three blocks down. Fair prices and a nice variety of goods. Tell him Sam at the Alamar sent you."

"Thank you, Sam, and good day."

Daman tipped his hat to the clerk and stepped outside into the turmoil that still ruled the streets. It made him long for the lake on his father's—now Edward's—estate. He spent many a pleasant day sitting on its banks fishing, whiling the afternoon away as he invented stories and characters to keep himself amused. Cynthia found him there any afternoon it wasn't too cold or raining and would bring him a sandwich or some of Cook's pumpkin bread or sand tarts to tide him over until teatime.

Daman shook off the sweet memories of his sister sitting beside him, reading to him from some volume of Shakespeare or Marlowe or Chaucer, her voice taking on different accents and tones as she portrayed each character in her own unique way.

Daman was done with the past. He had a train to catch. And no time to waste.

7

S erena made herself scarce once inside the crowded depot. Experienced taught her years ago how to blend into the background. It made her reminisce about the old days.

The first thoughts that came back revolved around the immense hunger. There never had been enough food. Mama always sick. Papa often out of a job. Uncle Ralph, selfishly eating more than his share as the adults turned a blind eye, the children too fearful of his fists to point out what he did.

The streets had been her home. Serena could still close her eyes and see the many vendors and their carts. She had made friends with old and young alike. One might spare an apple for her or an old, stale loaf of bread. She had been painfully thin then and knew she aroused sympathy in many with her long, gangly limbs that were bony and pale.

She swept up at a saloon in Five Points, Bill tagging along as usual. Working there taught her many a lesson. She quickly learned when and how to stay out of the way of drunks. The whores had actually been nice to her, even giving her and Bill candy. They all seem to have a sweet tooth and a particular fondness for peppermints. Serena's fascination with all the makeup they wore started when Ugly Annie painted herself. Serena thought Annie quite homely until she saw Annie in her full glory. Serena wondered how many other women in society hid their plain looks behind paint, albeit more subtly than the whores did.

The women treated Bill like a pet. Not one of them made fun of his limp—unlike others who rudely shoved him aside, calling him Clubfoot Charlie and worse. Serena wondered as she often did who chose Bill? Had he been taken at the next stop on the orphan train? Did he go to a good family—or did he arrive at the end of the line with a few stragglers they'd all heard tales about?

She had heard a lead about a man resembling Bill. He was a gambler in Denver. Serena was ready to pursue this when Charles Rayburn interrupted her life and turned her world upside down.

Revulsion swept through her. She could still remember the way the oily banker watched her. He had never leered openly but his gaze always remained on her when they were in the same room. She had only stayed with Rayburn's family once but the banker also visited when Serena boarded at his brother's house. It was hard being at the mercy of a community as a schoolmarm who didn't make enough to pay for a room. Serena did what every teacher on the Great Plains did—she lodged with her students' families for a week or two at a time.

She spent two different times with James Rayburn's house. They made her feel like part of their family during her stays, which rarely seemed to be the case. Serena especially enjoyed the company of their son, Ricky, who had come to visit her in the jail twice, despite the fact that she was accused of murdering his uncle.

The only hint of trouble occurred when Mrs. Rayburn commented on how Charles and his family rarely came to dinner at their place but had made an exception in coming two weeks' running while she was their guest. Mrs. Rayburn eyed Serena suspiciously as she mused aloud though Serena had done nothing to warrant any unseemly attention from the banker.

It was always like that, beginning with Franz von Wormer. His pig's eyes and sausage hands roaming over her. A wave of shame and humiliation blanketed Serena.

Enough. Think of anything else but that.

Naturally, her thoughts turned to Daman Rutledge. Why was this cultivated gentleman aiding her? With his tailored clothes and refined accent, he had appeared out of nowhere. Why would he help her, a total stranger, one about to be executed?

A sick feeling washed over her. He was a man. Like all the rest. The facade was dressed up but he still would want payment in the same way others had before him.

And yet Serena almost physically ached, yearning for Daman to be different from the rest. She wanted to trust him. Trust had long ago evaporated with experience, the same as her dream of having a permanent home and raising a family. She longed for a baby and a man to love, one to share her dreams.

Serena pushed these ideas aside. She was in more than a pickle now. She had no one to turn to, not even old Miss von Wormer, who had been an angel of mercy in a time of darkness, bucking her brother Franz and taking Serena in when Franz and his wife ordered Serena from their house. That woman saved Serena's sanity but Miss von Wormer had been dead for years now.

Access to Serena's meager savings had evaporated. Sheriff Parker saw to that. She could tell from his leer that he would have liked to take more than her money. Thank goodness she had often had visitors at the jail, even some of her pupils. She discouraged them from coming, knowing they often did so behind their parents' backs. Still, their cards and drawings touched her.

She absently fingered the locket around her neck as she looked at the clock in the depot. It was almost time for the Cheyenne train to leave. Where was he? Serena wondered why she believed she could put her faith in Daman Rutledge. He was a man, a foreigner, and someone she knew absolutely nothing about.

She needed more time to figure things out. Maybe she could get off at the very first stop instead. A good number of years had passed since she'd last picked a pocket but she knew instinctively she still had the skill in her fingers. She would lift enough to take a different train or coach and leave Mr. Rutledge behind.

Should she go back east? She had never thought about it in all these years. No one waited for her there. She'd grown to love the open spaces and friendliness of the west. No, she'd continue to head west. Westerners were a kind society. They actually treated women better, at least some of the time. Why, in Wyoming, women could even vote. Serena would love to march in and cast a ballot and keep people like Bud Parker out of office.

Most importantly, though, she needed to stay in the west so she could continue to search for her brother. Determination pushed her to reunite with her twin. Family was everything and Bill was all she had left.

Then she saw her rescuer sauntering across the lobby, whistling as if he hadn't a care in the world. He had changed suit coats. She'd give him credit for at least one smart move. Who knew if Parker's posse had already arrived in Abilene and whether or not they had linked the two of them?

She watched as he purchased a ticket and began to cross to the outer doors. He never looked left nor right, but he did tug on his right ear.

Cheyenne. Not Chicago.

Serena decided that she would follow Daman Rutledge, just for a little while. She wouldn't want him making a scene, coming back to look for her. She did want to head further West at any rate. Might as well do it on his dime and let Parker think she went to Wyoming.

Serena went to the ticket window as she glanced nervously at the Clock again. Five minutes before the train departed. She was slicing it close to the bone. At least the line had dwindled to nothing. She walked right up to the window. Moistening her lips, she smiled at the clerk as she stepped up. She knew she had looked far better at other times. At least she'd taken a few minutes to rinse her face and wash her hands in the facilities, trying to tidy her hair a bit.

She had never flirted before, though. Never wanted to draw that kind of unwanted attention. Serena didn't know if she even knew how to go about it. She remembered the picnic last summer on the Fourth of July. Sally Johnson, her prize student and all of sixteen, sprang to mind. Serena could see Sally cock her head to the side and smile sweetly, batting her eyelashes a bit. The boys flocked to Sally like flies to strawberry jam.

As she stood at the window, though, Serena chickened out. Flirting was simply not in her nature.

"One ticket to Cheyenne, please. I'm in a hurry."

The clerk, in his early twenties with oversized ears and crooked teeth, grinned at her broadly. "Yes, ma'am, one ticket to Cheyenne. You'll just make it if you hurry." He busied himself readying the ticket and took her money. "Are you going to see family?" he asked.

The question startled Serena. "Y-yes," she stammered, feeling her cheeks overheat. "My brother."

The clerk grinned at her again. "Have yourself a nice time. I hear Cheyenne's real pretty."

Serena relaxed and returned his smile. "I hope it is. Thank you."

She moved away from the window. In line behind her, two men eyed her appreciatively.

As she walked across the waiting area and out into the hot, late afternoon sun, Serena saw the platform packed with passengers. The lowing cattle added into their pens nearby brought a cacophony of sounds, making it hard for her to hear the conductor calling, "All aboard..." Serena rushed over and allowed him to assist her up the steps.

"Almost didn't make it, ma'am," he said as the train began to pull away from the station.

"I was held up unexpectedly."

"No luggage?"

Serena panicked. "No. Well, yes. My cousin came down earlier with it. I'll just look for him. Thank you."

She entered the narrow aisle and began walking down it as the train crept out of the station at a snail's pace. The rail cars were fairly crowded. Serena pretended to look for her cousin as she moved down the length of the train.

She reached the last car. Only two gentlemen occupied it, one engrossed in his newspaper and the other snoring openmouthed.

Then a touch on her elbow made her gasp. She turned to find Daman Rutledge beaming at her.

"Come on." He tugged on her gently, then slipped his hand around hers. "We need to hurry."

Serena needed to make a decision. If she rode to the first station, she put a good bit of distance between her and the sheriff. Or she could continue on with her charming benefactor and throw caution to the wind.

She allowed Daman to pull her quickly down the aisle, where he opened the door to the rear platform. The whistle blew and she could feel the train's momentum starting to pick up.

What should she do?

"Let's move rapidly, Miss Sullivan." Daman threw a leg over the rail and slid the other one over. "Steady your hands on the rail." He tightened his hand around her wrist.

Nerves fluttered wildly through her. Serena looked desperately at Daman. "This was the best you could come up with? I thought you promised me a different plan."

Daman shrugged, proffering a guilty smile. He gave her wrist another squeeze. "Come on, Miss Sullivan. I have faith in you."

Instinct took over. Serena lifted her skirt with her free hand and awkwardly climbed over the rail, stepping onto the other side. She clung a moment to the bars. Her mind told her to stay. She still had a little money and change from the ticket. And she didn't know a thing about Daman Rutledge.

But her heart told her she should trust him. If not, maybe she could shake him off at one of the stage stations.

With a leap of faith, Serena took the hand he offered. They let go of the railing and dropped to the dust. They landed in tandem, low to the ground. The impact stung her feet and Serena flung out her right hand and touched earth. She gave a grateful sigh as she watched the train chugging away.

Daman pulled her to her feet as the train moved on. Serena saw it started to pick up speed. Another half-minute and she'd probably have been too frightened to jump. A nervous giggle erupted from out of the blue. She tried to stifle it without success.

Her liberator smiled at her and laughed aloud. "We seem to be having all sorts of adventures, Miss Sullivan. Nothing like what I experience in London drawing rooms."

His eyes twinkled as he pulled out his handkerchief and dusted himself off before turning it on her and wiping it across her cheeks playfully.

Serena pushed his arm aside. "No, this is nothing like the schoolroom, either. Of course, that can get much rougher, you know."

Daman shuttered. "I cannot imagine what attempting to teach young American hooligans all in one place must be like. Boys, in particular. I was one myself once and I gave my governess, and later my tutor, fits. There should be some law against allowing more than a couple of boys together in any learning environment."

"I'll be sure to petition Congress with that Mr. Rutledge. Unfortunately, it will mean the death of public education in the United States, you realize."

He took her hand again and it seemed to Serena to be the most natural thing in the world.

"Come along then, Cousin. We need to head back to our hotel."

They began following the tracks back to the station. Serena saw they hadn't even gotten more than a quarter of a mile from the depot.

Daman waved his hand around. "See, look at the chaos. Why, no one will ever see or remember us, I'll wager."

Serena looked at the vast number of herding pens packed with cattle. Cowboys of every size and shape moved the animals, loading them through the gates, dust kicking up in every direction. She held her breath for long moments as they meandered through the confusion and made their way back to the station's platform.

"We won't go back inside. We shall skirt the perimeter and venture off to our hotel. It's as nice as could be found on a moment's notice. I think you'll approve."

Daman led her around the building and along a busy street. Serena finally began to relax for the first time that day.

And then she saw him.

She froze in her tracks a moment and then pulled hard on Daman.

"I say—"

"Shush!" Serena yanked him into an alleyway, her heart pounding loud enough to wake the dead.

Daman leaned around the corner and quickly moved back. "Bloody hell. It's that moron sheriff of yours. Riding quite a nice horse, I might add."

"Would you be quiet?" she hissed.

Daman chuckle. "As if he could hear you in this roaring crowd."

But Serena did notice Daman looked a shade paler under his tanned face as he inched back out for a quick glance.

"He's coming this way," he whispered in her ear.

"Do something!" She couldn't keep the hysteria out of her voice.

And then he did.

He pushed her against the brick wall, his body rock hard against hers.

8

Panic seared Serena, knowing Sheriff Parker would pass at any moment. He would see her and it would all be over. She fought to push Daman away but he clasped her wrists tightly and pressed them against the wall, his body leaning into hers, forcing her to stay in place.

She tried to protest but his mouth was suddenly on hers, insistent, hard and demanding. His tongue pushed into her mouth, keeping her from speaking, then even breathing.

And then the magic began.

Inside, her belly began to dance, as if she were riding in a buggy gone out of control. It bounced up and down and every which way. The tingling started, going from her scalp, down her nape, to where her breasts rubbed against Daman's muscled chest. It went lower. Past her belly. Weaving perilously downward. Causing a sensation of feelings that exploded within her.

Not knowing she did so, Serena answered his kiss. Urgency pushing her on, her tongue mating with his. Sweet sensations coupled with dizziness overwhelmed her.

Daman lifted his mouth a bare inch from hers. "Lock your hands around my neck," he commanded. "And lift up a leg."

Blindly, Serena obeyed him, her own free will shattered by his kiss. He released her wrists. She wrapped her arms about his neck, fastening her fingers together. He helped her raise her leg slightly. He stepped even closer to her than she thought possible.

"Wrap your leg around me," he whispered just before he began feasting on her mouth again. Serena felt him slide his hand along her waist and down her hip, gripping her thigh and stroking it sensually.

It was madness. They were practically on a public street, locked in an intimate embrace.

But it felt so right.

Daman's lips covered hers again, his tongue gliding along, outlining them. Serena opened to him, and he began to kiss her again, long, drugging kisses. An aching throb began steadily pounding as he cupped her breast with his free hand.

"Guess whores do it anywhere," a familiar voice said.

Serena froze. Parker must be at the entrance to the alley. Then she realized what Daman had been doing all along. Her mind had turned off to the danger with the beginning of his kiss but now she understood what he wanted Parker to think. She knew Daman blocked the sheriff's view of her with the way he stood over her. He was protecting her.

A small wave of disappointment filled her. She must be insane. Here Daman Rutledge was rescuing her for the second time today. Yet all she could think about was his kiss had been a false one though for very good reasons.

Serena threw herself into her performance nonetheless. Let Parker think her a backstreet tart in a busy cow town. She pushed her fingers into Daman's thick hair, playing with the curling ends at his nape. She rubbed her leg suggestively up and down his thigh, feeling his hand tightened on her. She pressed her breasts against him and his palm flattened, kneading one, causing her heart to race and her core to throb.

Serena kissed Daman Rutledge with every inch of her being as the pulsating tingles grew to a fever pitch within her.

Then he lifted his mouth, resting his forehead against hers as he breathed heavily, gasping in spurts. He turned his head slightly to look out at the street and then back again.

"He's gone," he whispered, his brow resting against hers again. She could feel his racing heart beating within his chest as if they'd melted into one person.

Daman slowly lifted his head and gently lowered her leg to the ground. He stepped back, shaking his head.

"Maybe you should go on the stage, Miss Sullivan. A command performance. Bravo." He wiped his sleeve against his forehead and swallowed hard.

A performance?

Is that what he thought just happened? In his mind, that's what they had given their audience of one. Daman had played the rutting stud, ready to take a loose woman in an alleyway. She had simply responded, playing off the cues he'd given her. She must remember that.

Serena ran her hands through her hair, which had come loose, falling about her in soft waves. She had just experienced her first romantic feelings ever—and her partner had only been acting. Of course, he had done so to save her hide. It did her no good to get her feelings hurt. Daman Rutledge didn't feel any romantic attachment to her. He only wanted to guard her from Sheriff Parker.

She gathered up her hair again, twisting it back and into a bun against her nape. Her cheeks burned. They must be beet red but she could do nothing about that. She looked up and saw Daman readjusting his shirt and coat.

He caught her eye. "I suppose that makes us kissing cousins?" he teased.

It was the right thing to say. It broke any tension hanging in the alley. "You do have a way with words, Cousin Daman."

"Ah, you're ready to actually use Christian names, Cousin Serena?"

"I suppose we finally know each other well enough now to do so," she said, her tone light and playful.

He offered his arm to her. "Then let us proceed to the Alamar, hopefully without further mishap."

He stepped to the alley's entrance and glanced the way Parker had gone. "Clear."

They walked rapidly the remaining two blocks in the opposite direction to their hotel. Daman escorted her up the back stairs and used his room key to let them in. He locked the door behind them and turned to face Serena.

She laughed. "We are ace high today," she proclaimed.

Daman frowned, a puzzled look on his face. "I beg your pardon?"

"It's an American expression. It usually refers to the top hand in poker but it can mean we've had luck on our side today. That everything's gone right."

Serena glanced at their surroundings. "And a beautiful room, to boot."

"Oh. Right." He took off his hat and ran a hand through his hair. "I need to make a trip to the general store. I shall purchase our coach tickets while I'm out." He pointed at her. "You stay here and rest a bit. Then we'll see to getting you a bath and some dinner."

She opened her mouth. "But—"

"No protests, love. I have a master plan right here." He tapped his temple. "Just follow my lead."

She pursed her lips. "Will I have any revision rights along the way as you write this tale by the seat of your pants?"

He grinned appreciatively. "I'll have to think on that." He led her to the sofa and took her foot in his hands. "Let's slip off these boots and have you lie down. You've earned a bit of rest."

Gently, he tugged off each of her worn boots. "No one should bother you. Lock the door behind me all the same. Close the bedroom door. If it has a lock, use it, too. I will return shortly."

Serena followed him across the room as he unlocked and opened the door. He brushed the tip of his finger against her nose. "Don't give the management a reason to throw us out. The streets are mean here. I do hope Denver will be tamer. I am certainly ready for a more civilized atmosphere."

Daman heard Serena locked the door behind him. He went down the convenient back staircase and set out for the general store the hotel desk clerk had recommended.

As he walked from the Alamar, his thoughts lingered on Serena's delectable mouth. He'd meant their kiss to be a ruse, hoping it would convince the sheriff that only a little sport went on in the alley. He hadn't wanted the lawmen to see her and make an arrest.

But his small deception turned on him. Daman had kissed numerous women over the years. Many gave him a sexual stirring. But Serena Sullivan had been dynamite in his hands, combusting into a blazing heat he had never known. Yet within that sexual heat was a yearning even more addictive.

Now, he not only felt the need to protect her but Daman desired her more than any woman in his past. Or his conceivable future.

A dangerous combination. One he would keep to himself.

Daman came upon the booth he'd seen earlier and purchased two tickets on the first coach out to Denver. Then he went another block down the thoroughfare and saw his final destination, Chaney's General Store.

For an American store in the middle of nowhere, Chaney's impressed him. Though stores with the finest of goods dominated London, Chaney's inventory amazed Daman. From quilts to canned goods, saddles to iron skillets, butter churners to seeds, Mr. Chaney had assembled quite a variety for his Abilene customers.

Daman ambled about the crowded store, perusing the goods. He came across a small corner of ladies' items and selected two sets of gloves, a hairbrush, and some rouge. He didn't think Serena Sullivan needed the latter but what he wouldn't give to run his finger through the pot and then stroke it across her lips or cheek.

"Bloody hell," he muttered under his breath, half wishing his randy thoughts would push off and half hoping they wouldn't.

"May I help you, sir?"

A young girl of perhaps sixteen stood in front of him, probably Chaney's daughter. She was plain. Long brown hair was pulled tightly back from her face and pinned into a neat bun.

Daman smiled at the girl, his most charming smile. He doubted she got many of them from strange men by the way she blushed and looked down at her toes.

"Yes, I do need some help. My cousin is in an awful bit of circumstances. She just arrived today on the overland coach and somehow the driver took off with her luggage."

The girl's eyes widened. "Oh, dear, what a mess."

"Exactly, miss. She's tidying up at the hotel now. The trip fairly did her in but I know she'll need all those feminine kinds of things which I know nothing about."

Actually, Daman knew quite a bit about feminine needs. He had bought lingerie and hats and perfumes, as well as all kinds of clothing for Daphne. She praised his every selection, claiming he had much better taste than she did.

"Sure, I can help you, sir" The girl hesitated and Daman realized she didn't know quite how to go about asking him how much he cared to spend on his cousin.

"I am so glad to have found your help. Please select everything my cousin might need. I've just come into my earldom and I have more than enough funds to see to her needs."

Why had he just said that?

Soon, though, young Miss Chaney had Serena set up with everything the store could provide for a female. Daman helped in estimating Serena's size by holding hands up here and there. If given a choice, he chose what he thought Serena might like. Knowing her as an underpaid schoolmarm, he doubted she had owned much in the past.

Her own clothes were tasteful but of a lesser quality. It made him want to lavish whatever he could find in Abilene on her. He had been assured that Denver was quite cosmopolitan so he hoped they could find a suitable dressmaker once they arrived so her wardrobe could be completed there.

His purchases made, he directed Miss Chaney to have them sent to the Alamar, including a large valise he'd seen in the far corner. Daman noted the time on his pocket watch as he stepped outside. The streets were slightly less crowded now. He supposed the action would start to take place more inside the saloons and whorehouses as the day wound down.

Then he remembered the coldness and the sheriff's eyes as he had stood next to Serena moments before her execution. Daman found himself turning around and walking back into the store. Miss Chaney gave him a broad smile.

"Nice to see you again, sir. Did you forget something for your cousin?"

Westerners all seemed to own guns. Daman wanted to be prepared for whatever came down the road. Especially with the Crombar Creek lawman present in Abilene.

"I'd like to buy a gun, Miss Chaney. I'd quite forgotten about that purchase for myself."

Her eyes widened. "Oh, I'll get Papa. He doesn't allow me to touch them."

Daman watched her summon Mr. Chaney from the back. The man parted a curtain and ambled over to him and Daman immediately saw he was an older, male version of the young girl. He had the same plain, broad face but like his daughter, his eyes shone with kindness.

"Lydia says you need a gun. Says you're an Englishman who's bought out the store."

"I am indeed. Here on business. I thought I might need a gun. For protection, you know."

The store owner looked him over. "Ever shot a gun before?"

Daman gave him a disdainful look. "Of course, my good man. Every English lad is raised to hunt, ride, and shoot."

He hoped his answer satisfied Mr. Chaney. Only Daman knew the lie in it. True, all gentlemen did learn these things. Except for Daman Rutledge. He might be the only exception in all of England.

It definitely caused a rift between him and his father. The earl was country through and through and lived for his horses and the hunt. Daman began life afraid of horses. He had made a poor rider. And he gagged at the sight of blood. Given a choice between fox hunting and being stretched upon a medieval rack, he'd choose the rack every time.

His father beat him, harangued him, and publicly humiliated him. Nothing changed Daman's mind. He thought it sickening that grown men would send their hounds to chase an innocent fox, all in the name of sport.

Eventually, his half-brother, Thomas, worked with him, teaching Daman to be a passable rider. He would never be a lover of horses but at least he proved competent in the saddle. After all, he had managed to ride from Texas to Kansas, no mean feat. Not that he'd enjoyed the lengthy trip, only tolerated it at best, since Edward needed him in America.

He could shoot. A little. At least he knew how to

load a gun. If pressed to hit a target, he probably wouldn't come close. Still, with Serena's dire situation, Daman believed he needed the threat of a gun at the very least.

He only hoped he never had to use it.

Chaney pulled some guns from a display case and set them on the counter. Daman inspected them, not knowing any of their names. Chaney rattled off a few facts that meant nothing to Daman as he handled several that were for sale.

Then one caught his eye. "What's this, Mr. Chaney?"

The man smiled affectionately and picked up the gun Daman indicated, stroking it lovingly as if it were a woman.

"That, sir, is a Colt Peacemaker. Has more firepower and less misfire than anything on the market. This here's a forty-five, single-action six-shooter. Seven and a half inches long with a nice walnut stock. I have one with nickel plating in the back but that costs extra."

Daman handled the weapon. Even he could admire the gun's craftsmanship. "It's range?"

"A hundred yards. And if it runs out of bullets, just pistol whip someone with it." Chaney cocked an eyebrow. "You know what they say, don't you?"

"I haven't a clue," Daman admitted.

Chaney leaned in, his voice dropping low. "God created man. Colonel Colt made them equal." He laughed heartily.

Daman nodded. "I'll take the Peacemaker and a box of ammunition with it, please."

"Good choice. Will you need a holster?"

Daman didn't want to wear one. He didn't want to

display that he had a gun. It was simply insurance down the line.

"No. I have one that is quite serviceable. Thanks all the same. "

He paid Chaney and slipped the gun into an inner pocket of his suit coat, walking out as the proud owner of a Colt .45 Once again, he hoped no one ever challenged him to use it. He couldn't guarantee the outcome if they did.

Daman eagerly headed back to the hotel. Something about Serena Sullivan drew him like Circe's siren song. Those amber eyes, which seemed to hold secrets she'd never shared with anyone, nagged at him. Daman thought he could get them from her. In bed. No woman ever resisted him there. He would love to see Miss Sullivan sprawled naked across his chest, her raven tresses silky between them.

Daman laughed aloud. Here he was, attracted to a schoolmarm. A woman who had killed a man.

It didn't matter. He had pledged his help to her. From what he gleaned from the other women who spoke before his rescue attempt, the man Serena had killed had made untoward advances not only to her but any female in a skirt.

Yet there seemed more to the story. Daman believed he'd get it from her.

In or out of bed.

As he reached the hotel, he realized his borrowed buckboard still sat in front. Daman gazed up at the setting sun and thought he better return it to its rightful owner. He was far later than he had anticipated in its return so he planned to tack on a bonus to satisfy the blacksmith.

Twenty minutes later, Daman walked back to the Alamar, the cart returned. He was hungry and tired.

Walking into the lobby, he wondered what type of food could be sent up to their suite.

Before he reached the desk, he stopped dead in his tracks.

Sheriff Parker stood in his way.

9

Daman's heart pounded so rapidly, he thought he might expire right there on the dark paneled floor of the Alamar Hotel. Terror seized him, rooting him to the spot. He had only experienced such fear once, years ago when he found Cynthia's broken body. He had suddenly realized she made good on her threats as she breathed her last breath. As a child he'd panicked, running from the house, his voice locked away, his lips moving silently. Only when he reached his beloved lake had his anguished cry filled the air.

Daman steeled himself. He was an adult now. No situation was beyond his grasp. Panic be damned. Rationally, the wheels in his head began to turn creakily again, frozen no longer. He had pushed the sheriff from the platform, blindsiding the lawmen, who toppled into the melee headfirst.

Daman had only been on the scaffold a few seconds, most of that with his back to the crowd as he cut Serena down. Then he had whipped her over his left shoulder, her body blocking his face from the crowd as he'd run like a madman.

Surely, this sheriff couldn't identify him as the man who'd freed Serena Sullivan. Daman had brilliantly thought to change his clothes, as well. It was reasonable to assume the lawmen wouldn't know him from Adam in the Garden of Eden.

At least he hoped so.

Putting on a bland expression, Daman strolled to greet the desk clerk, completely ignoring the fact that Sheriff Parker was conversing with the man. *Let him think me an arrogant Brit.*

"Good evening, Sam," Daman said, turning on his smooth charm. "I'd like to order up a bath and dinner for two to follow, around seven o'clock. You decide on the menu items. I've had quite a day, so I'll simply trust your good judgment. Have my packages arrived?"

"Not yet, Mr. Rutledge." The clerk then waved.

Daman turned and saw two men carrying in his bundled order from Chaney's.

"Ah, those must be for me. Rutledge?" he inquired.

The larger of the two men spoke up. "Yes, sir, Mr. Rutledge. Mr. Chaney said take good care of you. What room you in? We'll bring it up."

"I'll direct you. My cousin was napping when I left so we'll probably leave them outside the door."

Daman turned to leave, taking a half dozen steps before he heard, "Mr. Rutledge, is it?"

He turned, eyebrows arched. "And you would be?" he asked haughtily.

"Sheriff Bud Parker. Crombar Creek." The lawmen's eyes narrowed as he studied Daman.

Daman held his ground, allowing the silence to lengthen. One of the delivery men cleared his throat but nothing was said for a good half-minute.

Finally, Parker broke the void. "I'm looking for a gal."

"Aren't we all?" Daman quipped. "Mother thinks she has the perfect one for me back in London but as you Americans would say, I haven't quite sown all my wild oats yet. I don't plan on settling down for a bit."

Parker frowned. "This gal's an outlaw. A dangerous outlaw. Killed a man. One of the Creek's most outstanding citizens and my closest friend."

Daman shuddered. "A murderess on the loose? It's a good thing you're on her trail then, sir. I hope she will be apprehended within the hour."

Parker eyed him with interest. "She's supposed to be on a train bound for Cheyenne, best we can tell. I'll know soon enough. In the meantime, I'm just checking around town, seeing if anybody's seen her. Asking questions. You're a stranger here, you know."

Daman laughed. "You think a citizen of the British Empire would have stumbled onto this outlaw along the streets of Abilene?"

He turned to the hotel clerk. "Sam? Is this man actually serious?" He looked back at Parker. "It was difficult enough to walk down the streets of this rambunctious cattle town without being accosted in the chaos. Now, I'm on trial simply because I am a visitor to your country?"

"Oh, I'm sure Sheriff Parker only meant to ask for help," Sam gobbled nervously. "No offense intended, Mr. Rutledge."

Daman stared into Parker's beady eyes. "If this is the reception you give to out-of-town guest, then Abilene is much less accommodating than I first thought."

Parker began to backpedal. "I wasn't accusing you of anything, Mr. Rutledge. Just fishing for information."

Daman looked at him disdainfully. "Well, it certainly sounded accusatory to me. I'm not the only stranger in town. Abilene is full of them."

Parker shifted uncomfortably from one foot and

back to the other. "It's just she's a vicious cutthroat. Killed Charles Rayburn in cold blood, she did. She got away from her hanging today. I'm just trying to bring the witch to justice."

"Hanging? You hang women? How barbaric. Of course, having lost the Mother Country's good influence a hundred years ago . . . never mind." Daman shook his head. "Rest assured, Sheriff, I have neither seen nor want to see this woman. If the rest of the west is like this, my advice to my brother and my countrymen will be to invest in a more civilized society."

He turned again, hoping the two men from Chaney's would follow without question. Daman walked nonchalantly up the stairs though he found himself weak-kneed by the time he reached the landing and turned.

He could hear the sheriff's voice float up. "Damned uppity foreigners. Glad we cut 'em loose. We're better off without their snooty attitude. Keep me posted, Sam. Report any strange women you see directly to me."

A cold lump formed in Daman's throat as he walked the rest of the way to his room. He could hear the two men from Chaney's shuffling behind him. Daman paused in front of the door, not wanting to use their prearranged code and have Serena open the door with these two standing here. He wanted as few as possible to see her, especially now that he knew how Parker still searched for Serena here in Abilene.

"Please rest the packages against the wall, gentlemen," he said quietly. "My cousin will not appreciate us interrupting the chance to nap."

The smaller man nodded in agreement as he began setting items on the floor. "My father was the same way, Mr. Rutledge. I didn't dare wake him as a child, else he'd knock my block off. I'm even a bit that way myself before my morning coffee."

Daman listened to the chitchat as they finished and then tipped the pair handsomely. He waited until their steps retreated before tapping on the door as they had decided. Serena cracked open the door a slit.

He could see the relief on her face as she opened it wider. He decided he wouldn't tell her about the sheriff being downstairs in the lobby. She had enough to worry about without thinking Parker could be standing outside their door.

"My purchased items arrived," he told her as he began bringing in the wrapped bundles, depositing them on one end of the sofa and the table sitting in front of it. Daman proceeded to give Serena updates on buying the tickets and his visit to Chaney's general store.

She began untying the strings and going through the parcels, her eyes wide with amazement. "Why did you buy so much? How will I carry all of it?"

Daman produced the valise. "See, I thought of everything. Besides, you do look like a ragamuffin. We need you properly dressed to travel to Denver. The sheriff would never think to look at a woman in suitable attire. He must believe you boarded the train for Cheyenne dressed as you were for your hanging."

As Serena continued opening the packages and exclaiming at all he had bought, Daman left out mentioning the gun hidden away. He figured she'd notice it soon enough but the thought of it might make her nervous now. He chuckled. He should be the nervous one, in close quarters with a killer.

Still, as he watched Serena fingering some of her new possessions, doubt flickered in his mind. He hadn't known her all that long but Serena Sullivan seemed to be a fine woman, intelligent, possessed of good character and manners. He didn't believe Sheriff Parker's story of her murdering a man in cold blood, especially after what the other women had revealed about Charles Rayburn before the hanging.

Daman wanted to ask her about what had happened with Rayburn. He decided it best to walk gingerly around that subject for the moment. Besides, anyone deemed a close friend of the sheriff didn't rate high in Daman's book of reputable characters.

"I owe you so much Mr. Rutledge. I'm afraid you were generous to a fault. I've never owned so many clothes." She looked scared and overwhelmed. "I'm afraid it will take me quite a long while to pay you back."

"Don't think a thing of it. Besides, we'll do much better for you in Denver." He stood. "Here, let's take these things into your bedroom. You can set out what you'll need for tomorrow and pack the rest."

Serena helped him make several trips into the bedroom. "Seriously, I don't need another thing. I'm accustomed to a simple life. A teacher makes little income. As long as I have two serviceable outfits, I need nothing else."

Daman smiled. "Not even a few books? I'm sure you possessed a few personal things beyond your clothes."

Serena sighed. "I did own a couple of books. No more beyond that. I travel quite a bit from one position to the next. It pays to pack lightly. Less trouble that way."

A sudden knock startled her. Daman watched panic dawn in her eyes.

He laid a hand on her shoulder. "It's just the bath I ordered. Go into the bedroom and close the door."

Daman answered the door and directed where the tub should be placed and watched as several buckets of water were dumped into it by a flurry of hotel servants. The last left towels and scented soap with him. He thanked her and closed the door, locking it behind him.

Daman went to the bedroom door and knocked lightly. "They are gone."

Serena opened the door. She had several items in her arms and laid them out on the table next to the bath. Then she looked at him expectantly.

Daman nodded. "I suppose this would be my cue to exit the stage?"

Serena flushed prettily. "I would be most grateful if you did." She looked longingly at the steaming water.

"Then I will entrust these to you." He handed over the soap and towel and moved to the bedroom door. "I shall bide my time in here unless you'd like me to stay and scrub your back?"

"I believe I can handle things from here."

Serena watched Daman close the bedroom door and then turned back to the hot bath. Lord, it had been forever and a day since she had this luxury. Spit baths in jail would never compare. She quickly doffed her dusty clothes and slipped into the tub. A sigh of pure pleasure escaped her lips as the water enveloped her.

She lathered up the scented bar and first washed her long hair, letting it hang outside the tub as she scrubbed clean the rest of her body. While she did, she wondered about Daman Rutledge. She still was uncertain why she instinctively trusted him. He was at times flippant and still a stranger but she would not be alive except for his brave and unselfish actions.

She decided to think about it later as she sank into

the water. Soon, it would grow tepid but for now she would simply luxuriate in the water's remaining warmth. While she enjoyed soaking in the bath, her thoughts turned to their kisses in the alley. She found herself growing warm as she remembered the passion between them. She had never wanted a man's touch again, not after the von Wormers' abuse, but Daman Rutledge was quite a different story. She could feel his hand on her breast, his mouth insistent on hers.

Then a loud pounding sounded at the door.

10

Daman sprang to his feet at the loud rap, knowing he'd need to respond to it. He'd been careful not to refer to his cousin as female and wanted that information to remain private until they left on tomorrow's stage. Especially with Sheriff Parker in town.

Dread filled him. What if Parker were at the door now?

He stepped into the front room of the suite, his eyes drawn to Serena in her bath. She reached for both towels the maid had provided and was struggling to drape them over the tub. Tantalizing bits of milky flesh, coupled with the dark, wet locks streaming down her back and into the water, made his mouth go dry.

Yet he couldn't help but chuckle at the comical situation and the panicked look on her face.

"You look like a fox trapped by the hounds, Cousin," he whispered. He gave her a wink as he stepped to the door and turned away, giving her what privacy he could manage.

"Yes?"

"Mr. Rutledge? It's Sam."

Daman relaxed at the sound of the desk clerk's voice and opened the door a crack.

The friendly clerk fidgeted in the hall, rocking from side to side. "I know you said go ahead and order for you but some people are plain picky. Thought I'd ask your preferences before I had the meal sent up. Beef or ham?"

Daman smiled at Sam's eagerness to please. "Both."

The hotel clerk frowned. "Don't you want to consult with your cousin?"

"No need to do so, Sam. I am hungry enough to eat anything leftover."

"What about vegetables?"

"It doesn't matter. Please use your discretion. When in doubt, send it anyway."

Sam chuckled. "I'll be sure dessert is included. I've got a sweet tooth myself and I always say you can't go wrong with dessert. Or two."

Daman thought a moment. Though he wouldn't partake of any, he thought it might be nice to surprise Serena with wine. "Wine would be nice. Do you have any available?"

"I can rustle some up. Be back soon, Mr. Rutledge."

The clerk's steps receded and Daman closed the door, locking it for good measure. He turned and saw Serena's face and throat were flushed scarlet. The towels had collapsed and were now molded to the curve of her breasts. She squeezed her eyes shut as she clutched the towel to her.

"Relax, Miss Sullivan. Our enterprising desk clerk has vacated the hall."

She nodded furiously, her eyes still closed, her lips pursed much as the schoolmarm she was.

"I'm going back to the other room now. I would dress soon if I were you since our meal should be forthcoming."

Serena's head bobbed again. Daman stifled a laugh in respect for her tattered pride and returned to the bedroom. He closed the door noisily so she would know she was now alone. He sat on the bed, his heart racing. Many women had tempted him over the years and he had always given in to that temptation. Yet none had affected him as the shapely American schoolteacher sitting naked in the next room.

Daman hoped she realized what a gentleman he truly was. At this moment, he wished he were anything but one.

~

THEY SAT over what surprisingly was a splendid dinner. Serena remained in the bedroom while the meal was delivered and the bathing tub removed and now sat opposite Daman in one of the outfits he'd purchased at Chaney's. The blouse was a bit prim for his taste but the skirt showed off her small waist to perfection. She had left her raven hair loose in order to dry and it now fell about her in soft waves.

Her skin glowed in the candlelight but what stood out were those large, tawny eyes. He had never seen eyes so amber. Twice now, he had to fight to listen to what Serena said instead of remaining lost in their beauty.

"I know you're a playwright or at least you used to be one. What is the London theater like?"

Daman sniffed. "Most of it is bloody melodramas. Some Shakespeare. The *ton* all have their boxes and attending plays can become quite the social event during the Season."

"The Season? What's that?"

Daman thought a moment. How to explain the Season? "It's like a horse auction, I suppose. Young ladies barely out of the schoolroom are paraded about in their finery at balls and teas and such, while young gentleman look them over and decide which one they wish to make an alliance with."

"You mean marriage."

Daman nodded. "Yes, quite. Looks only play a part of it. Like horses, one must consider the breeding. Who are the young lady's parents? How prestigious a title does her father hold? What kind of dowry will she bring to the marriage? It's all a fine dance of flirtation, speculation, and negotiation. When the season is over, a flurry of weddings begins in earnest, pairing off the most eligible."

Serena regarded him with a slight frown. "Which young lady did you choose in the Season?"

Daman laughed. "I never did. Men usually sow a few wild oats. Then, in their mid-to-late twenties, they begin looking in earnest for the right match. I've reached the correct age but I do not have what a young lady's mama looks for."

Her frown deepened. "And what is that?"

"Mainly a showy title and the money and estates that go along with it. You see, Miss Sullivan, besides being a little disreputable, having entered the theater, I also am a third son."

She looked at him blankly.

"It's quite different here in America, I suppose. In England, the oldest son inherits everything from his father—the land, the title, the wealth. Everything went to my half-brother, Edward. A second is destined for the military. That would be my other half-brother, Thomas, who recently passed away."

Daman paused, sadness washing over him. "And the third son is destined to join the Church. Having no inclination to do so, I chose the sordid life of the theater."

He saw the concern on her face. "Don't worry. I liked it while I did it. For a member of the *ton* to be something as scandalous as a playwright brought a bit of novelty to my appearances at social events. It wasn't as if I were an actor, though. Performers are not well thought of in the proper circles, you see. That never would have been tolerated by Polite Society."

Daman took a breath. "But since Thomas recently passed away, I am now helping my older brother with the family estates and business. At least for now."

"I'm sorry for your loss, especially if you were close to Thomas." Serena's eyes were large in her face. "Do you have any other family?"

A tightness formed in Daman's chest, as it always did when he thought of his sister. "I did have an older sister who raised me after my mother's death. She passed on many years ago. What about you? Any family to speak of?"

Serena's jaw tightened. Daman could see her body tensing. "No. My parents are dead. They . . . were homesteaders." He saw her lips tremble. "How did you get the ideas for your plays?"

He wondered what in her past made her upset but decided not to press her about the rapid change of topic.

"Oh, I've been a scribbler since I was young. Short stories, bad poetry, a few novels. But I always liked plays. Reading them, at any rate. The concise language that must be chosen to convey the most impact."

She nodded, her gaze pinned to his face.

"A playwright only has an audience for two hours," Daman continued. "He must make them really know and then care for his characters in a short amount of time. He must place the audience in situations at the height of their emotions. I gravitated to the challenge of it all."

A dreamy look crossed Serena's face. "What is it like to hear lines you've written coming from someone else?"

Daman grew thoughtful. "It's funny because I had very little say about things once I sold the rights to my work. The producer, the director, the backers of the production? They all were more important than I, the writer, was."

He smiled. "But when my play was well cast, I must say it can be quite splendid hearing your words spoken aloud to a hushed audience."

Daman paused. "An actress in two of my three productions had a real grasp of the beauty of language. She possessed impeccable delivery and timing. She acted as much with her body and facial expressions as she did with what I had written. She was amazing."

He shrugged, locking thoughts of Daphne away. "That time in my life is over, however. Nothing seems to inspire me. Although I think I could crank out something of interest after spending a short time here."

Daman reached to a nearby table and held up a dime novel. "I read one while you were at your bath and dressing. Got it at Chaney's General Store."

Serena blushed as he handed it to her, lifting it to her face to cover her embarrassment. "Oh, it's Hurricane Nell, the Queen of the Saddle and Lasso." She lowered the book and met his gaze. "I just love her."

"You've read this one?"

"I've read several dime novels, including ones about Nell. They started about ten years ago. The women are intrepid heroines who can single-handedly thwart outlaws, Indians, and rise to any occasion. My favorites are Mountain Kate and Ben, the Trapper."

Daman leaned forward. "Why do you enjoy them?"

Serena smiled. "Even though the women sometimes resort to violence in defense of themselves or their loved ones, they are still ladies until the end. And every dime novel rewards its reader with a happy ending." She frowned. "Not quite like real life."

She must be thinking about her own life and how it almost ended earlier that day. As far as he knew, she had no family, no friends, and nowhere to turn. He desperately wanted to put a smile back on her face.

Resting a hand atop hers, he said, "Since you are such an expert on dime novels and western life and I am a writer by trade, perhaps we could write one together?"

His gaze held hers for a long moment. The very air crackled between them.

Then Serena broke the tension by reaching for her glass. "The wine is good, don't you think? I've only had it twice before."

Daman reached for the bottle. "Then have some more."

She placed her hand over the stemware. "No, this is enough. I'm not used to it." She wet her lips nervously. "I will take a slice of that cake, though. I've got a weakness for anything chocolate."

Daman set down the bottle, hoping his hand

didn't shake. "Chocolate cake. So, it is dear to you? My favorite dessert is strawberries and cream."

He sliced the generous bit of cake and passed it to her. "I love all sweets, though. Tarts, puddings, cakes, breads. Cook made the most fabulous pumpkin and cinnamon breads when I was a child. Like heaven on earth."

Serena took a bite of the sweet and sighed. "This is very good. I rarely have an opportunity to cook or bake. The families I board with handle all of the meals. I'm usually late getting in, after preparing the next day's lessons and cleaning and repairing things in the schoolhouse."

Daman's jaw dropped. "That is part of . . . your work?"

She nodded. "Yes. Families in the community put up the facility. The teacher is expected to maintain it. I sweep the floor, wash windows, bring in the buffalo chips for fueling the fire. It keeps me busy. By the time I arrive at my housing for the week, I might be given a menial chore, such as peeling potatoes or carrots for the evening meal."

Daman frowned. "What are these buffalo chips?"

He knew all about the chips from the fires Cookie built with them on the cattle trail, but he loved hearing her talk.

Serena laughed. "I'm not sure you want to know, Mr. Rutledge. You may have noticed the Great Plains don't have many trees. Instead of chopping wood for our fires, we use buffalo droppings."

Daman's nose crinkled in disgust. "Surely, you jest?" he asked, hoping she would say more.

"I wish I did."

She fell silent. Daman loved the sound of her

voice, low and throaty. He needed to hear more of it. He wanted this supper to go on forever.

"Tell me about the families you stayed with. Is it difficult moving about so often?"

Serena shuddered. "You are not treated as a guest. Not quite a servant either. And you have absolutely no privacy. The larger the family and the more children they had attending the school, the longer I stayed with them. Unfortunately, that was usually a situation where so many people meant little space was available."

Daman regarded her with awe. "I see we have led quite different lives, Miss Sullivan."

"Yes." Her amber eyes flickered with amusement. Then she pushed back her chair and stood. "I feel I should retire. We have an early start tomorrow."

He came to his feet.

Serena looked at him with sincerity and said, "I can't thank you enough, Mr. Rutledge. If not for you, I would now be dead for a crime I did not commit. I owe you my life."

Daman saw the truth in her eyes. Anger swelled within him, knowing that Sheriff Parker somehow helped frame her for what most likely had been an accident at the least or self-defense at the most. He determined to see Serena Sullivan's name cleared. He had no idea how to accomplish this, especially since she'd been so cryptic, but he felt he owed her that much. What had been done to her was abominable.

As Daman escorted her across the room, the protectiveness he had never felt toward anyone but Cynthia surprised him. At the door, he took her hand and raised it to his lips for a tender kiss.

"I wouldn't want you dead when I've enjoyed your company so much this evening, Miss Sullivan."

His tone was light but he knew a fire burned within him. For her. He wanted this woman with a passion that frightened him. Daman had chosen to be dead to the world around him since Daphne left.

And now a Yankee schoolmarm had brought him back to life.

11

Serena awakened early, never having had the luxury of being a lady of leisure. Rising early had been in her blood since childhood. She slipped from the bed and dressed in a dark blouse and skirt, courtesy of Daman Rutledge. She ran the new brush through her long tresses and then secured them with the pins he'd thoughtfully purchased. Last, she fastened her gold locket around her neck, rubbing a thumb along its filigree. It was the last link she had with Bill and she wore it every day.

She made the bed and tidied the room before placing the dark black hat on her head. It seemed the Englishman had thought of everything. She wondered about the love he had lost and how it drove him from the world of writing to what surely must be for him the rough and tumble American West.

She studied her image in the mirror. Even in the faint light, she could see the bruise on her cheek stood out against her pale skin. She wished she could cover it somehow.

That made her blush at the thought of the pot of rouge included in the many things Daman had purchased for her. Serena knew it was more common now for women to use rouge on their cheeks or lips, but as a teacher, she had always thought it unbecoming for her to try a cosmetic.

Still, it gave her a small thrill to know she possessed something of that nature. Daman proved far too generous in what he bought yesterday. She had no idea how she would begin to repay him.

She glanced at the valise and made a quick decision. She didn't want to seem ungrateful so she slipped her hand inside and retrieved the rouge. It wouldn't hurt to try a bit on her lips. Serena dipped the tip of her finger into to the pot and brushed a small bit of color across her lips.

A knock on the door made her blood freeze. She had dreamed of Bud Parker last night, barging in and dragging her from the hotel bed to an awaiting scaffold. She awakened in a cold sweat, shivering with fear. It took a while to calm her heart and fall asleep again.

Serena heard Daman's low murmur coming through the door, asking if she were awake. "It's safe to come out, Cousin Serena."

She quickly closed the rouge pot and slipped it into her pocket, smiling at his use of their supposed relationship. Serena opened the door and smelled the aroma of coffee. She saw biscuits stacked high on a plate with a bowl of gravy next to it. Other plates held sausages and eggs. Her stomach rumbled in delight.

"I took the liberty of going downstairs and asking for some breakfast before we left on our journey," Daman said when he saw her standing in the bedroom doorway.

They ate quickly, going over last minute items again.

"They say the Devil is in the details so let's have at it," Serena told him.

Daman swallowed a bite of sausage before continuing. "Remember your fiancé, Robert, was killed a week ago. We don't have to say how. As soon as people hear it was three days before your wedding, sympathy will blanket you."

He waved his fork for emphasis before stabbing at another piece of sausage. "Sam, the desk clerk, will certainly be curious about you so I want you to lower the veil when we leave this room. Say as little as possible. I'll do all the talking."

He paused, reaching his hand into his pocket and pulling out a handkerchief before plucking something from it. "You need to wear this."

Serena stared at the ring between Daman's fingers. "What? Why?"

"This is your engagement ring. It will help add credence to our story."

"I've . . . I've . . . well, I've never seen anything so lovely," she stammered. "I couldn't possibly—"

"You can and will." He took her left hand and slipped the ring onto her finger. "Your gloves will often cover it but it will be nice to have it to display on occasion if we need to trot it out."

"Where on earth did you get it? No general store would carry something so valuable."

Daman waved away her question. "Never mind that. Just drink up your coffee. It's almost time for us to depart."

He bit into a fresh biscuit, savoring the flakiness. Westerners did know how to make their biscuits. Even Cookie on the cattle drive could turn out one to rival any bread Daman had eaten in England.

Serena excused herself to find and attach the veil

to her hat. Daman chewed thoughtfully, wondering what Serena would say if she knew the ring belonged to his former mistress. He had retrieved the sapphire before Daphne left for Italy, with her corpulent count, along with every other piece of jewelry he had purchased for his muse.

She asked him to do so, explaining how it didn't seem right to go to one man adorned with another's precious gems. Daman protested strenuously but Daphne prevailed in the end. She fondly fingered the sapphire before removing it from her finger and placing it into her lover's palm. Daman had closed his fist about it tightly.

"Perhaps one day you will again give it to a woman —along with your heart," she had told him wistfully.

"You will always have my heart, Daphne," he had replied.

Sadly, she'd caressed his cheek. "I wish." She took his hand and pressed a kiss to his knuckles. "Think of me sometimes, Daman, for I will fondly remember you."

Daman kept the ring in his pocket ever since, through the nights of drinking, the voyage to Galveston, on the long drive to Kansas, until now. And he had just given it to another woman, one who stirred his blood even more than his blessed mistress ever had.

Daman figured he must be going mad. If London society judged a stage actress such as Daphne inappropriate for a Rutledge, what would they make of a Yankee schoolmarm who'd escaped from the gallows?

He consulted his pocket watch as Serena entered the room and finished attaching the veil to her hat.

"Ah, you look properly somber, my dear cousin. Let us make haste. It's almost time. The coach will pick us up in front of the Alamar. I did confirm that fact."

Daman retrieved her valise and his own portmanteau and they left the room.

"Carry your gloves in your hand," he instructed her, "so Sam can see your ring and confirm our story to anyone who might ask. If that sheriff comes looking for you, even he would have to realize that a schoolmarm would not possess a sapphire engagement ring, nor would she be related to British nobility."

They descended the stairs. As Daman expected, Sam idly pushed a broom at the bottom of the staircase, ready to investigate the mysterious cousin he hadn't seen before now.

Reaching the lobby, Daman took the bull by its horns. "Good morning, Sam. I must introduce to you Miss Rutledge, my cousin."

"Pleased to meet you, sir," Serena responded quietly.

Daman saw the man's eyes drawn immediately to her ring. Serena must have noticed, too, for she slipped her gloves on to ready herself for travel.

"I'll be outside, Cousin Daman, while you settle your affairs."

Daman set down the bags. "May I see our bill, please?"

The clerk went behind the desk and pulled out a few papers. "All prepared, Mr. Rutledge."

He handed it to Daman, who pretended to study it, waiting for where the conversation would surely lead.

"Lovely young lady, Miss Rutledge."

Daman glanced up. "My uncle's daughter. He was quite the adventurer. Left England and moved to the wilds of America. Married a local. My cousin was their only child."

Daman placed the bill on the desk and removed enough money to cover his stay and allow for a generous tip. He leaned over and lowered his voice.

"I was sent to represent my father's branch of the family at her wedding. A shame, you know." He paused and glanced down, waiting a moment as he fought giving into a smile, knowing Sam would press him for more information.

The clerk didn't disappoint him. "And the wedding?"

Daman met his eyes, shaking his head mournfully. "It never took place. Her fiancé, a banker, died three days before they were to be united in holy matrimony."

Sam gasped. "What a tragedy!"

He nodded in agreement. "I thought it best to remove her from such unpleasant circumstances. I hope I did the right thing."

"I'm certain you did, Mr. Rutledge," Sam said firmly.

Pocketing his copy of the hotel bill, he said, "We're headed to finish up some business for my father and then Cousin Ada will return to London with me."

Sam's eyes widened. "Is that so? Back to London, you say?"

Daman saw him filing away every tidbit, knowing Sam would spread the story like wildfire.

"Yes. Poor girl. Her parents passed away last year. She's been living on a small, fixed income, looking forward to a new life with her Robert."

"A generous man, I'd say," noted Sam.

Daman frowned. "Would you?"

"Well, her ring . . . that's quite a nice jewel."

He shrugged. "Quite nice, I'm sure. But she's never even met her English cousins. I've already cabled my father. He issued a formal invitation for Cousin Ada to come visit. I hope she will remain with us. I have a friend or two of marriageable age who might be interested in a match with her."

Daman winked. "Maybe we'll make an Englishwoman of her yet."

He bent to lift the luggage but Sam scurried from behind the counter. "No, Mr. Rutledge. I'll get those for you."

They stepped outside just as the stagecoach rumbled down the street and pulled up in front of the Alamar. The driver jumped down and Sam handed off the baggage to him to load on top of the vehicle. Sam then turned and hurried quickly to Serena.

"Miss Rutledge? May I express my deepest sympathy for your terrible loss?"

Daman watched Serena bow her head a moment, then lift it. "Thank you, sir. I appreciate your kindness."

Daman took her elbow. "Come, Cousin Ada." He handed her up into the coach and turned back to the clerk.

"A most hospitable place, Sam. I appreciate your every kindness." He tipped his hat, handed the driver their tickets, and climbed into the coach.

Two men already occupied the interior, both wearing long, dark coverings. Serena sat opposite them. Daman sat on the same cushion as Serena, leaving a space between them. Before he could settle himself, the driver opened the door.

"Here's some dusters for you." He handed a black bundle to Daman and slammed the door.

Daman frowned at the cloth. Why on earth would he wish to put on more clothing? It was already hotter than Hades inside the coach.

Serena reached for one and must have read his thoughts. "Believe me when I tell you to put this on. You won't want your fine suit ruined. It's called a duster for a good reason."

Daman remembered how dusty the trail from Texas to Kansas had been and nodded. He helped Serena into her duster and then put on his, as well. As the carriage pulled away from the Alamar and picked up speed, the dust kicked up immediately. He grinned at Serena.

"Hence, the name."

She nodded. "Wait until we leave town and really begin to make time. With the window open, you'll be covered from head to foot in dust." She smiled, a mischievous light coming into her eyes. "As it is, you'll simply wind up with grit in your teeth, Cousin."

The coach stopped three-quarters of a mile down the road for two more male passengers. Daman didn't want a stranger seated next to Serena so he slid over. He caught a whiff of vanilla, much as he had during their delightful dinner last night. If he had to ride in an uncomfortable stagecoach, at least he had Serena with him to make the trip bearable. He would insist they board a Denver-bound train as soon as he ventured it was safe to do so.

Daman settled back against the thin cushion, glad Abilene was fading into the distance. He hoped they would leave the disreputable Sheriff Parker far behind. He closed his eyes, a smile curling at the corner of his mouth.

He was ready to begin his adventure with the lovely Serena Sullivan.

12

Daman's mood could not have been worse. His head ached monstrously. His body no longer seemed human, having been jostled to the point where his innards must be a mass of quivering jelly. He sensed the carriage slowing and prayed it would stop in order for him to take a deep breath.

Minus inhaling the damned dust.

He wondered if they had passed a regular stage-coach on the post coach line. They rode in what the ticket agent termed the express coach. At the rate that currently made, by the time they reach Denver, his insides would be mincemeat and his brain scrambled for good. There'd be nothing left to conduct Edward's business.

The coach eased off the main road onto a side one. Daman spotted a small cabin and an unpainted barn that dwarfed it. Next to it was a large corral. The driver called out something and the team came to a stop. The dust swirled a moment and then hung in the air.

Daman heard the driver shout, "All out. Be quick about it."

Sweeter words had never been spoken. The last two times the coach stopped to switch teams, the process took only a couple of minutes at best, and the coachman hadn't allowed his passengers to step outside the confined compartment.

A man sitting next to the door reached over and turned the latch. He pushed hard against the door and it opened. It became a contest to see which traveler could get out the fastest. Daman jumped to the ground, his balance a bit wobbly, and reached out his hand to Serena.

The minute she touched the ground, Daman turned away and gulped a deep breath of the still, sweet air. He unbuttoned the duster and fanned it opened and closed in the searing summer heat.

Serena's eyes twinkled. "Watch," she said and cocked her head toward the horses.

Daman looked as the driver unhitched the team. Moving as one, without a command, they headed toward the stable. A man emerged from the hovel and followed after them. The team waited patiently as he opened the door for them and the horses disappeared inside.

"That is almost human," Daman proclaimed. I've never seen anything like it."

"It gets more intriguing," Serena promised. "But let's find something to drink. I'm parched."

They followed their fellow passengers, heading to the small house. A woman appeared and waved the group inside.

"Water and fried cherry pies," she proclaimed. "Or coffee if you want it."

Daman's stomach grumbled in reply as they entered the building.

"This will be a quick stop," she told him. "The driver wants his refreshments as badly as we do but he'll also need to stay on schedule. That means we'll leave promptly."

He asked, "How far have we traveled?"

Serena thought a moment. "The express usually stops every twelve to fifteen miles to switch horses. Then a longer stop such as this occurs after forty to fifty miles."

She took a tin cup the woman offered with one hand and a plate of pie with the other. Daman did the same. He looked around at the primitive shack. A small table contained two chairs that he doubted would hold the weight of a child.

He spotted a few hooks on the wall that held winter coats. No other clothing was in sight. Judging by what he had seen, the station's occupants wore the only clothes they possessed. He glanced about and saw three shelves which held cups, along with a few bowls and plates. Several rifles rested against the wall.

Serena said, "We make about eight miles an hour and it's after noon, judging by the sun. I'd say we've come forty miles so far."

She bent to rest her cup on the ground and began working on the pie.

"They've changed horses at each stop?" Daman asked.

"Yes. Since this is the express coach, it's a requirement. A fresh team is put into place frequently. Eat up. We probably won't be offered anything more until we stop for the night. At the remaining stops, they'll simply change the horses and move on."

Daman finished the pie in three bites and his water in a single, long swallow. The others were already starting to move back outside. He waited for Serena to finish and then escorted her to the stagecoach.

As they buttoned their dusters again, a new team emerged from the barn. No human led them. The horses walked straight to the coach and moved into place to be harnessed.

"That's uncanny."

Serena smiled at him. "Told you so. They do it so often, they don't need direction." She sighed. "I've often wished I could train my pupils as easily."

The travelers began boarding the vehicle. Daman's mood soured again. The noise made it impossible to carry on a conversation and they had no privacy in the small compartment.

He waited until the other passengers were inside the carriage and pulled Serena aside, facing away from the coach. He leaned close and whispered, "When can we travel by train?"

"That bad?" Serena chuckled. "I believe we threw Sheriff Parker off with our charade. I doubt Sam would think me a poor schoolmarm, much less an escaped murderess."

She gazed at Daman with pity. He recognized the look from the ones Mose gave him on the trail to Abilene.

"I would think as soon as we arrive in a city with a rail station, transferring to the train would be possible."

He looked her squarely in the eye. "That can't be soon enough."

With his words, they joined the others inside the coach. Just as they seated themselves, the driver called out to the horses and Daman's neck slammed against the hard cushion. He gave up further conversation and settled in for the duration, eyes closed.

Maybe if he were lucky, he would dream about walking along a country lane. No cart, no horse. Just his own two legs and the English countryside to admire.

A loud noise startled him. Daman's eyes snapped open. The man across from him wore a panicked look. Daman turned to Serena as the coach stopped, jolting the passengers from their seats. He pitched forward onto his knees. At least two others fell on top of him.

Quickly, everyone scrambled into their seats again. Daman looked questioningly at Serena.

"A robbery," she whispered. Her voice remained calm but Daman saw her mouth quiver slightly.

He reached and took her hand. She threw it off and slipped the gloves from her hand, quickly removing the sapphire ring and pocketing it. The gloves flew back on and this time it was Serena who took Daman's hand.

It touched him that she would try to protect the ring. He gave her fingers a squeeze.

"Git out!"

The door flew open from the outside and the passengers reluctantly filed from the protection of the stagecoach. Daman turned to wait for Serena but was roughly pushed aside. He started to lunge at his attacker but halted the instant he saw the rifle between them.

As the last one to leave the carriage, Serena paused at the top, seeing the robber aim his gun at Daman. She jumped down quickly and stepped between the barrel's end and Daman and nudged him away. As she pressed against him, she felt the gun in his right pocket. It surprised her. Daman took her hand again.

She saw an armed man on foot and another still on his horse. Both had their bandanas pulled up to disguise their identities. That meant they expected to leave the passengers alive—if no trouble broke out. A fast glance around the flatland told her only these two were involved in the robbery.

Unless one of the passengers was in on their game. The robber next to them motioned the six passengers with his rifle and they all stood away from the carriage in a huddled group.

The one on horseback hollered to the driver, "Throw down the boot."

Serena knew any valuable cargo would be in an enclosed compartment under the driver, from a payroll to gold bars. She wondered if it held anything or not. She supposed they were about to find out.

The driver stood, his hands held away from his body. "Nothing there, Mister. I ain't got no payroll this run."

The thief snorted in disdain. "Not what I've heard. Git down from there."

The driver squatted as if to jump down. The man on foot came and stood close by and the driver's foot shot out and kicked the man's rifle hand hard. The weapon went flying, landing a few feet from Serena, while the driver fell on top of the startled bandit.

With a cool head, the horseman turned and fired on the driver twice, pumping two bullets directly into his back. He remained motionless. So did the man underneath him.

"You." The thief motioned to Daman. "Climb up there and throw down the boot. Don't try anything or I'll shoot your pretty lady's head off."

Serena stiffened. She knew from the man's deadpanned tone he wouldn't hesitate to do so. She glanced out of the corner of her eye at the nearby gun lying on the ground, itching to pick it up.

"Certainly, I'll oblige you," Daman told the thief.

He climbed into the driver's seat and looked around, frowning as he did so. "Exactly what does this boot look like? Where might it be located?"

The brigand and spit into the dust. "It's a lock box, you British bastard. Pull up the driver's seat. It will be under there."

"Oh, right." Daman did as instructed, lifting the seat. "I see it. Where would you like this, sir?"

"Down on the ground. Throw it. You won't hurt it."

Daman lifted it. "It's quite heavy. I doubt you'll be able to carry it on your horse." He dropped the strongbox next to the horses.

"Git back down. Now," commanded the remaining thief.

Daman followed the directions and returned to Serena's side. Her gloved fingers sought his, gripping them tightly.

"No. Come back over here." The gunman looked at Daman.

Reluctantly, Serena released his hand. Daman walked to the boot. "How may I accommodate you now, sir?" he asked politely.

The robber snickered. "Git the key from the driver's pocket and open up the boot."

Daman went to the dead body, the tan shirt stained dark with blood. He dug through the man's pockets with his head slightly averted until he found the key and returned to the chest on the ground.

As he did so, the horseman looked back at the passengers. "Stan, collect their valuables, would you?"

A hand latched on to her wrist. "I'll take that purdy ring, to start."

Serena stared up into the amused eyes of the man who had ridden directly across from her the entire way from Abilene. She had caught him ogling her despite the hat pulled low on his face and was grateful that Daman kept his eyes closed for most of the trip. She couldn't guarantee what would have happened if Daman had seen it.

The man jammed his hand into her pocket, his body brushing intimately against hers. A wave of revulsion rippled through Serena, as it always seemed to when a man touched her.

Except for Daman. He was the lone exception in fifteen years.

Serena swallowed the rising bile as the man pulled out the sapphire and held it up between his fingers.

"This here is worth the entire trip, don't you think?"

The horseman grunted but Serena could see he seemed pleased. She looked back as Daman now had the lock box open. She could see the light glinting off and assumed either gold or silver rested inside it.

The thief named Stan called out, "Alrighty. Everyone empty your pockets." He jerked at Serena's brand new reticule and yanked it from her wrist. Opening the drawstring, he said, "Drop your goodies in here, folks. And no holding out on me."

The remaining passengers removed their valuables, from money clips to pocket watches, and dropped them into the reticule as Stan walked down the line. When finished, Stan returned to where he started.

"Hey, what about that?" he asked and pointed at her chest.

Serena looked down and saw what he wanted. "Not my locket." Her words came out in an anguished whisper.

Stan laughed. "Damned right." He ripped the locket from her before dropping it inside the reticule.

Anger boiled inside her. Everything had been taken from her. Her parents. Her brother. Her very childhood innocence. The locket remained her only link with the past. With Bill.

No guttersnipe would walk away with it scot-free.

Serena watched Stan begin to move toward his partner. She eyed the rifle of the dead gunman still lying on the ground. With a speedy movement, she took a single step in its direction and swept it up, jamming it into Stan's back.

"Move," she ordered, her voice low and threatening. She poked the gun hard to drive her point home.

Serena glanced and saw Daman still kneeling next to the strong box. The horseman had dismounted and was inspecting the find, his back to her. He turned as Serena approached with Stan. Daman locked eyes with her and nodded.

"Why, the pretty lady—"

"—will use this Winchester to shoot your partner in the back if you don't—"

But Serena had no need to complete her sentence. While she distracted the robber momentarily, Daman lifted one of the gold bricks from safekeeping slammed it down hard on the gunman's head. The robber crumpled into a heap on the ground.

Daman smiled winningly at the astonished bystanders. "Any of you chaps have a piece of rope or something to bind our prisoners?"

13

B ud Parker sat in the noisy bar, nursing the whiskey. Late afternoon sunlight poured through the saloon's door, bathing his table in a warm glow. A bitter taste lingered in his mouth, one that no whisky could wash out.

Serena Sullivan was in the wind. Everywhere he turned had been a dead end.

He sipped on the amber liquid, letting it trickle down his throat, the burning sensation trailing after. He'd have sworn on his own mama's grave that Serena Sullivan took the Cheyenne train from Abilene. The woman in question easily matched her description. And in a cow town where few women set foot, few could hold a candle to her beauty.

Parker knew with certainty that the trollop had bought a ticket to Cheyenne, simply from the drool practically oozing from the window clerk when Parker gave her description. That alone would have convinced him but two other witnesses in the rail station also saw her in the lobby and on the platform, boarding the train just as it pulled out of the station.

He immediately wired ahead and the authorities

boarded the train at the first scheduled stop. They fanned out both around the train and inside but their search proved futile. No stops occurred before. The only way Serena Sullivan could have left the train was if she sprouted wings and flew away

Parker wouldn't put it past the raven-haired witch. It was how he always thought of her. The Witch. The enticing body, the mouth made for sinning, and the unearthly amber eyes. No wonder Charles Rayburn lost his head over her, despite her prim and proper outward appearance and manners.

Dead. It was hard to think of Charles that way. They had been friends since knee britches. Had shared poker games. Bottles. Whores. All the good memories.

Now, The Witch had vanished into thin air and Parker couldn't accept that fact. He would find her if he had to search to South America and back just to bring the little bitch to justice.

Besides, the same disease infected him as had Charles. He needed a taste of her mouth and her cunt.

Then he'd kill her. Slow and nasty. And enjoy every moment of her suffering.

He drained the last of his whisky as his eyes roamed the smoky saloon. All his volunteer posse went home late last night. They'd searched high and low after word came that Serena wasn't on the train. Every inch of Abilene combed from head to toe. They came up empty. He'd sent every man home and stayed the night. Got roaring drunk. The rest was a blank.

Now, it was close to five o'clock. Over twenty-four hours after The Witch should have hanged. And the pounding in his head thundered on. What could he have missed? Nothing remotely indicated her whereabouts. She had no money, knew no one here, and yet she had fallen off the face of the earth.

Parker glanced at his pocket watch. He would return to Crombar Creek. Defeated. The bitterness and anger welled up in him anew.

"Bud Parker, you old son of a gun."

He glanced up and recognized the face of a big cattle buyer, probably in town to meet the incoming herds. He had met the man through Charles. They had played a few hands of poker together last summer.

"Can I buy you a drink?"

Sampson. That was his name. Parker leaned back in his chair. "Never refused one before. Besides, you owe me after I lost to you last time around."

Sampson chuckled as he signaled the barkeep. "Bottle and another shot glass," he called out over the din and took a seat at Parker's table.

The bartender hustled from behind the counter, bringing the order personally. He poured for Sampson first and then topped off Parker's glass before nodding deferentially and returning to his post.

The two men shot the breeze for a few minutes. "Business good?" asked Parker, not really caring if it was or not.

"Damn right it is. Last two days, I've picked me up the best herds coming in from Texas so far. Fat and sleek, just how I like him. Those Brits must know more than just tea and crumpets."

The comment got Parker's attention. "Brits, you say?"

"Yeah. Them English and Scottish gents are gobbling up land from Texas to Colorado faster than you can spit. They drive a hard bargain but they and the men they hire sure know cattle."

"One of 'em named Rutledge?"

Sampson nodded. "Daman Rutledge sold me the best of the best just yesterday morning. Here on behalf of his brother, some earl, though a trail boss named Jackson did the negotiating." The buyer snickered. "Figured he's the little brother who handles the family business while his lordship stays back on his throne in England and counts his money."

Parker granted. "Tall, good-looking, uppity fellow?"

Sampson looked surprised. "No, didn't seem uppity to me at all. Why? You meet him?"

Parker nodded. "At the Alamar. Said he was staying there with his cousin."

Sampson frowned. "Don't know about him. At least he didn't ride up with the herd from Texas like Rutledge did. Maybe they met up here before going to Denver. Jackson told me Rutledge was heading there next on business."

Parker digested the information. Something didn't add up to him. He emptied his drink and set the glass on the table.

"Good visiting with you, Sampson. Gotta head back to the Creek, though. Thanks again for the whisky. Maybe next time we'll swap stories over some cards."

Parker stood and strode from the bar. He squinted in the bright sunlight as he looked up and down the street.

Then he made his way straight to the Alamar.

He arrived fifteen minutes later, entering the darkened lobby. Immediate relief from the scorching sun caused him to pause a moment as his eyes adjusted to the dimness. The lobby was empty and quiet, a relief after the noisy saloon and loud streets.

Parker stepped to the desk and pinged the bell. A clerk rounded the corner from behind an open door. He recognized him from their encounter yesterday.

"Howdy, Sam."

"Good afternoon, Sheriff. Still looking for that woman criminal?" The clerk winked. "She ain't checked in here yet."

He ignored the attempt at humor. "You remember that English fellow?"

Sam smiled. "Oh, yes. Mr. Rutledge. A true gentleman. And his cousin was simply lovely."

"Lovely?" It sounded like this cousin was a woman.

The clerk frowned and shook his head regretfully. "Miss Ada was simply divine. Tall and with a figure that could stop traffic if you know what I mean. But in mourning. What a tragedy."

Parker narrowed his eyes. "In what way?"

"Her fiancé died just days before their wedding. She is still wearing the most gorgeous sapphire engagement ring to honor his memory. Mr. Rutledge is taking her to Denver on business and then home to London to recover."

"Denver. Is that so?"

The clerk frowned. "Denver was first on their agenda. I put them on the express coach myself this morning."

Parker grunted. It couldn't be Serena Sullivan, even if she vaguely resembled the physical description. What would she be doing with Rutledge, a total stranger, much less sporting an expensive engagement ring?

Still, talk of jewelry spurred his memory. The Witch wore a locket she refused to part with. He had taken every dime off her except for the simple necklace she always fiddled with. If the woman with Rutledge also wore a locket...

Parker decided he couldn't leave the Alamar without asking one more question.

"Did Miss Ada wear any other jewelry?" He hoped his casual tone would not betray the nerves now on edge.

Sam frowned, pondering a moment. Then a flash of recognition on his face had Parker tingling with anticipation.

"Now that you mention it, she did. Although it was nothing fancy, it must have meant a great deal to her. A small gold locket. The way she fingered it, I assumed it, too, was from Robert."

"Robert?"

"Her dead fiancé," the clerk revealed.

Parker nodded. Too much of a coincidence, two similar looking, locket-wearing women, despite the fantastic odds. His gut told him The Witch had worked her magic on the unsuspecting Englishman. How else would he have concocted an elaborate lie and passed her off as his grieving cousin?

He shifted his weight. "I'm looking for a locket for my wife. An anniversary present. What did this one look like? I don't know much about what women want."

Sam thought a moment. "It was oval, gold, some filigree on it. You know, the real delicate etchings. Women love that fancy sort of thing."

Parker cleared his throat. "Well, Sam, thanks for your trouble." He tipped his hat to the clerk. "Better luck next time, I suppose."

He exited the luxury hotel.

The Witch was definitely with the Englishman. He

was sure of it. Every bone in his body sensed it. They were headed to Denver. Same as he was now. He would find her. Use her up.

And then strangle her with his bare hands.

14

S erena watched as Daman helped the remaining passengers roll the dead bodies of their driver and one of the thieves into a tarp. After several awkward attempts, the men lashed the tarp on top of the stagecoach, along with the luggage.

They secured the robbers with strips from her petticoat. The men tossed the two thieves onto the floor of the coach.

Now, the passengers gathered around to discuss what should be done. After a few panicked moments with the men hollering questions about what to do next and who would drive the vehicle, Serena asserted herself. She thought they were acting like a group of whining, unruly children. At least she had experience with how to handle that kind of crowd.

Drawing on her knowledge of geography and transportation lines, she interrupted the confusion.

"We should be close to Ellsworth. That would have been the next stop to change out the team. It's a large enough town and will definitely have a sheriff. We can turn our prisoners over to him."

Her calm, authoritative voice settled down the men and she added, "I'm sure the express will find another driver for those wishing to continue by coach. Ellsworth is also along the southern branch of the Union Pacific. Those who wish to switch to the Kansas Pacific in order to reach Denver could do so then."

Daman flashed her a grateful smile. He also stepped up into the circle that formed as they talked matters over.

"I will volunteer to drive. I would ask that the rest of you ride inside the carriage and guard our prisoners."

Daman glanced at her. "Cousin Ada, if you will relinquish your rifle to one of the other passengers, it can be used to gently persuade the robbers not to attempt any type of escape."

General murmurings let Serena know that everyone was glad that someone had formed a plan and they would soon be on their way. She handed the gun to a capable look man, glad to surrender it.

"Cousin? I would prefer you ride with me," Daman instructed. "If everyone would help load the lock box before we leave, I'm sure the stagecoach company would be pleased with our actions."

"Of course," Serena replied, grateful not to be riding inside the confined carriage for the remaining time.

She watched the travelers lift the box containing the gold back up and Daman secured it in its resting place under the driver's seat. The men began dusting themselves off and climbing into the coach. Serena sensed the relief among them.

Daman came down from the top of the coach and reached over to pick up a pair of gloves from the ground. "The driver's gloves," he told her. "I removed them before we wrapped the bodies. I thought they'd come in handy."

He slipped them on. "Shall we?"

Serena walked to the front of the carriage and looked up to the bench. She laughed. "I have no idea how to get up there."

Daman smiled at her. He scrambled up and reached out his hands to her. "Yes, it is a long way, isn't it? Give me your hands and I'll hoist you up."

Serena braced one foot against the wheel for leverage and held out her hands. Daman gripped them firmly and easily pulled her up to the narrow platform as he took a step back. But his movement threw her off-balance and Serena pitched forward.

Straight into Daman's chest.

"Oh!" she exclaimed, her heart pounding rapidly. His hands tightened on hers as he helped her right herself in the narrow space. Then their gazes locked. Serena's heart skipped a beat before it began wildly hammering in her chest. She feared Daman would hear its thundering beat.

But what she feared most was that he might let her go.

His vivid blue eyes caressed her as much as a physical touch. Serena became lost in their depths, her knees weakening, threatening to collapse.

But Daman was there. She didn't know how it happened but she found his arms suddenly around her, holding her steady, her heart fluttering out of control. She didn't dare breathe else she'd break the spell.

And then he lowered his mouth to hers.

The kiss was tender, achingly sweet, his lips moving against hers, his hands pressing her closer to him. Then she sensed the change. His mouth became more demanding, more possessive, more consuming. A fire ignited inside Serena, burning brightly. She pushed her fingers into his thick chestnut hair, holding on tightly as the world began spinning around her.

A banging from the coach's interior startled her. Serena gasped for air as a voice called out, "Do you know how to drive or not?"

When Daman looked at her again, she trembled. He cupped her face, his gloved thumb running gently across her lower lip slowly. His eyes mesmerized Serena even as she longed for his mouth on hers again. She saw the regret as he dropped his hand and sat on the wooden bench and took the reins in hand.

"Your carriage awaits, Madam."

Serena shakily seated herself, realizing the small bench offered no room between them. Their thighs pressed closely together, as did their shoulders, and Serena took a deep breath and closed her eyes. She felt the flick of the reins and the start of the horses.

What had just happened?

They rode in silence a few minutes, her heart finally slowing to a normal beat. Yet her lips cried out for Daman's touch again. Every bone in her body longed to wrap around him. It startled her that in seconds her life could have changed so quickly.

But it had—and she had no idea what she could do about it. He had kissed her once before, in the alleyway when Bud Parker almost saw her, yet he hadn't attempted to do so since then.

And it was all she wanted in life now. His body against hers, his mouth on hers, lost in an embrace forever.

Serena opened her eyes and saw Daman struggling with controlling the team.

"Have you ever driven before?" she asked.

He grimaced. "Some. But it is always been a very sedate horse or two and then only around a London park on level ground at a very slow pace. Not with eight horses wanting to run like the wind over rough terrain."

Serena laughed. "I hate to tell you, but this isn't considered rough. She paused. "I have experience. I've driven both horses and oxen. Would you like me to take over?"

He smiled gratefully. "It will be said I acted in an ungentlemanly fashion but I accept."

He slowed the horses until they came to a stop. Peeling off the driving gloves, he handed them to her.

Serena put them on and took the reins. She called out to the horses and soon had them moving along at a good clip.

Daman chuckled. "You do everything well, Serena Sullivan," he proclaimed. "I so admire American women."

"Well, I can milk a cow and plant a row of seeds. I also try my best to teach unruly children how to cipher and add. But I couldn't hold a candle to the women in your circle of friends. Life on the frontier is rough. I'm afraid I don't possess the social skills of a London miss."

"I'm simply glad you agreed to ride with me. I did not want you in the coach with a group of strangers and criminals." He smiled winningly at her. "Besides, I've missed our conversation. I have only known you for a day yet I feel we are old friends."

Serena understood what Daman meant. She sensed a bond of trust between them.

And possibly more.

"Then maybe we should learn more about each other," she suggested. "Tell me about your family and your childhood."

Daman frowned. "I'd simply bore you to tears."

Serena gazed over at him. "No, really. I'd like to hear more than what you shared over dinner last night."

He shrugged. "My father's first wife was an heiress. Aren't they all? At least in our place on society's ladder, they seem to be. She gave birth to my half-brothers, Edward and Thomas. I've told you that Edward is the current earl. He's much older than I."

"How much older?"

Daman thought a moment. "I am twenty-eight, which makes Edward forty-six now. We simply have nothing in common. He was grown by the time I was born. Thomas was twelve years older than I. A dashing military man and quite the charmer. He taught me to ride. Never could get me to hunt, though.

"That made me deplorable in Father's eyes. He was a man's man. He drank, hunted, and drank some more. I heard the whispers about his drinking from the time I was young, from both servants and others."

He stared off for a few moments. Serena did not press him.

Finally, he seemed to shrug off his gloom. "Eventually, he married again. Who else but another heiress? Father became impossibly wealthy when he married my mama. She gave birth to Cynthia first."

Daman smiled. "My sister was absolutely wonderful. She played with me. Taught me to read. Sang to me. Invented all sorts of games."

"At least you had someone you were close with."

"Cynthia became my mother for all practical purposes, even though she was only six. Mine died giving birth to me. The servants said that father disliked me upon first sight since I had killed her. After that, he chose not to see me for two years."

Serena gasped. "How cruel!"

Daman shook his head. "At least they'd already hired a wet nurse so my survival was guaranteed. The servants all seemed to adopt me as some sort of household pet. But Cynthia took the best care of me."

His tone was light but Serena could hear the unspoken hurt in it.

"Besides, it was a blessing. I learned to lie low. Father did finally pay a bit of attention to me since I didn't live up to his idea of what a Rutledge should be. I didn't excel in the manly arts. I was most often clumsy. I suppose my feet grew faster than the rest of me and my social grace never quite caught up. Instead, my active imagination had me telling stories and acting them out. I was different from other children."

"He merely didn't understand you, Daman."

He laughed harshly. "That is the understatement of the universe. Well, it worked in reverse. I never quite understood him either. He was an excellent shot but I couldn't stand the thought of a gun in my hand. I would see the broken birds or the bloody fox hanging from his dog's mouth and the thought sickened me."

"Did you ever go away to school?"

"No. My brothers had but Father didn't seem to care much about my education. After all, he already had his heir and a spare. As he got older, he drank more. Spent more time alone. Cynthia pleaded with him to hire a tutor for me after my governess took a new post but Father told her she could teach me if she cared so passionately about my learning."

Serena glanced over and saw a shadow cross Daman's face. "She died when I was only eleven. Then Father died a month later and Edward became the earl."

Daman brushed the dust from his pants, as if he wished to brush away his past.

"That sums up the sordid little drama of the Rutledge family. Here I am now, a simple cowpoke in a
strange land, being robbed by grizzly gunmen while
sparing time to rescue damsels in distress."

Serena couldn't help but laugh. He had infused
the end of his story with humor, which she realized he
used to ward off more serious reflection. She knew he
ached deeply over the deaths of his siblings yet he hid
it even from himself.

"How about you? Shall we turn the tables and lay
your life out on the buffet? We can sample pieces of
your past and see how they compare to my own."

Serena felt uncomfortable sharing anything. How
could she explain being given away to the orphan
train and her separation from Bill? Much less what life
was like in the von Wormer household.

"I remember you said your parents were homesteaders who had passed away. What do you remember about them?"

Serena paused. Should she talk about her real parents in New York or should she pretend the von
Wormers were her parents? She didn't want to be
caught up in lies so she stuck as closely to the truth as
she could.

"I grew up in New York City in my early years in an
Irish community."

"A-ha! A city girl at heart. I've heard New York is a
sight to see."

Serena smiled. "It's full of people and buildings.
Everyone always seemed in a hurry. But I loved to go
to the street fairs and see the carts full of their vendors' wares."

"Then how did you manage to make your way to
the wilds of the Great Plains?"

Serena swallowed. "My mother was quite ill for

some time. My father was a drunk who wouldn't have managed to care for me even if he had lived. After he died and Mama grew worse, she decided to send me to her people in Missouri when she knew she had so little time to live. They ran a farm. So, when I said my parents were homesteaders, I was actually thinking of them. That's where I . . . grew up."

"That's where you learned to do it all, on their farm?"

Serena hid the bitterness creeping up. Oh, she had certainly learned to do it all, including making Franz von Wormer and his son happy on a nightly basis.

"Yes," she said, pushing the forbidden thoughts away. She had sworn never to think of that time again. "They passed away when I was sixteen and I went to live with an aunt, a Miss von Wormer. She was very kind to me and even encouraged me to become a teacher."

Serena rotated her head around, stretching her neck, trying to ease the tension that had built up as she lied about the von Wormers' passing on.

"There's nothing much to my story. I travel from community to community throughout the Great Plains. Probably a lot of the Irish wanderlust in me. I haven't really put down any roots. I suppose I enjoy meeting new people and helping different children each season."

"I see." She felt Daman's gaze searing into her but she focused on the road.

"Look!" she called out. "I see Ellsworth ahead."

15

They quickly located the sheriff's office. The town, begun as an army fort, was more compact than Abilene.

Daman told Serena, "Leave everything to me."

While the travelers stretched their legs, Daman entered the sheriff's office and smoothly explained the situation. At least conversation was one skill he hadn't lost, despite his previous weeks in the saddle, with only dust as his constant companion.

The potbelly sheriff sent a deputy over to the stagecoach company to inform them of the events and then showed Daman several wanted posters. He easily picked out the robbers. The lawman cackled in glee at the news.

"Why, you done brung in Lefty Randall and Stan Manning, Mr. Rutledge. They've been plaguing stage-coaches over a couple hundred miles."

Daman nodded brusquely. "It was quite a group effort, Sheriff. We're just all happy to be in Ellsworth safely and look forward to arriving at our final desti-nations."

The sheriff rubbed his large gut thoughtfully.

"Well, there's a reward. From what you say, you deserve it more than most."

Daman shook his head. "No, I cannot accept it."

The sheriff shrugged. "Suit yourself. The company will just keep it now. Won't do anyone good or any good at all."

Daman contemplated his words. "Perhaps I will take it after all."

"Then I'll wire it in immediately. Won't take no time at all." He hitched up his pants. "You're going out on the next coach?"

"No. I plan to purchase rail tickets to Denver. I've had quite enough excitement for one day. I feel the train would be more to my liking."

"No train out to Denver until tomorrow. About a quarter till noon. Why don't you stay over at the Foster Hotel? It's the nicest place in town. The best I can recommend. I'll have the reward delivered to you there."

"Agreed." Daman tipped his hat. "Thank you for your assistance, Sheriff."

Daman walked back out into the blistering Kansas sun. Was there no relief in this treeless land? He hungered for the lush green of England yet again.

Serena met him. "Mr. Dougal would like a word with you. He's from the switching station. And I have back both your ring and my locket."

"Slip the ring back on and give me your locket. I'll see about having it repaired."

Serena did as he asked as Daman walked over to meet with Dougal. He spoke briefly with the company representative, confirming the other passengers' stories. Then he asked, "Would it be possible to give the reward to our driver's family?"

The man squinted at him. "Didn't have any. Old Ben was a loner."

"I see."

"Well, let's gather everyone around." Dougal motioned for the passengers to come closer. "It's getting late in the day, folks. Ellsworth would have been your resting spot for the night. I can have a new driver ready to go first thing in the morning and you can all continue your journey to Denver then."

"Or there's a train coming through just before noon tomorrow," Daman added. "The sheriff mentioned that."

Dougal clucked his tongue. "No, no, that won't do, Mr. Rutledge. You have paid for your transportation. It's not necessary to do so again. These mishaps happen but all is well now."

Daman grinned. "Just the same, I think my cousin and I will take the morning train."

Dougal frowned. "Surely, you can understand that I cannot refund your fare."

Daman waved him away. "There is no problem, Mr. Dougal. We shall take our baggage and be on our way. Thank you for your every kindness."

The hotel recommended by the sheriff was only a block away. Daman took both his and Serena's luggage in hand and they walked down the street to it. The Foster was much smaller than the Alamar and not nearly as grand.

Daman walked up to the desk and asked the squinting clerk for a suite.

"Suite? We ain't got no suites, sir. I can get you a room."

"Make it two." Daman signed the register and asked, "May we have hot water sent up? And a light supper as well?"

The clerk whistled. "We ain't so fancy here, Mr. Rutledge. Bathhouse is next door. Supper'll be served in ten minutes." He gave them their room keys.

A voice interrupted them. "I'm Bob Rucker, the owner. You must be Mr. Rutledge."

Daman glanced at the man entering the hotel's small lobby. He had to be well over three hundred pounds and took up most of the remaining space.

"Sheriff figured you'd stay the night here. You're quite the hero, Mr. Rutledge. Them's two bad ones you brought in. We're obliged to you."

Daman shook his head, uncomfortable with the compliment. "It was most certainly a group effort, Mr. Rucker. Even Cousin Ada here helped in their capture."

Daman saw Serena flush and look down to the floor.

"Well, I see you got your room keys. Anything else I can do for you?"

"Actually, there is. My cousin and I would like to visit the bathhouse and then settle down for a late supper. Your clerk told me, however, that dinner is about to be served."

"You caught some rotten apples today, Mr. Rutledge. I think we can hold some supper for you and the little lady." Rucker smiled at Serena.

Daman thanked him and escorted Serena to her room. They retrieved clean clothes from their luggage and set off for the bathhouse.

An hour later, they returned to the Foster. Mr. Rucker met him and handed Daman an envelope as Serena walked into the small dining room for the dinner that awaited them.

"From the sheriff. Said it was the reward owed to you. I promised him I'd place it in your hands personally."

"Thank you, Mr. Rucker. Might I ask one more small favor of you?"

The hotel owner nodded. "Just name it."

Deming withdrew the damaged locket from his pocket. "My cousin's necklace was ripped from her throat in the robbery. It means a great deal to her. Would you know of someone who might repair it before we leave tomorrow morning?"

Rucker gestured for him to pass the locket over. He inspected it thoughtfully. "This ain't so bad. I know just the man to fix it. Your cousin needn't worry at all. She will have it back, right as rain, before you leave tomorrow."

The innkeeper slipped the gold locket into his pocket and told Daman, "Got some ham and corn and a good half dozen biscuits wrapped in the cup towels for you. Pie, too. Enjoy yourselves now."

Daman shook hands with Rucker and joined Serena in the dining room. He was glad the others had already eaten. More than anything, he was ready to spend time alone with her.

As they finished their meal, Daman pulled out the envelope from his jacket pocket. "For you."

Serena gave him a questioning glance and then opened it. "Oh, my. Why are you showing me all this money?"

"It's for you. It's the reward money for bringing in Lefty and Stan. I wanted to give it to our driver's wife and family but he had none. I thought you could use it, to make a new start for yourself."

She pushed the envelope back across the table. "No, I couldn't keep it. After all the clothes you bought me? Plus, my tickets on both the train and coach. I can't accept this."

The truth was, she didn't want to accept what it meant. To Serena, Daman Rutledge giving her the money meant he was freeing himself from her. She had lived from minute to minute for just under two days, not being able to or even wanting to think ahead to the future.

Yet somehow, she had deluded herself into thinking *he* would be her future. That she would stay under his protection while he conducted his business in Denver. And then just maybe, hopefully, he would ask her to remain with him.

The money he now dangled in front of her ended the foolish notion that she could have any life with this man. The passionate kiss they'd shared had meant nothing to him. She was simply a woman, a convenience, and he'd taken advantage of the moment. She had to realize that Daman Rutledge was no different from any other man. She had trusted in him —believed in him—too much. It had to end.

Now.

Daman placed his hand over hers. "Please, I want you to have it. The other things were a gift. This will help you, wherever you decide to go."

Serena slowly pulled her hand away, bringing the envelope back in her direction. She would take the money, the bribe to get rid of her. Yet his touch had started her heart beating noisily again. She looked at him to thank him but his gaze lingered over her in such a way that it brought a blush to her cheeks.

"Will you settle in Denver?" he asked.

Serena gazed at him, trying to divorce herself from the feelings rushing through her as she struggled to remain calm.

"It's far enough away from Kansas. But I will have to take a new name." Her nose crinkled in disgust.

"Possibly Ada? Does that name please you?"

Serena shook her head. "Not really. I think I will keep Serena but I shall change my last name."

It worried her that if she did, Bill would never find her. Of course, if word of Serena Sullivan and her notorious actions did reach Bill, she doubted he would claim being related to her. The thought of her picture on a wanted poster circulated throughout the west was a distinct possibility. She wondered if Denver would be far enough—or if perhaps she should go to California.

Daman's hand covered hers again. "Have you decided on this new last name?" He turned her hand over and slowly drew circles in her palm.

A burning sensation in her lower regions sprang to a life all its own, followed by a throbbing that startled her with its intensity. Serena's eyes widened at the sudden, new sensation. She knew she should pull away from him. They were in a public place even though no one was present at the moment. They were supposed to be cousins, not a couple romantically involved. Besides, she finally understood they could have no future together.

And yet this man's touch felt so good.

"Can I get you anything else?"

Serena guiltily jumped to her feet. Bob Rucker stood in the doorway with a light.

"No," she stammered, hoping he hadn't seen anything in the dim light. "This was lovely. So kind of you, Mr. Rucker."

"Then I'll light your way to your rooms, ma'am."

Serena looked at Daman, catching the regret in his eyes for the interruption. It mirrored the way she felt.

Yet she knew she was crazy for even dreaming of them sharing a life together.

She wanted something, wanted it desperately, and it was something she could never have. She longed for love, for babies, for a home to make her own. Why would a member of the English nobility want her? She was nothing but a convicted common criminal, considered no better than Lefty and Stan in the eyes of the law.

Even if Daman desired her in that way, his family would never accept her. He was the half-brother of an earl, part of the English nobility. Serena knew the glittering society in London was not the place for her, an Irish-American who grew up on the mean streets of New York and now had a price on her head.

Besides, Daman Rutledge would never make an offer such as marriage. No matter how kind he had been or how much he stirred her blood, she would never give herself away freely. It had been taken from her for so long. Serena didn't know if she would ever give herself to any man of her own free will.

So as much as she yearned for Daman's hands running through her hair and his lips against her throat whispering sweet nothings, it could never be. He was a free spirit that wouldn't be able to commit to her.

She determined to part ways with him once they arrived in Denver. It was the only path open to her. He would be relieved that she would no longer be his responsibility.

Mr. Rucker escorted him to their rooms. Serena refused Daman's proffered arm and walked stiffly up the stairs behind their host. She didn't think she could stand the touch she so longed for.

They reached her room first and they both

thanked Mr. Rucker, who reminded them when break-fast began the next morning as he departed. Serena reached into her reticule for the room key. Daman took it from her trembling hands.

"Allow me," he said softly.

Her gaze met his for a moment and she saw the confusion there. She quickly looked away.

Daman opened the door and handed her the key. His fingers burned as they brushed against her palm. Serena clutched the key tightly and said a curt good-night before hurrying into her room. As she closed the door and leaned against it for support, her knees buckled. She slid down the length of the door into a heap on the floor.

Serena might be able to stop any future advances Daman made but she could do nothing to stop the flow of tears that now came in a torrent down her cheeks.

Or the breaking of her heart.

16

They breakfasted at seven the next morning along with six other guests. Little conversation occurred between the gathered strangers beyond the occasional request to pass the plate of biscuits from one end of the table to the other.

Daman's confusion concerning last night lingered. He knew from Serena's eyes alone that she wanted him. Yet she had withdrawn and rather curtly bidden him goodnight. Not that he had gotten much sleep. Every time he closed his eyes, it was her image before him. Those bewitching eyes and the raven mane of curls, the slender column of her neck, the lush curves all beckoned to him as he tossed and turned.

So now, he was in a surly mood. Lack of sleep always did that to him.

They finished eating and adjourned to the small lobby.

"Have you asked for the luggage to be brought down?" Serena asked formally, as if they barely knew one another and had not shared anything between them beyond inquiring of the other how the weather might be.

So be it. If this were how she wanted it, two could

play the game at hand. Daman prided himself on knowing women but Serena was turning out to be a mystery to him. He would simply follow her lead and hope like hell to thaw her out once they left Ellsworth.

"I'm off to purchase our train tickets," he informed her. "If you'll kindly ask for our bags to be brought down, I'd like it done by the time I return."

He moved slightly closer to her and saw her stiffen. In a low tone he added, "We are still in proximity of the Kansas law. Please stay here and do not wander about."

She opened her mouth as if to make a sharp retort but closed it. He nodded brusquely and set off. He stopped to ask directions to the train depot and found himself there within ten minutes. Daman purchased their tickets through to Denver and then stopped at a general store, where he purchased paper and pencil.

He walked slowly back, knowing he needn't rush. Why did it matter? Serena Sullivan, despite her allure to him, was still a stranger. He had simply played Sir Galahad to her damsel in distress and helped her in a time of need.

Yet he felt more alive in her company than ever before. All kinds of ideas for plays ran through his head, which was why he had purchased the paper. A growing need to get down his musings pressed him harder and harder, as much as his desire for the charming schoolmarm.

Surprisingly, it was not simply a physical need he experienced. Oh, he wanted her, all right, his hands all over her, from that luxuriant hair to the tips of her toes. But he actually craved her companionship, as well. He had never really had friends, only plenty of acquaintances. Those were mainly from his time at university, now long past him.

Of course, Daphne had been his great friend. But after her, Daman hadn't wanted to get close to anyone.

Until now. He loved how Serena challenged him, entertained him, even inspired him.

He simply had to have her. He would convince her to stay with him somehow. Yet he was certain he would be fighting a losing battle. Serena seemed to follow rigid rules. Becoming his mistress would not appeal to her.

And offering her marriage was out of the question. He worshipped the ground Daphne walked on yet he hadn't been able to give her his name. Daphne had been an actress. How could he offer to marry an American, much less one wanted by the law?

Yet Daman knew in his heart Serena was guilty of no more than being beautiful and desired by a man who had tried to take advantage of her.

He sighed aloud, between the proverbial rock and hard place. With no answer insight.

He arrived back at the hotel, greeted by Bob Rucker, necklace in hand.

"Told you I wouldn't disappoint you, Mr. Rutledge. Your cousin's locket is fit as a fiddle. No charge at all. Just the thanks of the folks here in Ellsworth."

Daman placed the locket in his pocket. "I am much obliged to you, Mr. Rucker. Have you seen my cousin?"

"She went back upstairs. Got your rail tickets?"

"Yes, thank you. We're set to go."

Daman settled their bill. Returning to his own room, he heard Serena pacing restlessly next door. Her actions made him smile. At least he wasn't the only one suffering. Serena struggled with something. Whether it had to do with him or not, he couldn't venture to say.

But he hoped so.

He sat in the rickety chair and pulled some of the paper out, placing it on the equally unstable round table. Daman decided to pass the time with what he used to do best.

Write.

~

SERENA HEARD the bells charming the quarter hour. She couldn't see the town's clock from her hotel room but she knew it was now after eleven. The Denver train would come through in half an hour.

Where was Daman? Why hadn't he returned? For a moment, her stomach soured.

He had abandoned her. Left her to fend for herself.

She couldn't blame him. He had gone far above what any other man in her acquaintance would have done. And if caught together, she knew his British citizenship wouldn't save him from frontier justice.

Perhaps it was best. He had bought her clothes and given her the healthy reward for Lefty and Stan's capture. She would simply board the westbound train on her own and start anew in Denver or beyond. Change her name. Continue what would probably be the fruitless search for her twin.

And miss Daman Rutledge so bad her teeth hurt.

How could one man have such an effect on her? Especially after so little time together. And after Serena pledged to herself that no man would ever control her destiny again.

No, she'd been off-putting to Daman last night. Rejected his interest in her. She refused to indulge in some casual affair of the heart, despite longing desperately for his touch. She would use the opportunity at hand and march forward with her life, broken heart be damned.

Then she heard the sneeze. The paper thin walls didn't disguise the noise. Daman must be in his room even though she hadn't heard him returned.

Serena slipped from her own room and walked a few steps to his door. Silence. She boldly knocked. Nothing. She tried again. Harder. Nothing. Finally, she pounded the door until her knuckles hurt.

Still nothing.

Was he hiding from her? Thinking she would go quietly? Her anger stirred as a shaken hornet's nest. If he were cutting ties with her, then it would be on her terms, not his.

Shamelessly, Serena turned the doorknob and pushed open the door. She stepped into the room, ready for a confrontation.

Daman said hunched over a desk, writing.

"Daman?"

He didn't stir. His pencil scratched noisily along the paper. He was oblivious to her.

Serena studied him a moment. The tailored blue frock coat fit his broad shoulders snugly. Sunlight streaming in from the window burnished his deep chestnut hair and she caught sight of the dark, reddish flecks in it. He frowned at the paper a moment, totally lost in thought, his pencil poised in midair.

Then he smiled and began scribbling madly again.

Serena's breath caught in her throat. The white, even teeth against that tanned face brought pleasure to her in a way she'd never known. Daman Rutledge was beautiful. Perfect. Like a Greek god. Her heart fluttered wildly. She stopped breathing a moment, drinking him in like a desert traveler quenching a terrible thirst after a long journey.

She longed for this man physically yet she wanted more from him. She never let herself get close to anyone as she moved from town to town over the years, never opened up or trusted a soul. That attitude lingered from her childhood, when only Bill knew her innermost thoughts. Adults were never to be trusted and she had no confidence in a friendship with someone her own age in Five Points. They would as soon stab her for a crust of moldy bread, hunger greater than a bond of friendship ever could be.

But in a short time, Serena had talked with Daman, confided in him, laughed with him. She required his company as much as she wanted more of those dizzying kisses. She'd never let herself think about the loneliness that ate away at her.

Until now.

"Daman?" she called again, now knowing what he did. The only thing that she could imagine taking him away from this world was creating another one. She realized he was writing again. The notion gave her satisfaction.

Serena walked to him and touched his shoulder.

His head snapped up, his eyes disoriented for a moment as they focused on her.

"Serena?" His hand flew to his waist coat and the pocket watch there. He gasped and leaped to his feet.

"We've got to get to the station! Now. We'll miss our train."

"I had the luggage taken downstairs and over to the station," she said calmly. "Is it far?"

Daman scooped up the pages and folded them. He slipped them inside his coat's pocket along with the pencil, pulling out her repaired necklace.

"For you," he said, placing the locket around her neck and fastening it. "No, it's not too far. But we'll need to walk briskly."

He took her arm and hustled her down the hotel stairs and out into the street.

"I must apologize for losing track of the time," he said. "I had no idea it was so late."

"You were working again."

Daman shrugged. "A few ideas came to me. I thought I'd jot them down."

They walked a minute more before he said, "I'm being dishonest with you. They burned within me until I was compelled to commit them to paper. It hasn't been like that in a long time. It felt . . . exhilarating."

He smiled at her. She gave his arm an encouraging squeeze.

"Here we are."

He escorted her through the station and out onto the platform. Serena spied their luggage against a wall and pointed it out to him.

"I'll arrange for it to be placed aboard. I'll find a steward and return shortly."

Daman disappeared inside the depot. Serena heard the whistle of the train. She looked and saw it approaching in the distance. A calm washed over her. This train would take her far from Kansas. Away from Sheriff Parker and the murder charges. And hopefully, closer to finding Bill.

She watched the train pulled into the station and came to a halt. A few passengers spilled from its doors. Serena didn't imagine Ellsworth would be a long stop.

Daman took her elbow. "We should board. Our luggage is being placed on the train now."

Serena nodded. They walked to an opening and

the conductor assisted her up the steps. Daman followed behind her.

"Let's find a seat." He opened the door to a compartment and Serena stepped through.

She began moving down the narrow aisle. Most
seats were taken. She felt the train lurch and realized
it had already started up again. She stepped gingerly,
swaying slightly as the train started to pick up speed.
She reached and grabbed a seatback to steady herself.

"Nothing here together," Daman said. "Let's go to
the next compartment."

They came to the end and Daman reached around
to open the door for her again. Serena started through
it and froze in her tracks.

Sheriff Bud Parker sat inside the car.

17

Daman ran into Serena's back. He grabbed her waist as she pitched forward and steadied her. He leaned down to ask why she had stopped in her tracks, only to learn the answer himself.

That bloody Sheriff Parker sat not fifteen feet away from where they stood. Fortunately, his head tilted back and to one side as he leaned against the window. His mouth was open slightly and Daman could hear the snores emanating from the man over the train's rumbling.

Serena had stiffened under his fingers. He gently pulled on her waist and leaned down until his lips were an inch from her ear.

"Slowly turn around. We'll go as far to the front as we can."

She nodded shakily. Daman led them back the way they had come. They went forward three compartments and could go no further. Fortunately, he found two seats together at the very front of the car. He motioned Serena to sit and he slid in beside her.

She stared straight ahead at the wall in front of her. He saw her lips trembling. Then her shoulders began to shake. Even her hands, the fingers, locked tightly together in her lap, began jumping violently.

Daman wrapped an arm about her and drew her close. She clawed at his shirtfront, clutching it as a lifeline. He pried her hand loose and took it in his free one. Even through the gloves, her fingers were icy on this hot morning.

He slipped the glove from her hand and enveloped it in his, willing his warmth to reach her.

Neither spoke for a long time. Eventually, her tremors began to subside.

"How did he know?" she asked in a whisper.

"Maybe he played a hunch. He had to believe you were on the Cheyenne-bound train. We made certain of that. I'm sure he had it stopped and searched. When that proved fruitless, he probably decided to chance the Denver train himself."

"I hate him," Serena said, her voice low and menacing. "I think I could actually kill him."

Her deadly tone's intensity surprised Daman. "Did he hurt you while you were awaiting trial?"

Serena shuddered. "Not like you think. But he wanted to. He's as evil a man as I've ever known and believe me, I've known some who will rot in Hell."

Daman held her tightly, wishing he could have protected her from whatever haunted her from her past. He hadn't watched over Cynthia as he should have, and look what she had been driven to do.

He saw the desperation in Serena's eyes as she looked at him. "What should we do? Get off at the next stop? I can't even remember what it is. I can't think. Oh, what if he sees us?"

He felt her heart starting to race now, the violent thumps pounding heavily against her rib cage.

"We wait for now." He tried to look at her with a

confidence he did not feel. "Parker won't come this way anytime soon."

Serena smiled wryly. "I doubt even Bud Parker could sleep straight through the next six hundred miles."

Daman pulled her even closer. His lips brushed against her temple. "Close your eyes. Don't think about him. I'll find a way to get us out of this."

Serena laid her head on his shoulder. Daman's thoughts jumbled in a confused mess.

He wanted to scream aloud in frustration. Damn it, he was a *writer*. He put people in impossible situations and then figured out how to get them out of trouble.

Yet his mind was a blank slate. Either because he was out of practice in dreaming up solutions or worse —there was no way out.

Daman refused to accept that. He couldn't let Serena down in such a life or death situation. He had lived with guilt ever since Cynthia took her own life. He wouldn't allow another innocent woman to die.

Besides, his head was also on the chopping block. He had helped a convicted murderess escape her hanging. Daman wondered idly about the penalty for that crime. He envisioned a crowd gathered around a set of double scaffolds for the two of them and then shook the macabre thought from his mind as the conductor came by to collect their tickets.

"What's our next stop?" he asked as he handed over their tickets.

"Black Wolf, sir. Won't be but a brief one. Just enough for people to board or exit."

Daman thought a moment. "Is there a longer respite coming up?"

"Wilson. There'll be enough time to grab a sandwich at the station." The man chuckled. "You sound English."

"That I am," he replied.

"Then I shall warn you ahead of time in case you haven't been traveling much by train. I doubt you've seen the likes of this back home. It'll be pretty chaotic. We only stay about fifteen minutes. People tumble off the train and make a mad dash for food. Some of them look sedate now but they might have been on for a day without eating or relieving themselves. You wouldn't believe the elbowing and jabbing and poking that goes on." The conductor grinned. "That's why the wife packs me a lunch bucket."

Handing the torn ticket halves back to Daman, he added, "Enjoy your trip, sir."

Serena remained quiet throughout their exchange. Daman's mind began racing with the new information he possessed. If he could make sure Parker was in that crowd, maybe he could somehow force the lawman to miss reboarding the train.

But how could he accomplish that?

An hour went by as Daman furiously tried to come up with a way out of their predicament. He still hadn't thought of a solution when the friendly conductor went up and down the aisles announcing a fifteen-minute rest stop at the next depot.

Daman sensed the train slowing as they pulled into Wilson. It barely reached a stop when people sprang from their seats and poured from the doors. He remained seated, placing a hand over Serena's to keep her from rising.

They watched from their window as a crowd formed on the platform in front of several vendors' food carts. Serena stiffened as Bud Parker came into view, waddling along as he made his way through the throng. She quickly averted her face from the window.

Daman's thoughts still rushed as galloping horses. He didn't see how he could prevent the sheriff from getting back onto the train without being seen by him. He wondered if they should exit and take a later train. Yet it would be almost impossible to avoid their perse-cutor. The platform wasn't large enough. The man might spot them when they exited or spy them in the crowd or even inside the depot itself and give chase.

Daman figured they would have to risk it. There was no guarantee Parker would return to the same exact spot on the train. He could choose their car and they would be trapped.

"Let's go," he said quietly to Serena. He stood, his hand still wrapped around hers. Their gazes met.

"Trust me."

She nodded. "I do."

Daman could see her belief in him, shining in those tawny eyes. He led her to the rear of the first car and stopped just short of the door. Pulling his hat low on his brow, he leaned around, making certain Serena was totally out of sight.

"We're getting off. I can't trust that Parker won't move around the train in order to stretch his legs. Lady Luck has been with us so far in avoiding him. We've got to hope she'll stay with us a bit longer."

Daman continued watching the crowd and located Parker. He turned to Serena.

"We'll watch him board. We'll get off just as the train pulls away. If he doesn't spot us, we'll take the next train out. We shouldn't see him in the Denver depot since he would have arrived hours earlier."

Serena bit her lip. "All right."

She looked unsteady on her feet. Daman cupped her cheek. "I will see you safely to Denver, Serena."

Her trembling smile almost broke his heart, as did her words. "That's good enough for me."

He glanced at the clock tower above the depot. Ten minutes had already passed. He heard the conductor shout out of five-minute warning and the scrambling began. Old passengers along with new ones began boarding the train.

Parker lumbered back, a brown paper bag in one hand, munching an apple with the other. Daman panicked as he saw the lawman head their way. He grabbed Serena's hand and pulled her quickly past the door. They moved into the next compartment.

"Keep going," he said over his shoulder, walking as rapidly as they could against the wave of people coming on board.

They reached the last car and Daman heard the all aboard call. He released Serena's hand and stepped off the train, skirting another conductor at the back who gave him a puzzled look as Daman glanced about him.

He looked back up and explained, "My cousin has taken ill. I believe it's simply motion sickness. She needs to rest."

He reached a hand up to Serena, who certainly looked the part. She had turned quite pale and was trembling again as she stepped down next to him.

"I'm sorry, ma'am," the conductor called as the train started to pull away. "It affects some people worse than others."

"When is the next train to Denver?" Daman asked.

"About four hours, sir. It's too late to pull your luggage. Rest assured it will be waiting for you in Denver."

The conductor shouted the last bit as the train

moved away from them. Daman planned to remain rooted to the spot and let the train leave Wilson behind. He didn't communicate this to Serena, though.

As he watched the locomotive head down the tracks, she said, "I'm going to be sick."

She broke away from him and scurried across the length of the platform and into the depot.

"Bloody hell," he muttered. She hadn't put down her veil. His gut told him she'd made an awful mistake.

Daman hurried after her. He cringed as he heard a loud shout over the noise. He looked up and saw that bloated Sheriff hanging out a window, pointing and bellowing at Serena.

Parker's face disappeared and Daman knew the fool would do whatever it took to get off that train. Daman ran into the station, glancing over his shoulder. Sure enough, Parker jumped from the open doorway and landed hard in the gravel.

Even from a distance, Daman could tell Parker hadn't landed right. The lawman might have broken something, an ankle or even his leg. He realized that the train was pulling away and no one stood out on the platform to aid the lawmen.

Daman raced after Serena.

18

He *had to find Serena.*

Daman dashed to the side of the train depot, knowing he didn't have much time before Bud Parker called for help. And not just for himself. If the sheriff's injuries prevented him from doing so, he would demand someone hunt down his fugitives. As Daman turned the corner, he saw Serena hunched over. The awful retching gave his stomach a moment of queasiness.

She seemed to finish and Daman gave her his handkerchief. Serena wiped her mouth and pocketed the cloth, nervously glancing over her shoulder.

He couldn't believe the utter mess he was in. He had fallen in love with a beautiful stranger, besotted by her from the moment he laid eyes upon her. For that, he might swing from a gibbet. Wouldn't that amuse his father? He had always said Daman would never amount to a farthing.

Would Edward even know his half-brother had been executed? Did the American authorities contact a criminal's family or did they simply forget to extend such a courtesy? Daman's anger at the entire situation pulsed through him.

He looked at Serena, who still seemed to pale but began walking away from the train station. He fell into step alongside her as he heard faint shouts in the distance. Daman assumed Bud Parker had recovered enough to call for help.

She shook her head ruefully. "I'm sorry, Daman. We need to think fast—"

"Sorry?" he asked, cutting her off. "You're *sorry*? Sorry is if you accidentally bump into someone you pass on the street and offer an apology. Sorry is if you inadvertently interrupt someone in conversation. Not when you—"

But Daman halted his brief tirade. He shouldn't blame Serena. He had chosen to get involved. He would have to live with his consequences.

She waved his words aside, taking them in stride as they quickly moved down what appeared to be the main street of a town. Thank goodness it was large and crowded, allowing them to blend in.

Determination filled her face. "We need to move fast. Not on the train. Not a coach. We need to find horses."

Her color started to return, as well as her confidence. She added, "It's best if we split up. I've been an anchor around your leg long enough. You head to Denver as planned and complete the business for your brother. Your money can buy you new clothes and privacy from the law. Besides, they'll be looking for the pair of us, not you alone."

Daman arched his brows. "And exactly what direction would you head in, might I ask?"

Serena frowned. Daman could almost see the wheels of thought turning beneath her knitted brows.

"California," popped out. "I can forge a new life there."

"Why not England?" Daman countered.

Serena stopped dead in her tracks. Her face registered utter shock. He was glad he put that look there. A little smugly, he told her, "It's far enough so that obese sheriff might cease waddling after us. I doubt even he would cross an ocean to find you."

"You...you would take me to England with you?" A blush rose up her neck and colored her cheeks a bright pink.

Daman looked steadily at her. "I would take you anywhere. Everywhere." He reached for her, grabbing her shoulders and pulling her close. "Damn it, woman, I've fallen in love with you."

He saw the recognition in her eyes, the very moment she took in his words and believed in them.

In him.

Then he lowered his mouth to hers. He hungered for her. Needed her taste. Wanted her touch. Would die if they did not become one.

Serena broke the kiss, pulling away, those amber eyes large in her face. "Oh, Lord," she whispered. "I don't want to stop but, Daman, we need to keep moving."

He released his hold on her, one hand sliding along her arm to capture her hand in his. He tucked it through the crook of his arm and began walking again.

He turned to Serena as they continue down the street. "Any ideas?"

She calmly announced, "We're going back to Abilene. Parker would never expect that."

Daman laughed aloud. "Why the hell not?"

≈

"BLOODY ANIMAL," Daman muttered under his breath.

Back on a damn horse. He'd sworn never to be in that position again, saddle sore and fraught with tension. This obnoxious beast had a mind of its own. He had already been thrown twice and now held the reins in a deathly grip, his fingers sore to the bone from the pressure.

"I think we can stop and break camp for the night," Serena said. "The sun's almost set."

Daman looked to her. She was a natural in the saddle, much like his brother, Thomas. She looked perfectly at ease if a little rumpled. Wisps of hair had pulled loose from her chignon. Other than that, she was the picture of casual ease.

"It's about time," he grumbled.

Serena bit her lip and frowned but Daman saw her fighting a losing battle as the corners of her mouth turned up.

"Don't hide your smile," he warned. "I'd rather you laugh aloud at me than behind my back."

She grinned, her eyes alighting with mischief. "All right."

She dismounted and led her horse to a scraggly tree, knotting the reins loosely around its almost nonexistent trunk. Daman noted it was the only one in sight. God, how he longed for the lush, green hills and tall, endless forests of England.

He did likewise, leading his horse to the same place, although the mount nipped at him as he did so. Daman turned his back to the silly creature and managed to secure the reins.

"Bloody brute," he complained to the horse, looking it squarely in the eye. "Yes, you," he emphasized, just in case the beast didn't know whom he referred to.

Serena already sat on the ground, pulling open the drawstring of her reticule, retrieving some of the beef jerky they'd purchased earlier. He sat beside her and she offered him a piece.

"I'm sorry we had to go fast and frugal," she apologized.

He shook his head. "I realized there was no time to purchase bedrolls or coffee pots or any of the other paraphernalia for life on the road."

Daman eyed the jerky warily. "I had thought I'd never want to shovel another bite of hot beans in my mouth again." He shook his head and began gnawing on the piece of jerky.

Serena bit daintily into the jerky and chewed thoughtfully. "We really are lucky to have found Mr. Johns. It was Providence that he had two horses we could take off his hands. I think he was pleased at the price."

Daman grunted, thinking the jerky tasted like old shoe leather. No, that had to be tastier, even if it were splashed with grass stains and mud.

"Maybe you are happy with your mount. Mine seems to have left a sweetheart back some twenty miles ago and is determined to turn around at every step and return to her."

Serena smiled at him. "Why, Mr. Rutledge. What a romantic notion. A horse mated for life, separated from his loved one." She giggled.

Daman found himself infected by her good humor. "Yes. As a matter of fact, the two horses had been raised together in the same pasture. Their mothers foaled within a day of each other and so the pair grew up together, learning to stand and then run alongside one another, frolicking from one adventure to another."

Serena picked up the yarn. "Until one day the farmer had a buyer come to the property. He had seen an advertisement in the newspaper. The man absolutely knew he needed only one horse." She paused. "It just about broke the farmer's heart to separate them, as he understood how close the pair had grown."

"But he had hungry mouths to feed and couldn't worry about the feelings of a young colt and filly over his own brood of twelve."

"Twelve?" Serena laughed. Do farmers in England have twelve or more children?"

Daman stretched out, leaning on one elbow, his hand propped under his head. "Easily twelve. More if he has more land. It's all in the marriage vows, you understand. The wife is to produce a child to aid in laboring for every amount of acreage the farmer owns."

Serena nodded, mulling over his words. "So, that is the arrangement of the working class. What of high society? Do they, too, strike a bargain as to the number of children to be produced? Say, a child for each room in the castle?"

Daman stared into the depths of Serena's tawny eyes and gave her a lazy smile. He reached out a hand and wrapped his fingers behind her nape and gently pulled her in his direction.

"You would be surprised at the pact negotiated between a man and a woman."

"Would I?" she said softly.

"You have no idea," he said, the last of his words said against her mouth.

Her lips were meant to be next to his. If Daman had doubted the existence of Heaven before, he had found a bit of it on earth in Serena Sullivan's mouth.

He pressed his lips to hers, wondering that even the faint taste of beef jerky took on the taste of a fine delicacy as he traced the outline of her mouth with his tongue.

Her sigh sent a rush of desire shooting like lightning through him, even as she opened her mouth to him. Daman tasted deeply of her, leisurely exploring what he'd been dreaming of, wondering why no man had ever claimed her heart.

He pulled her closer as he turned onto his back, her breasts resting against his chest as he pushed a hand into her ebony waves, freeing them from the chignon. Daman's mouth left hers and trailed a line of hot kisses along her jaw as his hands slowly massaged his way down her back in circular motions. He nibbled at her earlobe, tugging playfully, smiling at the catch in her already erratic breathing.

Daman's hand reached Serena's lower back and slid down her thigh. His fingers found the tip of her skirt and slipped under it, stroking her calf, and then moving higher. He returned to her mouth, his kisses now hard and demanding. He couldn't remember wanting a woman as much as he did Serena.

His hand brushed up her leg and cupped her buttocks, the cheek sweet and round and so tempting. Daman longed to see her milky flesh before the evening sunset. He wanted to view every inch of her, explore every part, revel in the smile on her face after he pleasured her. Daman parted her fold, sliding a finger slowly into the velvet depths.

She stiffened in his arms. Began thrashing about and muttering incoherently. Yanked her mouth from his and pushed hard against his chest. Scrambled to her feet, panting.

She looked like an avenging goddess as she stood over him, her eyes trying to focus, her mouth trembling, her breath ragged, that gorgeous mane of hair spilling about her.

"Don't ever, ever touch me."

19

Serena looked down at Daman as the shock telegraphed across his face. Despite the desperate need coursing through her for his touch, that very touch went too far with one intimate gesture. It certainly brought Serena back to reality.

She was nothing more than damaged goods. Serena knew what Franz von Wormer had done to her almost nightly after he chose her from the orphan train. The German farmer amused himself with her in ways Serena could never forget.

He eventually shared her with his son. Serena could feel their rough, calloused hands on her even now, probing, pinching, mauling. Her skin remained bruised in various hues of the rainbow for years, from deep purples and blacks to shades of garish greens and faded yellows.

She fled once but the unsettled hills of Missouri proved confusing to a city girl. The von Wormer men caught up to her before she'd found even a single person to share her story with. The consequent beating she endured left her broken in body and spirit.

They never left her alone after that. Not even

during her weekly bath. Serena pleaded with words and finally her eyes alone but Frau von Wormer never acknowledged what went on behind closed doors in the pristine farmhouse.

At night, after the men were spent, von Wormer would lock her inside the pantry. Serena slept on the floor wrapped in an old quilt.

All the past came tumbling back when Daman touched her intimately. The ugliness, the shame, proved more than Serena could bear. Rationally, she knew men and women supposedly enjoyed those things between them. She had certainly relished Daman's kisses, the first she'd ever known in her twenty-five years.

But the one, painfully familiar move flooded her with obscene memories. She wouldn't have Daman become part of them.

Serena gathered her resolve, crossing her arms in front of her in a protective gesture. No words came. She could think of no excuse to give him.

Daman leaped to his feet. "My God, Serena. I'm a bastard of the first degree. I apologize for such for-wardness. I became caught up in my passion without thought for you, love."

He shook his head. "I haven't treated you as the lady I know you are." Daman reached out a hand and brushed a lock of her hair from her face. "My sweet, innocent schoolmarm."

His words hit Serena as hard as a slap in the face. Daman thought she objected because she was a virgin. The bitter irony pulsed through her. Yet she did not want to hurt or disillusion him. Let him think her pure and innocent if he would.

She looked into the face she had already come to love and saw his anxious eyes filled with remorse.

Serena knew she could never begin to tell him the horrors of her past.

Instead, she burst into tears.

Daman folded her within his arms as the sobs racked her body. Serena finally became aware of Daman smoothing her hair, the gentle whispers that murmured reassurances, the utter safety she experienced inside his embrace.

Why had her past unfolded as it had? Not just the terror of her life on the von Wormer farm but the wrenching poverty she was born into. Why did her father drink too much and her mother die in such a wretched way?

Most of all, why had the present cruelly brought her into contact with a man she might have only dreamed of, a real-life knight in dazzling armor who actually claimed he loved her?

Yet Daman had no idea who Serena Sullivan truly was or what squalor and misery she came from. If he ever learned what had been done to her, he wouldn't dream of touching her. Fate vengefully toyed with her yet again, dangling happiness and a charming suitor before her, knowing she must reject him.

Before he rejected her.

A part of Serena wished she had hanged and never been given the time with Daman. This magical experience would never repeat itself. She could live to be ninety and never have the rush of feelings and heady passion this English god stirred within her.

Daman slowly released his grasp on her. As he moved away, it seemed like a dream that receded upon wakening—the clarity lost to a fuzziness that grew until it swallowed up the illusion.

Her fantasy of being rescued from the gallows had

occurred, and by a handsome gentleman, all the sweeter because of his flaws.

But dreams fade and slowly die and Serena knew the time had come for the two of them to part.

"Daman—"

"Shh." He touched a finger to her lips, causing a bolt of fire to sizzle inside her. He cupped her face in his hands, smooth hands not hardened by farm labor, his thumbs gently stroking her damp cheeks.

"Daman—"

"There's no need to explain. Any unmarried woman of limited experience would have reacted accordingly. I regret my behavior, Serena. I am sorry I took advantage of you."

He raised her hand to his lips for a burning kiss. A flush of heat surged through her. Daman turned her hand over and placed a scorching kiss onto her open palm. He smiled at her, causing her heart to break in two.

"I'll refrain from more intimate caresses for now." His eyes glowed with desire. "Until we reach Abilene, that is."

Serena found her voice. "Abilene?" she echoed.

Daman grinned. "Yes. You'll be fully initiated there into the ways of love, Miss Sullivan. We'll be married as soon as I can arrange it."

Married?

Serena shook her head repeatedly, dumbstruck at the thought. "No, you don't know what you're saying, Daman."

He took her chin firmly in hand. "Look at me. I am perfectly serious. You have made an enormous difference in my life, Serena. I want to write again. Feel alive again. You have shown me I still have something to offer this world."

She could see the change in him. He shimmered with a confidence that hadn't been apparent when they first met.

"But . . . what will your brother, the earl, say?"

She saw something unreadable flicker across his face but it was gone before she could put a name to it.

Daman waved away her question. "Pish-posh. Edward will adore you. He will love your spirit and character."

Yet Serena realized Daman was trying to convince himself as much as her. She remembered the rigid, structured world he had spoken of and thought how he would be ostracized for such a marriage.

"But we don't suit," she said frankly.

He took her hands in his. "We suit nicely. Now remember, it's not as if I had a title. Or a great deal of money. I let a few rooms. Bachelor's quarters. We'll have to find something more appropriate for a married couple. And then we'll go and stay in the country for a while. I want Edward to get to know you."

Daman squeezed her hands. "Say yes to me, Serena Sullivan. I know leaving America would be a huge step but tell me you'll take it with me. Please."

Serena would give her life to do so. She refused to ruin his, however, and that's what a marriage between them would amount to. Daman wouldn't be received by fine society. Everywhere they went would be whispers and nudges and knowing winks. She wouldn't do that to him.

Because she loved him.

But he didn't need to know that now. They needed to get back to Abilene. She would figure out what to do and how to vanish on the way there. For now, she would pacify him. Serena thought how ironic it was to deceive someone because you loved them.

"Yes," she said quietly. "Yes. I will marry you. I will go to England with you."

His mouth came down on hers and Serena abandoned herself to the moment. She wouldn't have many after this. She might as well enjoy them while she could.

His kiss was achingly tender. Filling her with regret for what she must walk away from. All too soon, Daman lifted his lips from hers, a warm glint in his eyes.

"Let's try to get comfortable for the night. I want to break for Abilene as soon as it is light."

Serena watched as Daman removed the saddles from each horse and brought a saddle back with him. He then retrieve the blanket the saddle had rested against and smoothed it out on the ground in front of him. As he stepped back to survey his work, he tripped over the saddle behind him and fell hard to the ground.

Sheepishly, he jumped to his feet and dusted off before retrieving the wayward object and placing it on top of the blanket.

"Rest assured, Madam, I will never allow that saddle to attack you as it did me."

He lowered himself onto the blanket and leaned against the saddle.

"Come," he said, inviting her to join him. "This is how we slept on the cattle trail." He grinned up at her. "My arse is aching even as I speak. I am sure I will be concentrating on that throbbing pain for the next few hours so I promise I shall behave myself."

Daman grinned at her. "At least until tomorrow. Our wedding day."

Serena joined him on the ground. He placed an arm possessively about her and drew her to him. She rested her cheek against his chest, inhaling his masculine scent that she knew she would never forget.

"Sweet dreams, love."

~

BUT NO DREAMS came to Daman, much less sleep. He lay next to Serena, warm against him, her chest slowly rising and falling as she slept. He wrestled with his conscience as he listened to the noises of the night.

What had possessed him to tell Serena he loved her? He did, of course, but that wasn't something he'd intended to reveal anytime soon to her, much less blurting it out like a schoolboy wet behind the ears. He had only told his sister he loved her and that had been many years ago. Even Daphne, with whom he shared a grand passion, never heard those words escape his lips.

Yet he had proclaimed his love to Serena in the middle of a public street and then proceeded to blithely tell her he would marry her and take her home to England.

Was he mad?

Apparently so. If society would so cruelly reject as his spouse a talented actress such as Daphne, what would they make of an American outlaw and school-marm? Not that he would advertise either fact, but it remained to be seen what would happen once they returned to London. Despite Serena's beauty, her background was totally unsuited to enter the beau monde.

They would eat her alive.

He had very little money left from his playwright days. He lived in rooms that bordered on a questionable part of town. They simply wouldn't be suitable for a wife to inhabit, much less entertain guests. If anyone bothered to come calling. He had no current income coming in and no play to market, though he'd made a damned good start at one back at the hotel.

But a wife?

Daman had never desired one. He wasn't interested in domestic matters, such as what should be served for dinner or how often one should change nappies. Marriage had seemed like the proverbial anchor around his neck, dragging him down.

And yet as he looked at the slumbering angel in his arms, he couldn't imagine a life without her. Serena had utterly turned his world upside down. He doubted the Devil Himself could tear them apart at the end of time. The pull between them, the strong bond they had formed in a matter of days, would be one what would see him through until he was an old man.

He imagined himself with graying hair, a grandchild bouncing on his lap, glancing up as Serena entering the room. Her hair would have gone white by then but her face would be relatively unlined as those amber eyes pierced his. They would share a smile, secrets that crossed the years, as she came and took the child from him. His wife would rest her palm against his cheek and Daman would feel the utter happiness that had been ever constant between them.

Bugger Polite Society! He wanted a life with this woman in his arms, wanted to know every inch of her lush body, rain kisses upon her when awakening each day. He longed to know everything about her, from her favorite foods to what her childhood had been like. He wanted to spoil her, comfort her, and love her until the day he died. Yes, he had fallen hard for his outlaw muse.

Daman would deal with the future one day at a time. It was the only way he would have the courage to carry through with his plans.

The horses both whinnied at the same time and shuffled restlessly. Daman sensed a new presence among them. He looked up and saw glowing eyes slowly approach, coming closer at a steady pace. A chill rippled through him despite the warmth of the summer night. What on earth had such eerie eyes?

It had to be some animal, based upon its height. The horses acted more disturbed now, shifting and snorting. Serena sighed in his arms. He glanced down at her as she lay oblivious to the approaching danger.

Daman thought it must be a coyote. He had never seen one before, but Cookie lost a young dog to one on their way from Texas to Abilene. The old cook had brought the mama dog and one of her offspring on the long drive and Daman enjoyed playing tug-of-war with the pup, using an old sock.

One night, the dog simply vanished without a trace. A few small drops of blood dampened the soil. Mose told Daman that coyotes only went after small prey, biting them just behind the jaw and below the ear. The animal usually died of suffocation and shock, not loss of blood. No one in camp heard a thing. Cookie mourned the pup's death silently, never mentioning the canine again.

As the animal approached, Daman tightened his grip on Serena.

"What—"

"Hush," he warned softly. "Coyote."

Serena turned to look over her shoulder. She whispered, "They're very afraid of humans. I'm surprised this one's come so near to us."

"If it comes closer, I'll jump to my feet and yell at it.

Mose said they usually will run away from a loud noise."

They watched the wild dog drift nearer, dragging one leg behind it. In the moonlight, Daman saw the animal visibly trembled. It began a low growling, almost like a moan. Then it stopped, snapping its jaws and shaking its head.

That's when Daman saw the white foam.

"Rabies," whispered Serena.

Daman slowly removed his arm from around her and reached into his coat pocket for the gun he'd bought at Chaney's. He had thought if he ever used it, it would be in a shootout with Bud Parker. Never in his wildest dreams had he imagined confronting a rabid animal out on the prairie.

And he didn't really know how to aim and fire.

Daman pulled out the pistol and rested it against his thigh. He sensed his own hand shaking and willed it to be still. He had only shot a few times as a boy and never mastered the lessons. He loathed guns and everything to do with them.

But he needed to protect Serena.

"Daman?" her voice was low, barely audible. "Give me the gun."

He turned and frowned at her but steely determination marked her set jaw. Without arguing, he passed the Colt to her.

Serena raised a knee and braced the side of her hand against it as she narrowed her eyes. She wrapped both hands around the pistol and slid one finger against the trigger.

And fired.

20

T he noise was deafening.

Serena's ears rang as the bright light from the Colt revolver flashed against the dark sky. The recoil slammed her back hard against the saddle. Her arm reverberated with the aftershock.

"Hell's teeth!" Daman exclaimed.

He jumped to his feet and hurried to where the sick coyote lay motionless on the ground. Kneeling by the animal, he examined it. Serena noticed he carefully avoided coming in contact with the rabid coyote.

Looking back her, awe in his eyes, he said, "Bloody hell, Serena! You shot him dead between the eyes."

She watched his amazed expression turned to a frown as he started to process her skill with a pistol.

"Where on God's green earth did you learn to shoot in that manner?" Daman rose and returned to her side.

His question left the pit of her stomach cold and dead as the lifeless creature a short distance from her. Serena had simply known to take the gun from Daman when she saw his unsteady hand. Instinct took over.

Now, though, seeing his expression, she realized it

was time to pay the piper. He needed some kind of explanation. He deserved one, especially after all he had done for her.

Serena hesitated a moment, feeling the weight of the world upon her shoulders as she placed the gun on the ground, preparing herself for revealing the truth to him.

"Please. Sit," she said quietly.

Daman took a seat beside her. Wordless, he took her hands into his. Their warmth flooded her. Serena clung to them. She focused on their clasped hands as she began to speak, knowing she didn't have the courage to look the man she loved in the eye.

"I was born and bred in the bowels of New York City. Dirt poor. Irish Catholic. We never knew where our next meal might come from."

Daman squeezed her hands in silent encouragement. Serena's eyes grew moist at the comforting gesture. She wished being poor were her only crime.

"My mother authorized placing my brother and me on an orphan train." She dared a quick glance and saw the confusion in his eyes. It occurred to her that a foreigner, especially someone from his position in society, would have no idea what she meant.

"It was a government program to remove orphans and unwanted children out of inner city tenements and bring them into the American heartland." Serena heard the bitterness in her voice and did nothing to hide it.

"Papa was a drunk who more often than not found himself out of work. He died just before Mama got sick. Mama..."

Serena's voice trailed off a moment. She swallowed hard. "Mama took a long time in dying. She couldn't care for us so she made the difficult decision to let us go."

She gazed at the open sky sprinkled with a dusting of stars, something she had never seen in the city and had come to love on the plains.

"I thought it would be an adventure." She fell silent, unsure how to continue.

Daman finally spoke. "I assume it was not what you expected."

A harsh laugh erupted and Serena realized it came from her. "That would be an understatement."

She finally met his gaze. "Those in charge paraded us like cattle at each stop along the rail line. The local farmers checked us over thoroughly, much as one of your rank might investigate a thoroughbred horse for purchase."

Daman gasped audibly. "But . . . that sounds like, like . . . purchasing a slave. My God."

"The American public—and even the hundreds of children on the weekly trains—were sold on the idea by being told the participating orphans would enter loving homes. Become part of a true family who would care for them." Serena shook her head. "That is far from the actual truth."

She steeled herself for what she must now reveal to him.

"I was chosen by a stern German farmer with a wife and child." She fingered the locket from Bill as she spoke. "They did not want my brother and so we were separated.

"I never saw him again."

Daman's grip tightened on her hands. Serena continued before he could ask more about Bill. Her twin wasn't a part of the story that would make Daman hate her.

"They wanted me for manual labor. And for . . . other things."

Serena decided she must tell Daman the entire truth. Only by disclosing her sordid past could she set him free from her and the absurd idea that they marry. She would force him to see her for what she really was. She would save him from himself and his noble offer.

Quickly, she plunged ahead before her courage failed her.

"Franz von Wormer let me know that I was to be more than a milker and a plower. He quickly initiated me after hours into what he called the pleasures of the flesh," she said in a monotone.

Daman stiffened next to her. She pressed ahead without missing a beat.

"I was forced to become a sexual slave to von Wormer and later, his son. Eventually, I realized I would soon have a child. Frau von Wormer, who turned a blind eye for years, threw me out of her house when I could no longer hide my condition. Fortunately, Franz's spinster sister took me in. She suspected the abuse for years but I was terrified to share anything with her before then.

"Miss von Wormer sheltered me from her brother until I gave birth. The child . . ." she hesitated a moment. "The baby was stillborn. I'll admit relief flooded me because he was the spitting image of his father. Or the son. I never knew which man fathered him."

Serena shattered. "I don't know how I would have faced that child every day for the rest of my life."

She looked squarely into Daman's eyes for the last bit. "I swore I would never let a man touch me again. I learned to shoot. I didn't stop until I was satisfied I could protect myself in every situation."

Her voice remained as steady as her gaze. By this point, she had closed off all her emotions. "And no man ever has. Until you. I've been propositioned with words and looks alike. But no man came close to touching me. Only one man refused to take no for an answer."

Serena paused. "I killed him. Stabbed him with my sewing scissors and pushed him away. He stumbled and fell out an open window and . . . died. I was willing to hang for that. You prevented it. I'll come to terms with what I did. Eventually."

Needing distance between them before she could manage to get her final words out, she ripped her hands from his.

"You can see now why I can't marry you, Daman. I'm ruined. I'm a killer. I'm not the fresh English rose you deserve."

She straightened against the saddle and stared out across the flat prairie. "I would be grateful if you choose to accompany me back to Abilene and let us part ways there. If you'd rather wash your hands of me now and be on your way, I will certainly understand."

Serena drew her knees up, wrapping her arms tightly about her legs. Spent, she rested her forehead on her upright knees.

"Just breathe," she whispered to herself.

She forced air into and out of her lungs slowly a few times, trying to calm her racing heart. A part of her hoped that Daman would slip away while her face was hidden. Serena didn't think she could take whatever now lay in his smoldering blue eyes.

A hand gently caressed her crown. The touch sent a shiver down her spine. Slowly, he began to stroke her hair.

It undid her.

Tears began to flow in the silence. Serena thought by now she would have no more left to shed. These tears though, came from what might have been with this man, for the years they could have spent together as she tried to forget the haunting remnants of her past.

"Serena?"

Daman's voice was soft but full of authority. "Look at me."

She supposed she owed him this one last thing and raised her gaze to meet his.

"I love you."

The simple words left her speechless, as did his tender gaze. Serena shook herself from her spell and exploded, her hands waving wildly as she shouted at him.

"Did you not hear a word I said, Daman Rutledge? That I was raised a guttersnipe by a drunk? That I was literally given away to strangers? Raped every night for years from the age of ten until a child resulted?"

Her gaze fell to her feet. "I am worthless. I've wandered from town to town, trying to forget my past. I can't. I still see their faces in my dreams at night. I wake up with a scream on my lips, feeling as if I've been violated yet again."

She forced herself to be still and calm. "I've murdered for self-preservation. Not that society saw it the same way." She crossed her arms. "But I would do it again. And again. As many times as I had to. That's why—"

But Serena never finished her words. Suddenly, she found herself in Daman's arms, his lips silencing her harsh tirade. His embrace was protective, his mouth tender on hers.

As if someone else controlled her body, she submitted to him, allowing herself the luxury of giving in to his kiss one last time.

Daman's mouth finally left hers. His gaze sought hers but she refused to look at him. He took her chin firmly in hand and raised it until their gazes met.

"Don't you realize your past doesn't matter to me?"

His words shocked her.

He knew ... and he still loved her?

A flicker of hope surged through her yet she batted it down. She hadn't believed in anyone in a long time. If ever. She didn't know if she had it in her to start now.

"Serena? I understand. I truly do. My own sister suffered the same by our father's hand."

Her eyes widened even as she saw the pain of Daman's admission written across his face.

"I sat back and did nothing. I was a mere boy, six years her junior, but I have lived with the knowledge every day of what had happened to Cynthia."

He swallowed as the tears began. "She was a mother to me since mine died at birth. And I didn't protect her from that monster."

Serena's hand went to his damp cheek. "Daman, you were so young. Just a boy. You couldn't have stopped him."

He placed his hand over hers. "I realize that—and yet shame still fills me. I tried to tell my half-brothers but I was known for making up stories and writing all kinds of wild nonsense. They brushed me off. Neither lived at home since they were years older or else they might have realized what was going on. I have felt nothing but guilt since the day she ended her life to stop the pain."

Serena froze at his words. How Daman must have suffered.

He continued. "Like you, after Cynthia's death, I was alone. I essentially raised myself. I rarely saw my two half-brothers. My father drank heavily after her death, stumbling down a flight of stairs and breaking his neck a year later.

"I never mourned his death. I felt no loss. I merely escaped into my writing. I created worlds of my own making, ones I could control. I wrote light-hearted comedies because I couldn't face my darkest secrets."

Daman's hands came to firmly rest on her shoulders.

"So you see, my dearest, I am fully aware of your past and don't give a bloody fig about it."

21

She was about to be married. Nerves rippled through Serena as she stood outside of the small wooden chapel on the edge of Abilene. The hot noon sun burned into her back, but it did nothing to subside the chills that lingered. She bit her lip to still its quivering but didn't know how to begin to still her trembling limbs.

Serena took a deep breath, hoping it would calm her. It didn't help. Any minute, she expected her heart to leap from her chest and bounce along the dirt street like a child's rubber ball. Her vision went black for a moment as she became lightheaded so she grabbed onto a post, gripping it until her knuckles went white.

"We're ready, ma'am."

Looking up, she saw Lydia Chaney smile timidly at her. Serena took a few unsteady steps toward the girl she'd only met a few hours ago at an Abilene general store.

Lydia pulled a small bouquet from behind her back. "These are for you. Mr. Rutledge had me go pick them. Mama always kept flowers and I still plant some each year in her memory. I hope you like them."

Serena reached for the bouquet and wrapped her fingers around it. "They're lovely, Lydia. Thank you."

Lydia seemed to sense Serena's uneasiness and gently clasped her elbow. "Are you all right, Miss Serena?"

She cleared her throat. "Yes. It's just . . . hot. I'm a little dizzy from this intense heat."

That and the fact she was getting married at any moment. A dream she had locked away in her heart, wanting children desperately, and yet knowing she couldn't tolerate the act that would bring them. Marriage had been the last thing on her mind a week ago as she waited in her tiny jail cell for her execution.

Daman reassured her on the way to Abilene that he would not pressure her in any way regarding marital relations.

"We'll take things slowly," he promised. "You shall be in full control."

But then he swept her up in the instantaneous plans for their marriage. Serena thought she rolled along as quickly as a tumbleweed zipping across the Great Plains, pushed along by a strong wind, helpless to stop.

They arrived in the bustling cow town and quickly made their way to Chaney's General Store. According to Daman, Mr. Chaney was just the man to see. The store owner helped make the necessary arrangements in town while his daughter took Serena home with her for a much needed bath. She relished the luxury of sitting in the copper tub and having the girl help wash her long hair.

Lydia also had a simple blouse and skirt waiting for Serena as she dried off.

"Mr. Rutledge picked this out for you," the girl said, a twinkle in her eye as she held up the ensemble.

"He said both of you lost your luggage again! You sure have had a run of bad luck this week."

Lydia squeezed Serena's hand, which brought her back to the present and the wedding at hand.

"I have to go play the piano now. Mr. Rutledge said it wouldn't be a wedding without music." She glanced down at the floor, suddenly shy. "I only know a few hymns. I hope you don't mind. I'm going to play what I know best from memory."

Serena watched Lydia hurry up the aisle and seat herself on a rickety bench behind an upright piano. The strains of *Amazing Grace* filled the chapel and drifted out to the porch.

Daman and Mr. Chaney rose from the front pew and went to stand in front of the minister. Daman turned and winked at her.

Serena's feet were glued to the floor. Panic vibrated through her. Then suddenly, one foot stepped out on its own and planted itself inches in front of her. The other followed automatically and she glided the rest of the way, not quite sure who was in charge.

Lydia finished the verse just as Serena reached Daman. He took her icy hands in his warm ones and smiled encouragingly at her.

"Glad you could make it."

He slipped an arm about her waist, allowing her to lean into him. The minister, who had to be at least eighty, rocked shakily from side to side as he spoke of the sanctity of marriage. Serena had trouble focusing on his high, reed-thin voice.

Then she heard him call her by name.

"Do you, Serena Sullivan, take Daman Rutledge as your lawfully wedded husband? For better or worse, for richer or poorer, in sickness and in health, until death do you part?"

She hesitated a moment. Would she be ruining Daman's life with two simple words? Would marrying him be the most selfish act she'd ever committed?

Serena looked at him. Daman radiated confidence, love for her shining in his blue eyes. He nodded encouragingly.

Turning back to the aging minister, she said, "I do," proud her voice sounded so sure as it rang through the empty church.

Daman responded affirmatively to the vows before he removed the large sapphire she had been wearing while she played the role of his recently, almost-widowed cousin. He slid a thin gold band on her ring finger and then slipped the engagement ring back on top, saying, "With this ring, I thee wed."

"You may kiss your missus, Mr. Rutledge," the preacher proclaimed. "It's official."

Serena faced Daman. He placed his hands on her shoulders and leaned down. The kiss was lingering, full of promise and tenderness. It overwhelmed Serena with its simplicity and sincerity.

A nervous giggle broke them apart. Serena saw Lydia put a hand over her mouth, trying to hide her mirth.

Mr. Chaney slapped Daman on the back. "Congratulations, Mr. and Mrs. Rutledge."

Serena's eyes went wide at his words.

She was Mrs. Daman Rutledge.

She beamed at her new husband, love for him filling her to the brim and spilling over.

Daman took her hands in his and smiled. "Hungry, Mrs. Rutledge?"

"Famished, Mr. Rutledge."

"I could make dinner for you," Lydia offered. "Mama taught me how to cook."

Mr. Chaney put a hand on his eager daughter's shoulder. "That's a very nice offer, Lydia, but I'm sure the Rutledges might like to dine in private."

The store owner told Daman, "I booked you a room at Winston House. The hotels can get pretty rowdy in town with so many of the herds coming in during the summer months but Mrs. Winston's boarding house is always on the sedate side."

"That's because she'd sit on anyone and squash them if they don't follow her rules."

"Lydia! That's most inappropriate." Mr. Chaney glared at his daughter. "I'm sorry, folks. Lydia can be quite opinionated at times. I apologize."

"It's not necessary," Daman assured him.

Lydia grinned. "At least I can say in her favor that you'll get a good meal. She brings the best pies and fried chicken to church picnics."

"Winston House is not a far walk from here," Mr. Chaney added.

Serena said, "We can't thank you enough for all you've done, Mr. Chaney."

"Well, Mr. Rutledge has proven to be a good customer the last few days." He looked to Daman. "I'll get everything you requested bundled up and sent over to Winston House shortly."

"We do appreciate your every kindness, from finding the minister on such short notice to selling me Serena's wedding band."

Daman thanked the minister and Serena saw him slip the old man some money.

"Thank you again for the flowers, Lydia," Serena told the girl. "They certainly added a nice touch to the ceremony."

Daman offered Serena his arm. "Shall we go, Mrs. Rutledge?"

She blushed at the address, still not believing she had married the handsome man before her. "Of course, Mr. Rutledge."

They walked a few blocks down the main thoroughfare. Serena felt fortunate they would be staying where it was relatively quiet.

"It would have been nice to spoil ourselves and head back to the Alamar but I felt it best to avoid where we had been before. Just in case Parker doubles back and checks there when he returns to Crombar Creek."

Daman squeezed her arm affectionately. "Mr. Chaney assured me, though, that Mrs. Winston's place would be immaculate. She doesn't get many guests. I thought that best under the circumstances."

"I'm sure that's the right thing to do."

They saw the sign in the yard marking their stop and Daman opened the gate of the picket fence surrounding Winston House. Daisies danced in the hot breeze along the walkway as they made their way to the wide front porch.

Before they could knock, the door flew open. Serena hid a smile as she looked at Mrs. Winston's girth, recalling what Lydia said before. Serena estimated Mrs. Winston, who barely topped five feet, to be well over two hundred pounds.

"You must be Mr. and Mrs. Rutledge. Come in, come in." She ushered them into her home and seated them in her front parlor on a mohair sofa. "My, it's good to see you. And just married, you are. How delightful."

The woman studied them with a fond smile. "Mr. Winston and I were married nigh on thirty years before he passed last summer." She smiled at Serena, in particular. "Marriage is a wonderful thing, young lady.

And what a handsome catch you made!" She batted her eyes coquettishly at Daman, as if she were fresh out of the schoolroom.

"Thank you for taking us on such short notice," Daman quickly responded, obviously somewhat flustered at the attention. "Mr. Chaney had nothing but kind things to say about you and your establishment, Mrs. Winston."

"Did he brag on my pies?" she inquired. "I'm known for them, you see. Cherry, apple, peach. You name it and I do it best for six counties. Maybe further."

Serena smiled. "I believe Mr. Chaney's daughter, Lydia, was the one who praised your pies, ma'am. As well as your marvelous fried chicken. She said your food is always popular at church picnics."

Mrs. Winston chortled. "Good thing because fried chicken is what you'll be having for dinner." She stood. "Why don't I take you up to your room and let you freshen up a bit? Supper'll be ready in half an hour."

She led them up the stairs and along a corridor to a spacious room at the end. Organdy curtains framed the two large windows, while an intricate quilt with a star design graced the four-poster bed.

"This is lovely," Serena told their hostess. "But I'm afraid our luggage hasn't arrived yet." She glanced at Daman. "Would you mind if we sit on the porch and tried to catch the breeze?"

Mrs. Winston answered for him. "That's a splendid idea, Mrs. Rutledge. I'll bring you some fresh lemonade to cool your parched throats."

The three returned downstairs and stepped out onto the porch, where several rockers were positioned.

"Have a seat here or around to the side. It's a wrap-around porch. Mr. Winston wouldn't build any other kind. I'll get your lemonade."

She bustled into the house. Serena and Daman took a seat and she set her flowers on a table between them. Daman reached and took her hand that now wore his rings.

"This is the first day of the rest of our lives together."

He raised her hand and brushed his lips along her knuckles before playfully grazing his teeth along the same path. A flush of heat warmed her belly—and it had nothing to do with the summer day.

"May there be thousands more," he whispered.

22

Serena took the last bite of peach pie and told Daman, "I think this is the flakiest crust I've ever tasted."

Daman nodded. "Why do you think I had to eat two pieces?" he asked. "This puts to shame the cook I grew up with and I thought she was an undiscovered treasure."

Mrs. Winston appeared in the doorway. "Anything else I can get you two lovebirds?"

Embarrassed, Serena lowered her eyes and dabbed her mouth with the checked napkin in her lap.

"A wonderful meal, Mrs. Winston," Daman proclaimed. "You rather outdid yourself."

"You should see what I can do when the pressure is on, Mr. Rutledge. Why, at last year's three-county fair, I had seven dishes entered. The mayor of Abilene himself judged four of those contests." She smiled smugly. "Let's just say I have seven blue ribbons to show for my efforts that day."

"I'm sure every meal you prepare is worthy of a blue ribbon," Daman said politely. He gave Mrs. Winston a winning smile and Serena thought he could charm a woman of any age.

"May we help you clear the table?" Serena offered. "I could—"

"Not a chance of that, Mrs. Rutledge. You are guests at Winston House." Their hostess winked. "Besides, you have more important things to be about."

Fear pulsed through Serena at the woman's simple words. Her mouth went dry. She had almost forgotten about that part while she enjoyed her dinner and conversation with Daman, who proved as always to be a thoughtful and entertaining companion.

He must have realized how she felt as he whisked her from the dining room and out the front door.

"How about a leisurely stroll?" he asked, taking her hand and slipping it into the crook of his arm. "I feel I'm far too sated to retire just yet."

"That is a wonderful idea."

Serena would do anything to avoid being alone with him in the room where a large bed dominated the view. She fought her fear, knowing Daman would not ask her to do anything that she wasn't ready for.

Yet she knew men had urges that sometimes proved to be uncontrollable. The von Wormers proved perfect examples. She had met other men over the years who wanted certain favors from her which she was unwilling to give. She understood that men often acted on that impulse when a woman was near. In the case of the von Wormers, it always escalated into violence. She had experienced her fair share of bruises at their hands.

Yet she couldn't see Daman in that light. The kisses they'd shared were far from anything she'd ever known. They brought a pleasure to her that she would never have expected from contact between a man and a woman.

"Put it from your head, Serena," Daman said quietly as he opened the gate and saw them through it.

"What are you talking about?"

His gaze bore into her. "You need not pretend with me, love. Ever." He gently squeezed her hand. "I know how Mrs. Winston's words upset you and you've no cause for alarm. I promised not to rush you in any aspect and I am a man of my word. If you merely kiss me goodnight each and every night for the next forty years, I shall still be the luckiest man on earth."

He began to stroll down the road with her by his side, whistling softly.

Serena's galloping heart began to slow as they walked along. His tune had a calming effect on her nerves.

"What is that song?" she asked.

Daman shrugged. "I'm not sure. Mose used to play it on his harmonica. I don't know the words. He did tell me it was one his mother used to sing in the cotton fields when he was a boy."

"It sounds a little sad but it's comforting all the same."

"He told me a little about working in the fields of Alabama when he was a boy. Said that he gained his freedom just as he became a young man. Moved west to start over."

Daman paused a moment. Serena saw he was lost in thought.

Finally, he spoke. "I wonder if that's what I should do. Stay here in the States and begin a new life." He looked at her. "I suppose any decision is now one we both make together. What would you like to do?"

Serena felt honored he would ask her opinion.

Most husbands she knew did as they pleased, regardless of how their wives might view matters.

"I believe it might be hard to give up your native land. You've lived in England all your life and your family is there."

"I really don't have the ties you speak of. Edward is my only family now that Cynthia and Thomas have passed. We rarely see each other. Maybe it's time I forged a new life." He smiled. "With my wife.

"But" he continued, "we have got to get out of bloody Kansas. I'm tired of seeing flat prairie land in every direction. I miss the trees and green grass of England. I would like to view a hill every now and then. What do you suggest, Mrs. Rutledge?"

She thought a moment. "Let's continue on to Denver. Colorado is said to be green and mountainous. You can still do your business for your brother and then we can decide if it's a place you could grow accustomed to."

Daman leaned over and kissed her cheek. "I have married a wise woman. Good advice, my dear."

They continued their leisurely stroll until they got closer into town. It was just past seven in the evening and Serena saw that the night's activities in Abilene had started to heat up. The streets teemed with cowboys milling about, many with a bottle in their hands. Horses flew by as men raced in twos and threes, whipping their mounts with their hats.

"We should head back to Winston House," he suggested, trying to turn them in the direction that they'd come from.

But Serena remained firmly rooted to the spot.

"Serena?"

Daman's voice came from a long way off. She stared at the man coming down the wooden walkway, an ebony cane in his hand. The rim of his hat hid his eyes but something about his mouth and gait seemed all too familiar. A twinge of excitement built within her.

"Could it be?" she asked aloud, not realizing she spoke. She took a step forward and hesitated. No, not after so long a time. Not after she'd gone from place to place, searching for ten years.

Her fingers hand flew to her locket as she watched the man duck into a saloon. Her heart pounded wildly inside her chest. She had seen the man for maybe ten seconds but something told her that her long search might have finally come to an end.

She hoped beyond hope it had.

"We need to go inside that saloon for a few minutes," she said urgently, gesturing to the building across from them even as she moved in that direction.

Daman caught her arm. "Certainly not. You've gone mad, my darling. We are not going into The Wild Mare or any other establishment of that nature. I'll not have you thought of as—"

"I insist, Daman." She looked up at him, her tone growing serious. "You don't know how important this is to me. If I must, I'll go inside alone."

"Why on earth would you wish to go inside such a dreadful place, Serena? It will be full of drunken hooligans and worse."

"I'll explain everything later but please escort me inside at once."

Her husband shook his head. "This is not a good idea. But then again, it's not mine—it's yours. Just stay close and don't let go of my arm. That's an order."

Serena took the lead without thinking, hurriedly heading toward The Wild Mare. She prayed that she was right, that her eyes hadn't deceived her.

Daman snatched her back as a trio of cowpokes came blazing down the street and passed them. She looked both ways this time as he hustled them across the thoroughfare and onto the covered porch.

"You really want to do this?" he asked.

"I really need to do this," she replied.

They entered the crowded venue. Immediately, the smell of beer, perspiration, tobacco, and cheap perfume hit Serena like a punch to her face. The air was thick from the smoke of the cigars. Someone played Stephen Foster's *Camptown Races* on a piano in the distance.

Her eyes took in a back bar of rich mahogany with elaborate carvings. A massive mirror ran the entire length of the bar, reflecting the images of hundreds of whisky bottles lined in front of it. The opposite wall held pictures of nudes and she quickly cut her gaze to the center of the room. Small, round tables filled the main area and she scanned each eagerly, looking for the man she'd briefly glimpsed in the street.

A young man with a scraggly beard step between her and Daman, separating them.

He grinned widely. "Busier than a cat covering crap on a marble floor, I'd say."

Serena's jaw dropped. "I beg your pardon?"

"Quite a crowd tonight. Heard some cowpokes from South Texas came in this afternoon. Them's always the wildest boys, my mama said."

The cowboy grinned again and she could see he had more gaps than teeth in his mouth.

"A course my mama married one of them and had eight boys, to boot, so I'd say she knowed about South Texas men."

Daman pushed the man aside. "Excuse me, Sir, but you've maneuvered between my wife and me."

"Damn, that's an odd way to talk. Say something else."

Her husband glared at the stranger. "Are you quite finished? You nosed in between my wife and me. Now, scurry off."

"Well, don't pee down my back and tell me it's raining." The young cowboy shot a stream of tobacco juice from his mouth and walked off.

Daman looked grim. "I told you this wasn't the best of ideas."

"One more minute, Daman," Serena promised. "Just a quick turn around the room."

She walked quickly around the perimeter, her eyes constantly searching. Men talked, drank, and ate all manner of foods, from Limburger cheese to pickled eggs and beef stew. One man even sat in a barber's chair in the back corner, getting his hair trimmed while he read a newspaper.

But there was no sign of Bill.

Serena reached the far end of the saloon and saw a set of batwing doors. She moved to push through them until a man stepped in front of her.

"Going somewhere?" he asked.

Her eyes continued upward until she met his gaze. He must have been close to seven feet tall, with the jaw chiseled from granite.

"I believe I know someone who just went in there," she said, not willing to believe she'd come this far and would now be stopped by a giant bully.

"Sorry. Private gaming room. And I don't see your invitation anywhere."

Anger flared and Serena sensed her cheeks going red. She glared at the man wordlessly, her thoughts a jumble.

"Would this suffice as an invitation?"

Daman's outstretched hand shot past her. She caught a glimpse of the gold coin it held. Thank goodness, Daman had come to her rescue yet again.

The man raised the coin to his mouth and bit into it. Smiling, he stepped aside and pushed on the swinging door. "I believe you may be admitted after all," he proclaimed as he pocketed his quick profit.

They quickly hurried through the entrance before the guard changed his mind and found themselves in a back room of gaming tables. Most men held cards in their hands although a few tables shuffled around dominos. Women in scanty attire draped themselves over the men with the most chips in their piles. A roulette wheel whirred in the almost silent room as players concentrated on their cards and quietly placed bids.

Then she saw him. Her breath caught in her throat. She couldn't be wrong. His hair was still black and wavy as ever. Her own amber eyes peered from his lean face. A slim, black mustache graced his upper lip.

A moment later he smiled. Any doubts Serena had fled. She walked the length of the room, Daman close on her heels, and stopped in front of his table.

"Bill?"

W*ho the hell was Bill?*
        Daman glared at the handsome man before them, seated at a full poker table. A ripple of jealousy curled in him, threatening to spring out and tear into this broad-shouldered stranger Serena sought out.

The gambler viewed his cards, an engaging, confident smile on his face. Coal-black hair, long sideburns, and a thin mustache completed the picture.

"Bill?" Serena repeated, a little more insistent this time.

Instead of looking up, the man rearranged the cards in his hand.

"Hey, Bill. One of your fancy pieces wants you."

"Not now, darling," he murmured.

"William Mahoney Sullivan! Put those damned cards down right now or else!"

Daman watched the startled look appear on the poker player's face. He dropped the cards in his hands and zeroed in on Serena, shock causing the color to drain from his cheeks.

But his expression turned instantly to pure joy as he focused on her. He leaped to his feet and gathered

Serena in a bear hug, rocking back and forth with her, murmuring her name over and over as he caressed her hair.

Waves of possessiveness—and jealousy—jolted through Daman, seeing his wife in the arms of another man. Daman's fists balled at his side as the anger built.

Suddenly, he stopped himself from pummeling the man's face to a bloody pulp as he studied the stranger again. Serena's amber eyes rested there, and Daman realized he witnessed a family reunion.

Hadn't she mentioned a brother? She had. He remembered her agony as she spoke of the orphan train. She had been separated from her brother and taken by that German monster.

Daman relaxed, certain he was right.

Serena's hands clutched her brother shirtfront. Tears of happiness streamed down her cheeks.

"I have looked everywhere for you, Bill," she proclaimed. "It's been—"

"—fifteen years. I know." Bill's eyes shone with love. "Oh, Serena Sullivan, you are a sight for sore eyes." He squeezed her tightly as if he worried she might vanish into thin air.

"Gonna play poker or not?" growled the dealer seated to Bill's right. "Ain't got all day, you know."

Bill stood. "I'll join you at a later time."

He swept the chips in front of him into his hands and pocketed them before placing an arm around his sister. Gripping a black cane in one hand, he began to move them away from the table. That's when he finally noticed Daman standing nearby.

"And you would be?" He gave Daman a guarded look.

"I'm Daman Rutledge. Serena's husband."

Bill's eyes cut to his sister. Serena blushed. "I'm so sorry. I got caught up in the moment." She gestured toward Daman. "Bill, this is Daman. We were married earlier today."

Bill shifted the cane to his left hand and took Daman's in his right, shaking it firmly. "Mr. Rutledge, it's good to meet you. I'm sure you've discovered that Serena is the best of the best."

"Likewise, Mr. Sullivan. The pleasure is most certainly mine."

Bill led them away from the tables to a corner. "Actually, I go by Chance now. Bill Chance."

Serena's eyes widen. "I've heard of Bill Chance, the famous gambler." She laughed. "No wonder I've had trouble locating you."

Bill shrugged. "Changed it a long time ago. After the orphan train picks." He grew quiet. "Went through some hard times, Sis. Ran away from a few places. Then found a terrific set of parents, only to lose them within the space of three weeks. I came out of those bad years, but I didn't want any reminders of the past."

Daman tensed as he watched his wife's face fall. "Not even me?" she asked, her mouth trembling.

Bill looked at her fiercely. "You'll always be a part of me. Thoughts of you got me through everything bad."

Daman relaxed at Bill's words, watching the smile return to Serena's face. "I'm glad to hear that," she said.

He glanced about the room. While play at the gaming tables had continued, everyone present seemed incredibly interested in the situation unfolding, straining to overhear what was said between the Sullivan siblings.

Quietly, he suggested, "Would you like to accompany us back to Winston House? We're staying there at present. Mrs. Winston has a parlor where we could speak more privately."

Bill nodded. "Agreed. Let me speak to someone for a moment and then I'll meet you outside." He indicated a door to their right. "You can use this side door and avoid the saloon crowd."

Daman took Serena's arm and escorted her from the back room out into the sultry summer night. The sun glowed a deep reddish-orange as it sat lazily on the horizon.

Serena beamed at him and Daman easily read the pure joy on her face. "Just think—to be married and find my long lost brother in a single day." She sighed contentedly. "I couldn't be happier."

He touched his palm to her cheek. "You are radiant. I'm glad you found your brother."

"We're twins, you know. It's been fifteen years since we last saw each other but I just knew when I saw him. It had to be Bill."

She frowned. "I've pursued every tip I could scrape up for years now, trying to locate him. I had a wonderful lead about a gambler with a severe limp and eyes like a jungle cat that spooked his opponents. He was last seen in Denver so I was eager to travel there."

She hugged herself tightly. "That was just before . . . the incident in Crombar Creek." Serena swallowed hard. "It set off things with Charles Rayburn, the local banker who'd shown me what I considered inappropriate attention, him being a married man and all. Word must have reached him that I was leaving the Creek because he came to see me a few hours before the stage departed."

Her mouth tightened. "I told him I was heading for Denver. He tried to convince me it would be to my benefit to stay in the Creek. Not only could I remain as the local schoolmarm, but he thought I would enjoy being what he termed his *special friend*. When I reminded him of his wife, the mayor's sister, he forced himself on me."

She looked up at him, her amber eyes glowing with rage. "I didn't tell you any of the details before. He threw me onto the bed and held me down with his weight. He shoved a hand up my skirts and I snapped. All I could think of was von Wormer and all those nights of misery."

Daman watched Serena fight the memories as they flickered across her face but he sensed she needed to tell him the complete story.

He rested a hand on her cheek. "Go on," he encouraged.

"My sewing basket sat on a table next to the bed. While he slobbered on me, I lifted the lid and found my scissors." Her mouth trembled. "I clutched them as tightly as I could and slammed them into his back. He yelped in pain and jumped from the bed, trying to reach around and pull them out.

"That's when he stumbled backward and fell through the second story window. I'm sure he would have survived the fall with nothing more than a broken leg or two but he landed on his back. It drove the shears through his heart."

She shuddered. "I'll never forget the look of horror etched on his face."

"And the trial?" Daman asked gently.

Serena shrugged. "There wasn't much to it. I admitted to Rayburn's best friend, the sheriff, that I had stabbed Rayburn in self-defense. The reason didn't seem to matter to him or the good citizens of the Creek. They also incorrectly assumed that I'd pushed a pillar of the community out the window. Case closed."

Her eyes, bright with tears, focused on him. "Until you appeared."

Daman smiled at her. "I often find I must rescue damsels in distress. It gives me quite a few good ideas for my plays," he said teasingly. Then he grew more serious. "But what's important is that you found your twin after all this time. I know you will have much to catch up on with Bill."

"I can't wait to hear where he's been." Serena smiled knowingly and said with a hint of pride, "I can assure you Bill Chance has quite the reputation at cards. He's known as the luckiest gambler on the Plains and beyond. Of course, he always showed promise of that when we were children."

Her words took him aback. "He gambled as a *child*?" Instantly, he regretted his words. He knew so little about this wife of his and realized that her childhood in New York must have been abominable, living in abject poverty as her dying mother literally gave her twins away.

He squeezed her shoulder. "I'm sorry. I don't mean to sound judgmental. I know your early years were as difficult as the later ones." Daman felt her relax with his words. "But I can assure you the years to come will be quite remarkable."

He bent and brushed his lips against hers briefly, pulling away since they did stand in public, albeit in an out of the way place.

The door opened behind them and Daman turned. Bill came out, scowling. For the first time, Daman noticed his pronounced limp and realized he had a clubfoot.

"I'm to be delayed, Serena. Some important business I must take care of immediately."

Her eyes flashed in anger. "What? I've searched for you all these years—yet you can't spare an hour for me? That's cruel, Bill." She turned her back on him.

Her twin took a step toward her and laid his hands on her shoulders. Serena stiffened at his touch.

"Sis, you are the most important thing in this world to me. You always have been, from the very beginning. But I didn't know you would drop like manna from heaven tonight."

He turned her to face him. "It's business of a type that cannot be put off. Surely, you can understand that?" he pleaded.

Then he turned and glanced at Daman. "Besides, you have a hale and hardy groom here. I'm sure that you both are looking forward to your wedding night." He grinned. "I think I'd make a fine uncle, you know. Much better than Uncle Ralph, at any rate."

Daman saw Serena soften at Bill's words. "When will I see you?"

"How about I come around for breakfast at this Winston House? I've heard the Widow Winston makes a fine meal."

Serena nodded. "All right. But you have to promise me the entire day. I refuse to settle for less."

Bill looked at Daman. "Only if Mr. Rutledge agrees."

"Daman, please. We're now family. And I would do anything that would keep a smile on Serena's face."

Bill laughed. "I see she has you wrapped around her little finger." He kissed his sister's cheek. "Please, Serena. Go back to Winston House. This area is no place for a lady to be. I swear to you I will see you first thing in the morning."

He fingered the gold locket at her throat, a smile on his face, and then shook hands with Daman again and took his leave.

Daman and Serena walked back to Winston House and contented silence. He sensed the happiness that radiated through her. Although he selfishly wished he had been the cause of it, he was happy her spirits were so high.

They arrived at the boarding house and informed Mrs. Winston of a guest for breakfast the next morning.

"Good thing you told me. I'll be sure to have more bacon and biscuits."

"And griddlecakes if possible?" asked Serena. "Bill has always been fond of them."

Mrs. Winston smiled. "That I can do, Mrs. Rutledge."

"Then we thank you for everything, Mrs. Winston," Daman said, "and will bid you a good night."

He escorted Serena up to their room. Mrs. Winston thoughtfully had lit a lamp that glowed softly. She'd also turned back the bed and plumped the pillows. In the corner rested a trunk and valise.

"I see Mr. Chaney sent over my request," he said. "We should each have a few changes of clothes and some night attire. Some personal toiletries, too. Lydia was to pack everything for us."

Serena's eyes glowed appreciatively. "You always think of everything."

He grinned. "Isn't a writer supposed to?"

He didn't want to make her uncomfortable so he added, "Why don't I step out for a few minutes and let you dress in your night rail?"

Color bloomed on her cheeks. "All right," she agreed, turning away from him.

Daman stepped from the room and closed the door gently behind him. He had promised Serena all the time in the world but he didn't know how he'd keep to such a crazy pledge. He had always been a man of honor, his word being sacred, and he had not taken his wedding vows lightly. He'd let his new wife make the first move in the bedroom.

But it didn't mean it would be easy.

After ten minutes, he figured it was safe to return. He tapped lightly on the door before entering the room. Serena sat at the dressing table.

She turned and looked over her shoulder. "Would you mind helping me remove my pins?"

"Certainly."

Daman crossed the room and stood behind her, looking at her image in the mirror. While primly cut, her white nightdress could not hide the fullness of her breasts. He forced his eyes upward and began slipping the pins from her hair, letting the raven curls cascade down her back.

When he finished, Serena picked up her new brush.

"Allow me."

Taking it from her hand, he stroked the brush through her silky tresses. The motion soothed him. He loved the very nearness of her, her alabaster skin, the faint floral scent from her recent bath, the dark locks that belonged to the only woman he would love.

Daman finished and handed the brush back to her.

"Thank you," she said softly.

Rising, she went to the bed, slipping underneath the coverlet and closing her eyes.

And not a moment too soon. Daman's reaction to seeing her briefly against the lamp, when the gossamer material became transparent, occurred all too quickly. He took a deep breath and let it out slowly, trying to control his very physical reaction to his wife.

He moved to her side of the bed and blew out the lamp before returning to his side. He stripped off his clothes and got under the bedclothes, turning away from Serena. No sense in alarming her with his growing erection.

He lay in the dark for several minutes, his eyes open, finally adjusting to the faint moonlight that peeked through the frilly curtains. To be so close, almost touching, was sheer agony, he decided. And another thousand or more nights like this might lie ahead.

Serena's voice broke the silence.

"Daman? Would you make love to me?"

24

Serena lay in bed with her heart racing as Daman extinguished the light and crawled into their bed. Then nothing.

Even though Daman promised her that he would not ask anything of her, a part of her hadn't believed him. Men made all sorts of promises which they failed to keep. She witnessed this from childhood. Her father would promise her mother he'd be able to keep the next job. Or the next. Uncle Ralph would swear each drink would be his last. She heard men on the streets of New York vow all kinds of things, none of which they intended to keep.

It continued with the people who organized the orphan trains, those hypocritical Christians who broke their sacred word and did not honor her mother's request. They separated her from Bill. And on to Franz von Wormer. He pledged to give her all kinds of things, from pretty dresses to chocolates in the light of day for a sweet little cooperation under the sheets at night.

Serena saw even more men break their word as she aged. Whether in business or pleasure, it seemed men guaranteed one thing and yet proposed quite another. She gave up counting the number of times she was told—often in writing—what her annual teaching salary would be, only to have unnamed problems occur in the community, shorting her every time.

She expected Daman's manly urges to break the promises he'd made to her, despite his best intentions.

Yet he hadn't.

As they lay together in the darkness, her amazement grew. Had she finally found a man of his word? He said he loved her. She knew she loved him. He stirred urges in her like no man, feelings she thought she'd never experience.

A certainty took hold of her as never before. Serena realized she didn't want to keep Daman waiting some arbitrary amount of time while she got used to the idea of marriage. He had thrown his lot in with her from the very beginning, never once wavering in his support of her. How many men would have done so in the same circumstances? With every ounce of courage she could muster, she asked him, "Daman? Would you make love to me?"

Serena heard his quick intake of breath. Yet he remained motionless.

Finally, he asked, "Are you sure?"

He still faced away from her, as if he feared her skittering off if he turned in her direction.

Serena bit her lip and took a calming breath. "I'm sure I love you."

Daman rolled to face her. In the narrow bed, she could feel the heat from his body, its very nearness causing her chest to tighten in fear.

"I love you," he whispered. "I always will, Serena. It pleases me to call you my wife. I have no greater need than that." He brushed his knuckles against her cheek. Don't think this is something we must do tonight," he added. "We have the rest of our lives together."

He gathered her up in his arms, his chin resting atop her head.

"You have had an emotional day, love. You need some rest. Go to sleep."

Serena's heart pounded as she lay nestled against his hard, muscled body. She had never felt more protected or loved. This man put her first in every way.

She had to show him the depth of her feelings.

"Daman?"

"Huh?"

She reached up a hand to stroke his face. "I really want to do this. With you. Now."

She slid her hand down to rest against his heart. It beat rapidly against her palm.

"I will admit I have some fears," she said softly. "But none that cannot be conquered. All I know is how my body craves your touch. How your kiss sends me to another place in another time. How I want to experience what real physical love is and only with the man I love. I want to please my husband."

"I want nothing more than to please you, sweetheart." Daman caressed her cheek. "We will go slowly. Stop me if you feel uncomfortable or afraid in any way. Promise me?"

"I promise. Now, kiss me like there's no tomorrow, Daman Rutledge."

"That is something I will gladly do, Mrs. Rutledge."

He pressed his lips to hers and Serena's hands wound around his neck. Daman held her fast as he lazily ran a tongue around the shape of her mouth. She pulled closer to him and he deepened the kiss. Serena's insides immediately turned to jelly.

Timidly, she touched her tongue to his and smiled at the growl she heard. More boldly, she swept it around, teasing with him as he did her. His hands stroked up and down her back, causing little ripples of sensation where he touched. She imitated his gesture, admiring the sleek muscles that bunched under her fingers.

Daman broke the kiss to ask, "Are you all right?"

She heard the concern in his voice. "I'm fine. A little nervous. But in a good way," she assured him.

Serena decided to make the next move. She eased away from him so she could glide her hands down his bare chest. He shuddered as she moved them up and down and her confidence grew.

Daman copied her gesture now and her breast ached as he did so. She moaned a little and he stopped.

"No, don't stop. Please, don't stop."

"Yes, ma'am."

He began kneading her breasts, rolling her to her back and slipping her night rail over her head before he bent and placed her breast in his mouth. The instant his tongue touched her nipple, a jolt of fire spread downward and she gasped.

"Are you all right?"

"Yes," she said breathlessly. "Very."

Daman continued to lavish attention on first one, then the other breast, causing needles of electricity to begin zinging through her.

"I had no idea this could feel so good," she blurted out.

He chuckled. "Oh, wait. It gets better."

It did. Daman continued to touch her, stroke her, caress her. New sensations appeared every few seconds. Her body tingled everywhere as he found each nook and cranny and explored it with his knowing lips and tongue and hands.

Then he moved lower, tracing his tongue around her navel. Serena tensed.

"Wait," she said, panic starting to override the other delicious feelings.

Daman rested his head on her stomach and stroked her hip and thigh. The good sensations returned and Serena tamped down her fear.

He lifted his head and gazed deeply into her eyes. "You can trust me. I'll stop whenever you tell me to."

"I know," she said, her voice quavering with emotion. "I do trust you." She closed her eyes. "I'm yours. Make me whole again, Daman. Set me free from the dark shadows of the past."

"With pleasure, my love."

He kissed her belly and down along her thigh. Serena willed herself not to tense but go with the feelings and new sensations he brought to her body. His mouth moved along the inside of her thigh and Serena exhaled slowly as new sparks began.

"I'm going to pleasure you, Serena Rutledge," her husband promised. "You will enjoy this."

She bit her lip and clutched the bedclothes next to her. She fought the nerves as Daman moved lower and a fierce throbbing began. She kept her eyes closed, not wanting to see what he would do next.

Daman knew the next few minutes would determine the course of his relationship with his wife. He wanted to help her conquer the ugliness of her past and bring her joy. He took a calming breath, knowing everything must be about her now.

Carefully, he slid a finger inside her. She tightened around it instinctively and then relaxed as he eased the finger out and then back in again quickly. She gasped.

"Oh!"

"Does that feel good, Serena?"

He moved back and forth, first with one and then two fingers, stroking her deeply. Her hips started to rise and meet him.

"Yes. Oh, yes!"

He smiled at her answer. "Would you like to feel better, love?" He stroked her sensually.

"Yes," she whispered.

"Don't talk, love. Just feel."

Daman's touch was beginning to drive Serena into a frenzy. Something was building inside her and she had no idea what. He continued speaking to her softly but she no longer was capable of understanding his words. One hand continued its magic where her drum pounded more wildly at each stroke. The other caressed her belly, reached up to her breast, and playfully tweaked her nipples.

Serena thought she might go mad.

Then a quick rush swooshed through her and wildly she pressed her hips against his hand, harder, faster, need now exploding through her, vibrating out of control.

"That's it. Ride it out, Serena."

She did as he instructed, as wave after wave crested and crashed. And slowly, she came back to an awareness of her surroundings, of Daman and their room at Winston House. She grabbed him and pulled him down on her.

"That was amazing," she said, her voice full of wonder.

"It gets better," he told her.

Serena smiled up at him. "Show me."

25

S erena awoke with a delicious sense of satisfaction permeating through her. Last night changed her in ways she might never understand. She'd leaped off the mountain of doubt and fallen willingly into Daman's open arms.

Her husband.

It didn't seem possible. He had rescued her from the jaws of death only days ago, but more importantly, he had liberated her soul from the unseen chains that had kept her from finding true happiness.

Now, she lay nestled against him, his arm wrapped protectively about her waist, holding her close even in sleep. Never had she felt safer. Or truly loved.

Serena smiled. The physical act of love between a man and a consenting woman had proven most interesting. Daman made love to her twice and they'd fallen asleep, exhausted yet satiated.

And she was ready for more.

It surprised Serena how one man and his love for her changed her outlook overnight. Of course, she returned that love and knew she would do anything for Daman, even give her life for him, so powerful was the bond between them.

She stroked his arm, almost bursting with the love overflowing in her heart. She supposed the same feelings would be created anew when they had their first child. She wondered if they had already started a new life within her with their lovemaking last night. She hoped Daman wanted children. She imagined him holding a small child in his lap, telling him or her stories he would invent about far-off places or magical kingdoms and fairy princesses.

His arm tightened about her as he stirred from sleep. Serena shivered as his lips caressed her neck.

"Already awake?"

"Habit," she told him. "Farmers rise early and so do their families and houseguests such as me. I always arrived at the schoolhouse a couple of hours before the children did. Wood needed to be chopped. A fire lit. The floor swept and lessons planned. The list of tasks was never ending."

Daman nibbled on her earlobe. "That is all in your past, Mrs. Rutledge. I intend to finish the play I've started and stage it in London. It will be my comeback production. I now have my new inspiration and you'll keep me on my toes and my writing fresh. I intend to give you every luxury known to man. You need never do physical labor again."

Serena turned toward him. "I have the only luxury I need. You. No, you are definitely a necessity, Daman Rutledge."

She pressed a soft kiss on his mouth. Yet a flicker of doubt crossed her mind as she did so. She had found Bill only yesterday. How could she leave him and leave the country for London? Serena pushed the thought aside. She would deal with it later. She couldn't even think now. Daman's touch had that effect on her.

He kissed her back slowly, thoroughly, deepening the kiss until her heart fluttered wildly and the new, yet familiar urges took hold of her.

"It'll be day soon," she whispered against his lips, feeling the smile that began to curve on them.

"Scandalous, isn't it? Making love to my wife in the morning sunshine."

Daman pulled away from her and jumped from the bed, a wicked smile playing about his lips. "I say we let the light come in so I can see just how beautiful you really are. I want to see every inch of your lovely body, Serena Rutledge."

He stepped around the foot of the bed and walked to the window, pushing the curtains aside as he smiled at her over his shoulder. Serena admired every inch of him, no longer afraid of the contours of his body, rather reveling in his broad shoulders and sleek muscles.

Daman grew eerily still for a moment as he looked out the window. He snapped the curtains shut and turned back, an urgency on his face.

"Get dressed. Fast."

The light, playful tone had been instantly replaced as if Daman were a military man issuing orders on the battlefield.

"What—"

"Now, Serena. Clothes only. Carry your stockings and shoes."

He picked up his own clothes and rapidly threw them on as she leaped from the bed and did the same, fear tightening her throat.

He spoke quietly as he slipped into his trousers. "Three riders are approaching Winston House. They have a look about them that tells me they are on business."

"They found me." The words came out a bitter whisper. Her hands rose, her fingers too numb to move.

Daman hurried over and began buttoning up her blouse. He threw the skirt about her and fastened it before gathering her shoes and stockings and pushing them at her.

"I'll go downstairs and see if I can head them off." As he spoke, he pulled a roll of cash from his pocket and pressed it into her skirt's pocket. "Take this. Slip down the stairs and out the back. Go to Chaney's store. I'll find you there."

"But—"

"Go!"

Daman opened the bedroom door just as a loud pounding sounded on the front door below. He grabbed her free hand and Serena found herself being dragged along the hallway and down the stairs. When they reached the bottom, Daman pushed her toward the kitchen. He turned and headed toward the front of the house, fastening the remaining buttons on his shirt as he walked.

The pounding went on relentlessly. Surely, Mrs. Winston would have heard it by now. Daman wondered why the landlady didn't come down and see what was happening on her own front porch. He decided he had better open up and let the trio in. Serena would be ready to move away from Winston House by now and he needed to distract the men who came for her. What better way than inviting them inside?

"May I help you?" he asked in his most formal tone once he'd opened the door. "I do believe it's far too early for Mrs. Winston to be receiving guests."

The men pushed past him and spilled into the

small foyer. They looked around quickly and Daman knew they searched for Serena.

"If you would have a seat, I will awaken Mrs. Winston. If you've come for breakfast, she serves at seven-thirty. You should have seen that on the sign posted at the gate. I do hear her biscuits and ham are delightful."

Their leader, a balding man in his early forties, took a threatening step forward. "Is this the one, Claude?" he asked, looking at a thin, short man with yellow teeth and a crooked nose.

"Yep," the man nodded sagely. "He was with her when they came in. I overheard him say this is where they'd be. Told that Chance fella."

Daman's gut tightened. He had to stall in order to give Serena more time to get away from the property.

~

SERENA HEARD the front door open as she turned the knob on the rear one in the kitchen. She closed it gently and turned, running into Mrs. Winston.

"Oh!" she gasped, startled to see the widow standing in front of her with a deep basket filled with eggs.

The elderly woman looked her up and down, concern written across her face. "Did you have a fight with Mr. Rutledge, dear?"

"No. Nothing of the kind. But I must leave, Mrs. Winston. Now. There's . . . trouble. I don't want you involved."

Mrs. Winston nodded. "I see. Then I'll go head it off. Do what you must, Mrs. Rutledge. I haven't seen hide nor hair of you."

Serena took off running, praying that the woman

wouldn't become more involved in their complicated affair than she already was.

She cut around the side of the property and angled toward town, wincing as the rocks cut into her tender soles. She decided Daman would delay the men by at least a few minutes so she plopped to the ground and thought it best to put on her stockings and shoes. Already disheveled in appearance, she would be far too memorable in case she saw anyone at this early hour by traipsing into town with bare, bleeding feet.

Her boots buttoned up, Serena pushed herself to her feet and continued toward Abilene. The sun finally slipped above the horizon, bringing light to the early morning. Birds sang lustily in the summer breeze as she walked quickly down the lane. She saw no one and thought the night's revelers had stumbled home drunk, while the town's businesses would not be open for a few more hours.

Serena wondered what time the Chaneys arrived at their store and decided she would to wait for them in their back alley. Part of her wanted to be grateful for having a place to run. The other part of her knew the kind store owner and his daughter would be in trouble with the law if they shielded her in any way, even for a short while. Maybe she could simply leave a message with him of her whereabouts, which they could pass along to Daman.

But where she could she hide?

As Serena hurried along, she decided to slow her pace a bit. She had a little distance between her and the men at Winston House now and she didn't want to be noticeable in any way. Besides, she could see a man walking up ahead in her direction. She wanted to appear as normal as possible.

She watched him as the gap closed between them and even from a distance, she knew it was Bill by the cane he carried and the unsteady gait. She forgot all else and ran to meet him. Serena saw his surprised look as he recognized her and he called out a greeting as she came closer.

"Hey, Sis. Here I thought I was going to be early to breakfast. Guess you thought I wasn't coming and decided to meet me, huh?"

Serena threw herself at him and Bill grunted. "What's wrong, Serena?" He held her at arm's length, frowning at her. "Have you and Daman had your first fight already?"

"I can't explain now, Bill. I have some men after me. Daman stayed behind to give me a chance to escape."

She slipped her hand through the crook of his arm. "Come on. I'll explain along the way but we've got to get to Chaney's General Store."

She tried to catch her breath as they walked together. She realized already that having Bill on her arm would help. If the sheriff's men were looking for her, they wouldn't think she'd be with someone else.

"Is it far?" Bill asked.

Serena thought as she got her bearings. "It is a ways down the main street. Can you make it that far?" Worry kicked in, knowing how too much walking caused his clubfoot to ache.

Her brother gripped her arm. "I can go wherever you need me to, Serena, but talk to me as we walk."

"It's a long story, Bill."

She felt tears pricking her eyes and pushed away the sadness, holding on to her anger instead.

"I was accused of stabbing a man and pushing him

out a window. He died. I stood trial in Crombar Creek, a little town not far from Abilene."

"You are the woman that was to hang?" Bill asked, astonishment in his voice. "I heard tell of you when I arrived in Abilene."

"I stood blindfolded on the scaffold, a noose around my neck, when Daman rescued me. Sight unseen—and he risked his life for me."

Her twin whistled. "And he really did marry you?"

Serena nodded. "Yes. But only after our coach to Denver was robbed and we decided to take the train. Then the Creek's sheriff was on the train and we abandoned that route. We wound up back in Abilene and were married yesterday. We were planning to leave for Denver today and I was going to look for you."

She sighed. "It's been the biggest mess but I love him, Bill. Now I don't think I'll ever have a future with him." She felt the tears coming again. "And I've only just found you again."

Bill squeezed her arm. "I'll get you out of this, Serena." He stared at her intently. "I promise you that. You and Daman will have the life together you deserve."

Then a crooked smile graced his face. "After all, what are brothers for?"

26

"Where are we headed again?" Bill asked as they continued along the dusty main road.

"Chaney's General Store. The owner helped arrange our wedding but . . ." Serena's voice faded in doubt.

"What?"

"I feel guilty dragging him and his daughter into my mess. I don't know the penalty if they're caught helping me escape. They've already been so kind."

"We won't endanger them. We'll go to my hotel instead."

"How will Daman know where I am?"

"Don't worry. I'll get word to him. Getting you out of Abilene unseen is the most pressing need now. He can follow."

"But how? This is the third time—"

Bill cut her off. "Just trust me, Sis. Let's head for my hotel room. I'll leave you there out of sight. I'll make all the arrangements as fast as I can." Bill paused. "You do ride?"

"Yes." Her voice broke as her frustration bubbled to the surface. "There's so much we don't know about each other. So many lost years."

"Don't think about that now. We'll have all the time in the world to catch up." He winked at her. "Preferably not in Kansas. Do you have a destination in mind?"

"Not back home. Nothing's there for me in New York."

Bill nodded. "Same here. The west is home for me now."

They continued walking in silence. They passed a boy throwing buckets of water along the walkway in front of a saloon. As they passed, Serena smelled why. It needed to be done. Bill had them cross the street to avoid the stench.

As they did, a man stepped from a building and automatically tipped his hat to her. Serena knew he seemed familiar but she couldn't place him. Her nerves were at the breaking point as they passed him.

Then the man called out from behind her. "Why, could it possibly be Miss Rutledge?"

Serena reluctantly turned around, afraid if they continued on it might cause a scene. As she did, she remembered him. The nosy clerk from the Alamar Hotel.

She smiled sweetly at him. "I'm surprised you recognized me without my veil, Sir."

He closed the distance between them. "I spied that lovely engagement ring on your hand, Miss Rutledge. It certainly is a sparkler." He shook his head sadly. "I'm sorry I brought that up. But what a pleasant surprise. Fancy seeing you back in Abilene." He glanced at Bill speculatively. "I thought you and your cousin were headed for Denver."

Serena nervously fingered her locket. "Cousin Daman had a change in plans along the way, Sam. You know how business can be." She wished she sounded more confident and looked less disheveled.

Sam studied her. "Well, I should pass along to you that the oddest thing occurred not soon after you departed for Denver. Sheriff Parker from Crombar Creek —that's a little town about six miles to the west of us —came looking for you. Or at least someone who looks an awful lot like you."

Bill quickly spoke up. "I doubt that, Sir. Miss Rutledge is one beautiful woman. I don't see many women who match her beauty, much less resemble her."

The clerk tittered. "I suppose you're right. Besides, the sheriff was chasing some adulterous murderess that escaped the hangman's noose. And we both know Miss Rutledge is a respectable lady mourning the loss of her fiancé." Sam paused a moment. "You do know about that, sir?"

Serena prayed Bill wouldn't flinch. He'd already picked up on the story Daman had invented for her while at the Alamar. After all this time, her twin must still have part of the con man in him. And his legendary status as a poker player gave him that air of cool civility he now used.

"I do." Bill stared hard at Sam. "I don't believe Miss Rutledge would like further mention of this upsetting incident. He turned to Serena. "We must be on our way. Daman sure doesn't like being kept waiting."

Sam took a step back. "My best to Mr. Rutledge, ma'am. Sir."

They moved away from the meddlesome clerk. When they were out of his hearing range, Bill said, "It's not far. Just ahead. The Crystal Palace."

Bill pointed and Serena saw a three-story building a block ahead on the right. Her heart still pounded furiously from their previous encounter. What would Sam do? Did he suspect anything? Would he seek out Sheriff Parker and let him know she had suddenly returned to Abilene?

Once they reached the hotel, Bill walked past it and Serena knew exactly why. They'd used misdirection many times in the old days. He led them past another block then they doubled around and entered a side door of The Crystal Palace. If Sam still lingered on the street, he would not have a clue where Bill was staying.

They went down a long corridor and then entered a spacious lobby. It was still quite early and thankfully, no one was in sight. Bill let her up a flight of stairs, slowly swinging his clubfoot around to move up each step. They walked down a silent hall. Bill inserted his key and they entered the room.

The room was actually a suite. A large sitting room with a camelback sofa and two wing chairs took up most of the space in the outer room. A small oak writing desk sat in a corner.

"Lock the door behind me," Bill instructed. "Go into the bedroom and lock it, too. I'm off to find the best way to sneak you out of town. Once I do, I'll drop by Chaney's place and give him a message to pass along to Daman."

Bill wrapped her in his arms and held on tightly. Serena couldn't believe she'd put Daman and now her brother at such risk. She pulled back and looked into his eyes.

"Do whatever is necessary but don't include yourself or Daman in the travel plans, Bill. I've put everyone I love in jeopardy. I won't do it anymore."

Serena touched her palm to his cheek. "I've dreamed about you for years. I wondered where you went. What you were doing. I prayed I would recognize you if I ever found you. But I will not get you killed. The Creek's sheriff has a vicious streak, Bill. He won't rest until I'm swinging from the end of a rope."

Bill took her hand in his. "Serena, don't talk like that. I know you're in trouble but it's not anything we can't handle. And you also have Daman in your corner. Hell, we need to get you out of the country with murder charges hanging over your head. You two need to go to England. Get as far away from this mess as possible."

Serena nodded. She didn't trust herself to speak. Her emotions threatened to erupt in a volcano of tears.

Bill thought a moment. He squeezed her hand. "Stay safe. I may be gone a few hours but I will be back. Don't open either door for anyone. Understand?"

He limped to the door and paused. Looking over his shoulder, he said, "I love you, Sis."

"Take care," she managed, fighting back her tears.

Bill left and Serena locked the door.

"WHERE IS SHE?" the trio's leader growled at Daman.

"I wish I—"

"What is the meaning of this?"

All four men turned to the shrill, accusatory voice. Daman breathed a sigh of relief, seeing it was Mrs. Winston, an egg basket resting over her arm. He wondered if Serena ran into the woman as she exited the house.

"And you!" Mrs. Winston glared at Daman. "Coming down in your bare feet with your shirt misbuttoned and no frock coat? I run a decent place, sir. Please return to your room until you are properly attired. Do not reappear for breakfast in this sorry state or I shall have to ask you to vacate my premises."

Daman managed to look sheepish as she dismissed him from the room. Something told him Mrs. Winston might hold her own with the men recently arrived. He also believed that the landlady was covering for Serena, as well.

As he retreated up the stairs, he heard her light into them and hovered a moment, listening to the conversation.

"And as for you, Jimmy Barrows, what are you bringing these men to my place at the crack of dawn? You've tracked mud in on my newly waxed floor. I declare, good manners have gone out the window. I don't know what Abilene's coming to."

"Ma'am, we're aiming to find a young gal said to be staying here."

Mrs. Winston sniffed. "Well, you won't be finding one here. That gentleman who just left is my only guest at the moment."

Their voices faded as Daman reached his room and hurried inside. He went through the room quickly and threw the few items not already in their luggage into it. He glanced around and saw that the room bore no trace of Serena having spent the night there. Thinking two pieces of luggage might be considered odd for a man, Daman pushed one flush against the bed. From the doorway, the bed obscured it.

"Just in time," he said to himself as he heard heavy boots bearing his way.

Daman quickly corrected the buttons on his shirt and picked up his coat, tossing it on as the men rapped loudly on his door.

He sat on the bed and said, "Come in," busying himself with getting something on his bare feet.

"Where is she?"

Daman looked up. "Might I inquire whom you seek?"

"You know," the man called Barrows said, his eyes narrowing. "Serena Sullivan."

Daman frowned. "I believe I've heard that name." He paused a moment then brightened. "Yes, indeed. Isn't she the one who's to hang for some murder? No, wait. That should already have occurred." He tried to sound exasperated. "Well, if she's already dead, why are you looking for her here? You Yanks are—"

"Cut the malarkey. Claude here saw you with her. Last night at The Wild Mare."

Daman scratched his chin thoughtfully. "I was at that very establishment last night. Oh, wait." He looked over at Claude. "Do you mean the beauty with the dark hair and amber eyes?"

Claude's head began bobbing up and down. "See, Jimmy. I told you he knew her."

Daman pursed his lips. "Well, that couldn't be this Sullivan woman if she's already dead. That was a . . . what do you call them here in the States? We," Daman smiled, "would call her a lightskirt. I'm sure, Mr. Barrows, that even you might have needed of the services of a woman from time to time. I'm a long way from home and Dixie Lee was most accommodating."

"Dixie Lee?" Barrows frowned at Daman.

He shrugged. "That is what she informed me her name was when I engaged her services. I'm sorry but she never gave me a last name." He smiled broadly. "She did give me a grand time, however. Expensive— but worth every penny. I would highly recommend Dixie Lee to any of you chaps."

Barrows cut his eyes to Claude. "Could you be wrong?"

Claude shuffled his feet as he looked at the ground. "Didn't think so, Jimmy. Could have sworn it looked like her. And she really seemed to know Chance. That gambler. They hugged and hugged like there was no tomorrow. Then I heard this feller say they'd be here."

Daman cleared his throat. "Dixie Lee did accompany be back to Winston House. Mrs. Winston had naturally retired for the evening before this occurred." He lowered his voice. "I would be most appreciative if you did not advertise to her that I had brought a trollop back here for a few hours' romp. The room rate is quite reasonable and Mrs. Winston is a fantastic cook. I think she might throw me out over such an incident."

The third man, who'd remained silent until now, finally spoke up. "Jimmy, why don't we go check out this Chance fellow? See how he knows the girl. He might know if it's Serena Sullivan or not. Then we can let Parker know the score."

Daman prayed that's exactly what these men would do. Bill would probably pass them in the street and no one would be at his hotel room when they arrived. It would be another dead end. When he arrived at Winston House, Daman would warn Bill not to return to his hotel for the rest of the day. By the time these men came back to Winston House to pick up the trail, Daman would be long gone to Chaney's.

And hopefully far outside Abilene's city limits, with Serena in tow.

27

S erena sat on the edge of the hotel bed, doubt flickering in her mind as she toyed with the gold locket that hung around her neck. Bill had been gone for at least half an hour, she guessed. She hadn't had time to pin her new watch to her dress in her haste to exit Winston House.

She didn't know if Bill could set a plan in motion to help her escape. She had no idea how long he'd been in Abilene or what connections he might have formed. Despite her warning him to arrange for her to leave town alone, she knew he would never turn his back on her.

Neither would Daman. The two of them had forged far too great a connection in the short time they'd known one another. Serena knew without a doubt that Daman would risk his very life to protect her.

And she decided she couldn't allow that.

She stood and began pacing the chamber, trying to work out in her mind what to do next. She loved her husband and brother and she would not have them pulled into a quagmire of her making. Bill seemed to have fashioned a successful life for himself. Daman was writing again. He would have great success once more, she was certain. If not for his American wife, the albatross hanging around his neck, he could easily re-enter and charm London society.

Serena pictured him peering from behind the drawn curtain at the full house, waiting for his new production to begin, full of eagerness. He would catch the attention of the beautiful lady seated on the corner of the first row and wave to her, proud of his delicate English wife and her standing in society.

That's what he deserved. Not someone who would shame him before the London elite, much less a convicted felon who might very well drag him into losing his own life.

She determined to do the only thing she could under the circumstances. She would turn herself in to the authorities. Once in custody, events would proceed quickly. Her execution date would be reset. They wouldn't gamble this time. Sheriff Parker would not twice be made a fool.

And Daman and Bill would be safe. They would mourn her for a time but they would be alive. They would go on with their lives. It was the greatest gift she could give them. Protecting them from Parker and harm's way.

Yet Serena could not picture handing herself on a silver platter to the corrupt sheriff of Crombar Creek. She managed to live through Franz von Wormer. Daman had given her a chance to continue to live. She'd be a fool to go willingly to the gallows again.

No, she would escape on her own and keep Daman and Bill out of it. She had been in more than a few tight pinches in the old days back in New York and had gotten out of those scrapes. She would be re-sourceful enough to skip town this time, too, using whatever deception and skullduggery was needed.

Serena walked to the window and pulled the curtain aside, ready to search the streets and decide on her next move. Abilene had awakened since she and Bill entered the hotel. The streets buzzed with activity. Riders galloped down the thoroughfare in front of the hotel. Passersby walked on both sides. Customers already entered the saloon directly across the street.

Then she spotted three men who approached The Crystal Palace with purposeful strides. Only Daman saw them before but Serena's heart told her these men had somehow made the connection between her and Bill and now came for her.

She dropped the curtain and hurried to escape the hotel room. She refused to be found in Bill's suite when it might implicate him in some way.

Serena unlocked the doors and fled down the hall. She had no idea where to run, only that she must. She doubted she would find a back staircase since Bill had led them to the room up the main staircase. Did she have time to make it to the lobby and out the side door?

Her skirts flying, Serena sailed down the stairs, reaching the bottom just as the front door of the hotel began to open.

She whipped her face away and turned to go down the hallway leading to the familiar side door. She reached the door and pushed it open. Her hand immediately came up to shield her eyes from the bright sunlight.

Strong fingers latched onto and twisted her wrist. Serena was spun about, throwing her off-balance. As she tried to steady herself, her arms were roughly jerked behind her and handcuffs locked tightly around her wrists. She winced in pain, biting down on her lip, too proud to make a sound.

Her captor turned her toward him and she recognized the balding man in his mid-forties as one of Parker's cronies. He must have been one of the men who approached the hotel.

"Thought you might try to give us the slip." He cleared his throat to state his official business. "Serena Sullivan, I'm here to arrest you on behalf of the town of Crombar Creek."

The man's fingers locked around her upper arm, biting into her flesh. A sardonic smile graced his thin lips as he studied her.

"About time we caught up with you. You gave the sheriff and his posse a hard time. Now, you'll dance to his tune."

Serena remained wordless, knowing she had nothing to say in her own defense.

~

SERENA SAT in the cell she hoped she would never see again. She stared at the tally marks carved onto the wall by some long ago prisoner. Her fingers traced them as she wondered how long she had to live.

She assumed her hanging would occur quickly. No one had spoken to her since they arrived back in Crombar Creek. Serena rubbed her wrists, still sore from the handcuffs she'd worn. She rotated her shoulders one at a time. They, too, pained her from having her hands locked behind her for so long.

The men who'd come for her had placed her in the

back of a wagon. Without her hands to brace herself, Serena had been jostled back and forth for miles. She doubted she'd live long enough to see the bruises form.

Still, her life was already much richer than the last time she awaited death in this cell. In the space of a week, she had fallen in love. She'd experienced physical passion and Daman fulfilled desires she hadn't even known were embedded deeply with inside her. He had become husband, lover, and good friend all in the matter of days.

She had also found her twin, her goal for the past fifteen years. It pained her that their reunion was short-lived but she had accomplished it all the same. The authorities could hang her now. She would die at peace, blessed to have known what some might never find.

Serena heard the heavy, familiar tread of boots scuffling along the corridor and steeled herself. The jingle of keys came next, taunting her. The lock turned and in stepped Sheriff Bud Parker.

He slammed the door behind him and hobbled over to stand in front of her cell, leaning heavily on a cane. Daman thought the sheriff had injured himself when he leaped from the train after them. She knew the lawman would blame his injury on her.

Serena rose from the bunk and stepped to the bars to face him. Her legs began to shake so she tightened her fingers around the iron bars for support. Parker eyed her for a long moment.

"Tsk-tsk," Parker mocked, shaking his head. "The bird that flew the coop has now returned. No worse for the chase, though. Unlike me."

Parker's hand snaked through the bars and

wrapped around a thick lock of her loosened curls. He wounded it around his hand tightly, holding her firmly in place.

"Seems like we have the place all to ourselves."

He bent toward her menacingly. Serena tried to turn her face from his but his hold kept her in place. She stared into malevolent eyes and thought that hanging might be easier than what lay ahead.

"You'll die tomorrow, you little bitch. No doubt about that. And no one's here now but you and me."

Her gut tightened. She forced herself to show no fear.

He grinned. "I can't bring Charles back but I can inflict a few lessons for you to remember him by. Broken ribs. A bruised kidney. I can be awful clever. Nothing will show. But you'll think of poor old Charles with every gasping breath you have left."

His grin broadened. "Let's get started."

He twisted his grasp until Serena's scalp burned in agony. Tears sprang to her eyes. She saw her pain only fed his rage at having lost his friend.

So, she spit in his face.

Parker laughed aloud, unwinding his hold on her hair. Serena scrambled out of his reach, knowing he would enter the cell momentarily. Still, she would bite, kick, and scratch as hard as she could. He might not leave a visible mark on her but she planned to make her imprint on him.

The lawman shook his head. "Still a feisty one. I told Charles you were. Lord, how that man wanted to bed you." He stared at her intently. "Did he before you stabbed him and tossed him out that window?"

Serena stared back. "Rayburn fell out that window on his own. I told you that over and over. Not that you ever believe me."

Parker shrugged. "Doesn't matter. Whether it was an accident or not, Charles is dead. You might as well pay for it and for making my ankle get all twisted out of sorts pursuing the likes of you."

The sheriff licked his lips in anticipation and inserted the key into the cell's lock. Serena knew to scream would only anger him so she stood her ground. She would launch herself at him the minute he stepped through the door. She'd defended herself numerous times as a wild child growing up on the streets of New York. She knew to go for his balls first and claw his eyes next. She would not go down without a fight.

"Sheriff? Sheriff Parker?" a high voice called. "You here, Sheriff?"

Serena almost fainted with relief. Nine-year-old Ricky Rayburn's voice floated out from the front room. Bless his heart. He had been her most frequent visitor from among the school children, despite the fact that she had been charged with his uncle's murder. It saddened her when his visits ended abruptly. His friend, Jimmy, told her Ricky had been sent to stay with his grandparents on the other side of Abilene.

Parker grunted and removed the key from the lock. "Back here, son." He glared at Serena. "I'll get rid of him quick so we can continue our fun."

He turned and greeted the boy as Ricky opened the door to the cellblock. "Well, Ricky Rayburn, what brings you here to see me?"

The boy quickly pulled his hat from his head, nervously clutching it in his hands. "I came to see Miss Sullivan, Sheriff."

Serena calmed her racing heart and gave the boy a smile to reassure him his presence was welcome. "It's good to see you, Ricky."

"Does your pa know you're here?" growled Parker. "Seems to me he told you not to come around no more."

"Mama said it'd be fine," Ricky replied, staring down at the hat in his hands. "That is, if Miss Sullivan don't mind me being here."

"Of course not, Ricky," Serena chimed in. "I'm sure the Sheriff will leave us be." She stepped closer to the bars, willing Parker to go away.

"Ten minutes," Parker spat out. "No more." He limped off, shuffling his feet. "I'm locking the door, Ricky, so you just holler when you want out."

The lawman opened the steel door and then slammed it shut, turning the lock. Serena held a hand up to Ricky to silence him, waiting to hear Parker leave before they spoke. She heard the sound of the sheriff's boots fade away and nodded at the boy.

Ricky thrust his hands through the bars and captured Serena's in his. "I thought you was a goner, Miss Sullivan."

"Were a goner," she responded automatically. They both smiled. "Yes, I thought so, too." Serena paused a moment. "Do you really have your mother's permission to be here, Ricky?"

He shook his head. "No, ma'am. Neither Pa nor Mama knows you're back in jail, Miss Sullivan. Pa will be hollering about seeing justice done for his brother the minute he finds out."

Ricky gazed at her earnestly. "He and Mama sent me away before the hanging. That's why I stopped coming to see you, Miss Sullivan. I went to stay at my granny and pappy's place the other side of Abilene."

Serena squeezed his hands. "I know. Jimmy Nichols told me where you were. Don't worry about that now."

Ricky pulled his hands from hers. "But I do worry, ma'am. I came to the hanging anyway. Walked a good eight miles and hitched a ride on a wagon another fourteen or so but I had to be there."

He bowed his head. "I heard what them other ladies in the crowd said about Uncle Charles."

Serena bit her lip, hating that the boy had learned his uncle was such a scoundrel. "I did, too, but it was too late. Maybe if they would have testified at the trial, their words would have carried more weight."

She sighed, not wanting to think about the other women and if they'd spoken up earlier, whether their testimony might have made a difference in the outcome of her trial or the punishment rendered.

Ricky raised his eyes to hers. "What if you got a new trial, Miss Sullivan? Could they testify then?"

Serena thought about it a moment. "I don't think so. I think it takes new evidence to hold a second trial. I don't see how any would surface at this point."

Ricky swallowed hard and took her hands in his again, tightening his fingers around hers. "What if it did?"

Serena was puzzled by his question. "I suppose the Sheriff would have to be informed. The circuit judge would then be notified. If he thought it critical to the case, he might reopen it."

"Really?" Hope filled the boy's face.

Serena pulled her hands away and wrapped them protectively around her. "If you don't mind, Ricky, I'd rather not talk about things that won't ever happen. I can't afford to hang on to hope when none is there. I need to resign myself to my fate."

She sank on the bunk, willing herself not to cry in front of the small boy.

"Miss Sullivan?" Ricky's voice was barely a whisper. "I have new evidence."

"What?" Serena jumped to her feet and grabbed tightly onto the bars. "What are you talking about?"

28

D aman waited in his rented room for several minutes. He had to admit that the visit from Parker's men had shaken him badly. He sat on the bed and took deep, calming breaths as he wished he could simply drown his worries in a bottle of whisky as he had done after Daphne's death.

A few months ago, that would have been the easy answer. Things were much more complicated now. His life had spiraled out of control the moment he had laid eyes on a beautiful woman in the jaws of death and acted to rescue her.

But he wouldn't have it any other way. It might have seemed like impulse at first as he had acted so rashly for a hooded stranger, but Daman believed fate drew him to Serena Sullivan, the woman who now claimed to his heart.

His wife. His life.

Daman knew nothing sweeter than to have the woman he loved nestled in his arms. She brought out the best in him and he would do what it took to ensure she remained alive.

He stood, knowing he'd given the men enough

time to leave the premises and head back to town. He didn't want to lead them to Serena when he left for Chaney's. In fact, he would take a circuitous route there to be safe, in case one of them remained behind to monitor his movements. He thought he'd been convincing in his story about Dixie Lee but as a writer he knew to play all the angles.

Daman left the rented room and went down the narrow staircase. As expected, Mrs. Winston waited for him at the bottom. He knew he owed her an explanation.

He reached the bottom. "Mrs. Winston, I—"

"I don't give a pie in the sky for whatever sorry excuse you're going to share with me, Mr. Rutledge." She frowned at him. "If in you were in trouble, you should have told me."

"Madam, I assure you—"

She smiled, which startled him into silence. "No assurances are necessary, young man. I seen how the two of you looked at each other. Just like me and my Mr. Winston, God rest his blessed soul. Whatever that bunch of overgrown bullies think you or your missus have done, I don't believe it. You're a gentleman, pure and simple, and Mrs. Rutledge is as sweet as a summer day is long. Tell me what I can do to help and I'll do it, young man."

Her words brought him relief. "There has been a bit of trouble, Mrs. Winston. Nothing that we can't resolve. I'm off to meet Serena now and see if we can straighten things out. If we must leave town abruptly without saying our goodbyes to you, know that we appreciate every kindness you have shown us."

"I'll keep your luggage if you need me to, sir. Just send word where you want it sent."

"You are a wise woman, Mrs. Winston. And one fine cook."

She blushed at his praise. Daman tipped his hat to her and exited Winston House.

Three-quarters of an hour later, he found himself at Chaney's General Store. It had taken him twice as long to arrive at his destination but he felt certain he hadn't been followed. He stepped up onto the walkway, glad to be out of the hot morning sun and once more longing for the lush grass and dampness of England as he removed his hat.

Daman entered the store. A few women placed items into the baskets they carried over their arms, gossiping as they did so. Lydia stood behind the counter, finishing up a sale. As her customer stepped aside, she brightened.

"Why, Mr. Rutledge. How good to see! Did you get everything Father and I packed for you?"

Daman nodded a greeting. "Yes, we did. You and your father are very considerate, Lydia." Daman glanced over his shoulder. "Is he here? I'd like a word with him."

"He's in the back, sorting some new canned goods that came in. Shall I get him for you?"

Daman thought a moment. "If you don't mind, I'll just go visit with him as he works. Is that acceptable?"

"Sure, go ahead. He'll be pleased to see you."

Daman walked around behind the counter and pulled a thin curtain that separated the back storage room from the rest of the store. He doubted Lydia had seen Serena this morning. The young girl's face registered her every emotion. He hoped he would find Serena in hiding in the store room. As he stepped through the opening, Daman immediately spied the

shop owner bent over, counting goods and making no-
tations on a pad he held.

Serena was nowhere in sight.

"Good morning, Mr. Chaney."

"If it isn't Mr. Rutledge. Good day to you, sir, good
day." He rose to his feet and winked at Daman. "Hope
you two had a pleasant evening."

Daman's heart began to pound. Unless Chaney
thought a shopper might overhear them, the man
wasn't hiding Serena.

He whispered, "Is Serena here?"

Chaney frowned. "No," he said quietly. "Did you
two lovebirds already have a fight?"

Panic swelled instantly, racing through Daman's
veins. "No, nothing of the sort. There was some . . .
trouble, though. I thought Serena might be here."

"No, son. We haven't seen her since the wedding
yesterday afternoon."

Daman saw the concern on the store owner's face
and held up a hand. "Don't ask, Mr. Chaney. It's better
if you know nothing. But if Serena does stop by, will
you have her wait here? Preferably in this back room?"

Chaney nodded slowly, his hand rubbing his chin
in thought. "Of course, Mr. Rutledge. I'll help in whatever way I can."

He swallowed hard, trying to keep his voice from
shaking. "I'll stop by again in a little while. Thank you
for your time."

Placing his hat back on his head, he returned to
the front of the store. Lydia was occupied with another
customer so Daman slipped around the counter and
stepped out into the heat.

Where could Serena be?

His gut twisted painfully. He should have gone

with her. Protected her. What if Parker had more men than those he had sent to Winston House? What if they'd captured Serena as she fled?

Daman stepped off the porch and smacked into Bill. He grabbed the gambler's shoulders to keep them both on their feet.

"Change in plans, Daman." Bill informed him quietly. "I ran into Serena on the way to Winston House. I have her tucked away safely where no one will find her and it saves the Chaneys from being involved. She was worried about them."

Daman steadied himself. "Thank God. When she wasn't here, I thought Parker or his men had her."

His new brother-in-law slapped him on the back. "She asked me to leave word with Mr. Chaney for you but I'll just take you back with me now. We've cut out the middleman."

Daman fell into step with Bill, noticing up close his clubfoot and awkward gait. Remembering how the two siblings have been separated on the orphan train, he realized what severe blows life had dealt the both of them.

"I left Sis and went to make arrangements to get her out of Abilene." He eyed Daman. "Can you ride a real horse? I mean, I know you English dandies ride to the hunt and all, but—"

Bill broke off and shook his head. "That came out all wrong. I'm trying to extricate both feet from my mouth now."

He laughed. "Don't bother. I'm sure they're comfortable in there. And yes, I can ride. Hate it, but I can do it. Rode up from Texas, driving cattle to Abilene. Longest weeks in my life, spending sixteen hours a day in the saddle."

Bill looked puzzled. "I thought you English folks drank tea and ate crumpets and whatnot. How in hell did you wind up on a cattle drive?"

"My half-brother is the titled nobleman in our family. I'm a lowly third son. Edward invested in Texas cattle. It's all the rage in London now. I was sent to check up on his investments, as well as buy some land for him in Colorado. Another passing fancy with the English."

Bill frowned. "You're telling me you don't have a dime to support Sis on?"

"I wouldn't say I'm destitute. I'm a playwright, Bill. I write for the London stage. Not too shabby if I say so myself. I took a bit of a break to aid Edward in his business but I recently started a new play, thanks to Serena. She seems to inspire me to new heights."

"I suppose you two will head back to London once your business is over."

Daman heard the hurt in the man's voice. "Actually, I've grown quite attached to America. Serena told me that Colorado is a little like England, with hills and green grass."

Bill laughed. "Tired of the flat prairie, Daman?"

"You could say that. I know how happy Serena is to have found you. As long as we stay away from Kansas, I think she'll be safe. I would eventually like to take her back to England for a visit but I believe we will make our home here in America."

Happiness spilled across Bill's face. "We do have playhouses and opera houses here, Daman. Maybe you can write for one of them."

They turned left and Bill indicated the hotel on their right. "That's The Crystal Palace where I'm staying. I know Serena will be happy to see us both. She was mighty nervous when I left."

Daman stopped in his tracks. "Oh, no, Bill. Not your room." His mouth went dry. "Tell me Serena isn't hidden here."

"Why, sure she is. Best place for her to be. I've got it covered. We're leaving after night falls. I'll tell you the details when we're all together."

He groaned. "You don't understand. Parker's men know you're connected to her somehow. One of them witnessed your reunion at The Wild Mare last night. When they didn't find Serena at Mrs. Winston's, they returned to town to look for her. With you."

Bill swore softly. "And the first place they'd look is the Crystal Palace. I made no secret of where I was staying."

The men hurried down the block and entered the spacious lobby that buzzed with conversation. Daman was ready to tear up the stairs but Bill took his arm.

"The desk clerk is a friendly guy. Knows everything happening in this place. We don't want to walk into a trap upstairs. If Serena's been taken into custody, it won't do her any good if we're locked up, too."

They walked to the desk and the young clerk on duty spied Bill coming. He pulled an envelope from a slot.

"Mr. Chance, your letter came. The one you've been expecting. But you missed all the excitement!"

"What excitement?" Daman asked quickly.

"The woman. They took her."

"What woman?" he demanded.

"Why, the Sullivan woman. She's a convicted murderess. Escaped from her hanging about a week or so ago. Made a big fool of the sheriff out Crombar Creek way."

The boy's asked gleamed with excitement. "I seen them put her in the wagon. They was right out front of the Palace, three of 'em. Tossed her in the back and took off for the Creek. I'll reckon she's dead this time tomorrow."

Daman turned to Bill.

"Let's go," they both said in unison.

29

S erena's hands shot through the bars and grabbed Ricky by his shoulders.

"What do you mean, Ricky?"

Her voice rose in hysteria. Serena saw the instant fear in the young boy's eyes and bit her tongue. She loosened her hold and tried for a more calming tone, the teacher's voice that Ricky would recognize—and hopefully respond to.

"When you say you saw it, tell me what you mean, Ricky." Serena's eyes searched her young pupil's face. "Please," she pleaded.

Ricky swallowed hard. "Just that . . . I just . . . saw, Miss Sullivan. How Uncle Charles was . . . hurting you and . . . how you stuck him with the scissors to get him off you. How he was cursing at you and tripped and fell."

Serena gasped. "You know it was an accident?"

The boy nodded. "Yes, ma'am. That's what I told Pa."

Her hands fell to her side. "You told your father this?"

"Yes, ma'am. I ran to get Pa since Mama had gone to help Mrs. Bonner have her baby. I didn't think

Uncle Charles would be bad hurt. Heck, it's not that far. Jimmy and I done jumped off the roof a few times when no one was looking. I thought he'd get bruised up or maybe break his leg and be mad.

"But when I came outside, I saw he was still. Then you came running out and hollering. And then Pa came running from the barn." He flushed a dull red. "I got scared and hid in the root cellar."

Serena brushed back a lock of hair from Ricky's forehead. "That's all right, Ricky. We all get scared. I've been scared more times than I could tell you about."

"Really?" His eyes grew enormous at the thought of a teacher experiencing fear.

"Really," she assured him. "But you want to do the right thing now, don't you? It's always important to do what we know is right in our heart, Ricky. Can you do that for me?"

Ricky's lips quivered and she saw tears puddle in his eyes. "I tried to, Miss Sullivan. I really did. I told Mama what I saw and she told Pa. They had a long talk with me about family and how important family is. They told me to trust them, that they'd fix things up right.

"Then they told me Granny and Pappy wanted me to go stay with them since I was family. They told me not to worry about nothing at all but family, and they'd take care of things for me."

Serena suddenly understood what the Rayburns had done. They had sent Ricky out of town while her trial occurred and kept the knowledge that Charles Rayburn's death was an accident to themselves.

"But they didn't." Tears began to stream down his face and Ricky wiped them away angrily with his sleeve. "I heard Granny talking to Pappy about it. I just knew I had to come back and help you but I was too late. If that man hadn't saved you, you'd be dead, Miss Sullivan. I know the sheriff will hang you, for sure. He won't care that it was an accident."

Dropping to her knees, she gathered Ricky as closely as she could, despite the bars between them.

"That's not going to happen, Ricky. You're going to be a brave boy and help me. I know you can. I—"

They both heard the key turn in the lock without warning. Parker must have tiptoed back and listened at the door. Ricky froze in fear.

The door swung open. Parker's eyes gleamed in anticipation.

"Go on home, Ricky. Don't be stopping nowhere. Go on. Git now."

Ricky looked from the sheriff to Serena. She saw the helplessness dissolve his posture. He looked much younger than his nine years.

"Thank you for coming to see me, Ricky. Please go home now. I'll be just fine."

Ricky's jaw dropped. No words came out. He closed his lips, pressing them tightly together to keep from crying, and nodded.

"Goodbye, Miss Sullivan."

Parker patted the boy on the head as he passed. Ricky flinched at the lawman's touch. He scurried out the door, which Parker shut quietly.

He turned to face Serena and grinned wryly. "Who'd believe a boy? I'm sure he's just confused about what he saw."

She stared daggers at him. "You knew the truth. And did nothing about it."

Parker shrugged. "It's like the boy's father told him. Family is what's important. Not some stranger passing through town. If only Charles had let you get on that train." Parker shook his head. "But I think my fun has started now. I knew the boy would tell you."

The sheriff smiled broadly. "I wanted you to know what he knew and have hope for just a moment. Before I dashed it on the ground and broke it into a thousand pieces.

"Just like I'm going to break you."

~

DAMAN AND BILL rode at breakneck speed on the horses Bill had purchased for that night's escape from Abilene. Daman took the lead since he knew exactly where to go. As they galloped along the dusty road, Daman's heart ached as if it had been torn in two.

What if Serena were already dead?

From what he knew of Sheriff Parker, the lawmen wouldn't take any more chances. Would he immediately send Serena to the hangman's noose? Or would his ego demand the townspeople of Crombar Creek be there to see his handiwork come to fruition?

Daman prayed it was the latter.

They reached the Creek and tore down its main street, headed for the sheriff's office and jail. As they reached it, a small boy came walking out. His body shook with wrenching sobs. The two men leaped from their saddles and threw their reins over the hitching post.

Daman raced up the steps. His gut told him this child was somehow linked to Serena. He knelt in front of the boy.

"Is Serena Sullivan in there?"

The boy nodded, wiping away tears. He stared at Daman, his eyes widening in recognition. "You're the one. You're the one who saved her." His voice quivered in awe.

"Yes. And I want to save her again."

The boy's head bobbed up and down. "I can help you. I really can. I told her I saw it. I can tell the judge it was an accident."

Daman grabbed the boy and held him tightly.

Bill's voice rumbled above them. "Does the sheriff know about this?"

The boy nodded. "He was listening, but he don't care. Can you help me find the judge? Please? Before they hang Miss Sullivan?"

He looked the boy in the eye. "Of course, we will. This is Miss Sullivan's brother and I'm Miss Sullivan's husband, Daman Rutledge. What's your name?"

"Ricky Rayburn."

Daman glanced at Bill. He looked back at the child. "Are you related to Charles Rayburn, Ricky?"

The boy nodded, clearly miserable. "Yes sir. He was my uncle. But I still know what I saw and Miss Sullivan didn't aim to kill Uncle Charles."

"I'll see if there's a telegraph office nearby. We've got to let the authorities know so we can stop the hanging," Bill said as he untied his horse and jumped back into the saddle.

"Don't got one in the Creek. You'll have to go to Abilene, Mr. Sullivan."

Bill look to Daman. "I'll be back as soon as I can, with a damned good lawyer in tow. Hold the fort, Daman." He took off, kicking up dust as he headed back toward Abilene.

He stood and took Ricky's hand. "I'm going in to see Serena. Why don't you head home, Ricky? When I'm done, I'll come talk to your parents."

Ricky shook his head furiously. "No. I don't want to go home by myself. Can I just wait here for you?"

Daman knew he'd need to speak to the boy's parents to convince them to let their son come forward, so he agreed.

"Then wait here for me, Ricky. I'll visit a bit with Serena and then we'll get you home. We'll work out all the details so when Bill returns with the lawyer and the judge, we can get Serena out of jail."

He hoped he sounded more confident than he felt. Daman knew it would take quick action to prevent Serena from swinging at the end of a rope. He gave Ricky a reassuring smile and opened the door to Sheriff Parker's office.

It was deserted. Daman guessed Parker was the only man on the payroll in such a small town so it didn't surprise him to find no deputies in sight.

Then he heard a shriek and shouted obscenities coming from the back. Parker must be with Serena.

Like a crazed man, Daman threw the door open and ran down a small corridor. He opened the door at its end and saw Parker standing inside a cell with Serena. The lawman held a handkerchief to his bleeding face. Daman guessed Serena had clawed it.

Parker turned, an evil smile lighting his craggy features as he dropped the handkerchief and pulled his gun. "I do believe I've seen you before, sir." He turned and gave Serena a quick shove in the stomach with his cane. She slammed against the wall and slid down it as the sheriff stepped out of the cell.

Parker leveled the pistol at Daman's heart. "I believe you are the cause of all of my woes. What is your name?"

"Daman Rutledge. Citizen of Her Majesty's government of Great Britain."

"Damn. That might complicate things a tad."

Parker motioned with the gun to his right. "You are under arrest, Mr. Rutledge, for aiding and abetting a fugitive from the law. Now, git into that cell while I figure out what to do with you."

He knew it was useless to fight back at this point. He had the Colt Peacemaker on him, tucked into the inner pocket inside his suit coat but he could never get it out in time to shoot the Sheriff—if he could even hit him. Even if he did so, it would be an attack on a lawman, honest or not. If a gunfight broke out, he couldn't guarantee that one of his wild shots would actually hit the sheriff and not Serena.

Still, if the fool forgot to search him, so much the better. Daman walked a few feet to the cell adjacent to Serena's and stepped inside. Parker rushed to slam the door and inserted a key in the lock. He went and did the same with Serena's cell door.

"I got me some thinking to do, Daman Rutledge." The sheriff stared at him in hate. "But I guarantee I'll do my best to see you hanging, too. Maybe not tomorrow, although a double hanging would sure bring out the crowds. But you are finished, boy. Nobody bests Bud Parker."

30

D aman waited until Parker's steps receded. He hurried to the bars connecting their cells.

"Serena? Are you all right?"

His wife opened her eyes and used the wall to push against to get to her feet. She walked the few steps that separated them and clasped his outstretched hands reaching through the bars. Daman saw a trickle of blood oozing from the corner of her mouth. He whipped out a handkerchief and gingerly pressed it against the wound.

"I don't have to ask if he hurt you," he said quietly.

Serena grinned wryly. "You should ask what I did to him."

She took the handkerchief and dabbed her mouth and then handed it back to him.

He attempted a weak smile. "It appears you caused a bit of damage. The ladies may never see Sheriff Parker in the same light again," he said lightly, hoping to alleviate the despair radiating from her.

She took hold of his hands again. "I'd hoped you wouldn't see me trapped in this cage." Her amber eyes loomed large. "I'm sorry they found me but it's even worse now that you are imprisoned, as well."

Daman saw how that fact alone caused her spirits to drop as she spoke.

"We'll get out of this, love."

He moved as close as he could to the bars and pressed a kiss against her forehead. "Bill is still on the loose. We ran into the boy outside and he told us his uncle's death was an accident. Bill's riding back to Abilene for a lawyer and hopefully a judge."

Serena shook her head. "You think Parker might allow a new trial? Even if he did, the Rayburns will never let Ricky testify. They hustled him out of town to prevent that the first time." Her voice fell to a whisper. "It's over, Daman."

His hands cupped her face. "Have faith, Serena. Bill would swim to China and back to save you. Parker has no idea Bill is out there working in your behalf. Don't give up now."

Daman tenderly brushed his thumbs against the tears that spilled down her cheeks. "We have a lifetime of love to give each other. I refuse to believe it will end in death in a dusty town on a godforsaken prairie in the middle of nowhere."

Serena's lips trembled. "This isn't one of your plays, Daman. You can always write a happily ever after ending. Real life is more like a Shakespearean tragedy."

She pulled away from him. "Parker said he was arresting you for aiding and abetting me. He didn't mention he knows you are the one who originally rescued me."

She wrapped her arms around herself. "You mustn't clue him in, Daman. Let him think you only helped me while I was on the run. And under no circumstances let him know we are married. He will drag you into the mire."

As she turned away from him and walked to the far side of her cell, Daman sensed her emotional withdrawal as well as experiencing the physical one. It caused an ache he had never known as despair filled him.

He tightened his fingers around the cold bars that divided them. "Serena, I know you think to save me but don't do this."

She kept her back to him.

His mouth was dry but the words poured from him like a river. "I have never needed anyone as I do you. You have brought joy and purpose back into my life. You have given me the chance to know real love. I do not want to live in a world without you. Every breath I draw is for you. Every thought and deed I perform, I think of you, because you are my whole existence now, Serena Rutledge."

"If Parker means to have your death on his conscience, then I willingly go to the gallows by your side. We are no longer two, Serena. We are halves of a whole. As surely as the sun rises in the east each morning, I would wither and die if you are no longer a part of my world."

Daman's knuckles turned white against the black bars. "I love you, Serena. I will die with you. You won't be alone."

Serena turned toward him and Daman saw the anguish on her beautiful face. More importantly, though, he read the love that shimmered in her golden eyes. She quickly closed the short distance between them, her hands covering his.

"You are a romantic fool, Daman Rutledge," she said gruffly. "But I wouldn't have you any other way."

Their lips met in a fervent kiss. He pulled her as close as the bars would allow as they whispered affirmations of their love for one another between kisses.

Yet even as they touched, Daman sent a fervent prayer for Bill Sullivan to hurry.

～

RICKY RAYBURN WAITED PATIENTLY for Mr. Rutledge to return. As the minutes passed, he grew uncertain. Had the sheriff killed Miss Sullivan's husband? Surely, he would have come out by now if he weren't dead.

Ricky heard the front door of the jailhouse creak open and he scrambled off the side of the porch, dropping to his knees next to the raised platform. The door slammed and Sheriff Parker strode down the steps and mounted his horse. He turned it in the direction of Mrs. Harvey's.

Ricky figured since it was late afternoon, the sheriff must be headed over to the widow's house for a piece of her pie. Everyone in town knew the sheriff was a sucker for good pie and Mrs. Harvey baked two every day. Ricky heard grownups talking about how the sheriff and Mrs. Harvey were special friends and how he liked getting some pie every day. They usually laughed when they said it but Ricky didn't think there was anything funny at all about pie.

Especially if it involves Sheriff Parker. Ricky was scared of him. Most people were. It had taken all his courage to go visit Miss Sullivan today but he was glad he did so. He wanted to tell her about how he'd seen what happened. He thought she might be grateful and marry him someday but he didn't think she could because she was already married to Mr. Rutledge now.

Again, he wondered where Mr. Rutledge was. He hadn't come out and Ricky knew the sheriff wasn't stupid enough to leave with Mr. Rutledge still inside. That meant he had to be dead.

Ricky thought if he went in and saw the body, he could tell someone what the sheriff had done. Then everyone could see what a bad man Sheriff Parker was and maybe they'd let Miss Sullivan out of jail. Ricky doubted the sheriff would give Miss Sullivan a new trial, even if her brother did bring back some fancy new lawyer from Abilene.

He looked up and down the street but no one was in sight on a hot summer day. Ricky crept back onto the porch and pushed open the door to the sheriff's office. He closed it quietly behind him and looked around the small room.

Nothing. Ricky decided to be brave enough to look in the back. He opened the door and tiptoed down the hallway to where the cells were. He turned the knob on that door and opened it.

His eyes widened as he saw Miss Sullivan kissing Mr. Rutledge. He knew married people kissed but he never saw his parents do it. He heard that was how you made a baby. That's probably why he didn't have a little brother or sister. A wave of disappointment swept through him, even if he did think kissing was for sissies.

He wondered what he should do. Mr. Sullivan would need to get both of them out of jail now. He wondered what Mr. Rutledge had done wrong.

Ricky cleared his throat loud enough for them to hear. His mama had said that was good manners when you wanted to interrupt people.

"Ricky!" cried Miss Sullivan.

She broke away from Mr. Rutledge and held out a hand to Ricky. He walked over and let her squeeze it. She ruffled his hair like ladies liked to do. He didn't mind when she did it, though.

Mr. Rutledge stuck out a hand and Ricky shook it. "Sorry I kept you waiting, Ricky, but you see I've been tied up in here."

"Is the sheriff gone?" Miss Sullivan asked.

"Yes, ma'am," he told her. "Looks like he's done gone down to Mrs. Harvey's for some pie."

"Ricky?"

"Yes, Miss Sullivan?" She beamed at him, making his insides go all squishy.

"First, I think you can call me Mrs. Rutledge now. I understand you've already met my husband."

He lowered his eyes. "Yes, ma'am."

He looked back up and saw Miss Sullivan looking at Mr. Rutledge. Her eyes glowed at him and Ricky felt a pang of jealousy. Still, she was his favorite teacher ever. He knew she couldn't really marry someone his age.

"I'm going to ask you to do something for me," she continued. "If you don't feel comfortable doing it, that won't be a problem."

"Anything for you, Miss Sullivan."

"I'd like you to let Mr. Rutledge out of his cell."

"Serena—"

"No protesting, Daman. If you're free, you can accompany Ricky home and talk to his parents about what he saw." She laid her palm against her husband's cheek. "If you can convince them to let Ricky testify, Bill might be back by then with a lawyer. I don't want to add fuel to the fire and be a runaway for a second time. I'll stay put."

"I don't want to abandon you, sweetheart," Mr. Rutledge protested.

He looked at Miss Sullivan so strangely and Ricky understood in an instant how hard it would be for him to leave her behind. They must really, really love each other a great deal.

Ricky decided he had to help them, no matter what trouble he got into.

"I can let you out, sir. Keys are hanging right over there."

Ricky walked over and reached up, stretching as tall as he could, just able to touch the keys dangling from a silver ring. He jumped a few times and knocked them from the hook. He retrieved him from the floor and went to unlock Mr. Rutledge's cell.

The door swung open and Mr. Rutledge bent down to him.

"Thanks, Ricky. Do you feel like taking me home to talk with your parents?"

"I suppose so."

Ricky didn't think that would go very well, knowing Pa's temper, but they had to try. He appreciated how Mr. Rutledge talked to him like he was grown and not as if he were some stupid little kid.

Mr. Rutledge took the key from him and opened the other cell and hugged Miss Sullivan to him.

I'll be back," he promised her.

He opened his jacket and handed her a pistol. "Hide this in your pocket. Parker forgot to search me, probably because I'm not wearing a holster. If you feel he's threatening your life, use it."

They kissed again and Ricky watched, fascinated. He realized he had a lot to learn. Mr. Rutledge didn't seem to think kissing was for sissies at all. Miss Sullivan seemed to like it, too. Maybe he could ask Mr. Rutledge for advice about it.

Mr. Rutledge closed and locked the cell and returned the keys to their hook. He turned to Ricky.

"Ready?"

"Ready, sir."

They left the sheriff's office and Mr. Rutledge hesitated.

"Do you know how long the sheriff might be gone?"

Ricky shrugged. "After he eats his pie, he'll come back here for a while. Then he usually goes to the saloon and drinks and visits."

Mr. Rutledge nodded. "Then we'll leave my horse. If it's missing, he'll know for sure that I'm gone. With it still here, he might not think to check on me. It could buy us some time."

"It's not far," Ricky told him. "But I have a few questions to ask along the way if that's fine by you."

"Sure, go ahead."

They fell into step together and had walked a full minute before Ricky finally asked, "When did you start thinking that kissing was fun?"

31

Daman continued down the street with the boy. Each step closer to their destination brought dread. If Ricky's parents had known of Serena's innocence before and deliberately withheld the truth, why would they change their minds now?

Ricky glanced up at him nervously yet Daman saw the hero-worshipping look in the boy's eyes. He gave Ricky a smile with confidence he somehow mustered from deep within.

"We're going to save Miss Sullivan. I mean, Mrs. Rutledge. Aren't we, sir?"

Daman stopped and laid a hand on Ricky shoulder. "We will, Ricky. Don't doubt that."

His own words renewed the determination within him to save his wife's life by whatever means he could find.

They walked along in united silence another ten minutes when Daman sensed Ricky's steps starting to slow.

"This is it," the boy said, his voice thin and shaky.

Daman squeezed Ricky's shoulder reassuringly, realizing just how very young a child he really was. "Then let us take care of business."

They opened the gate and walked toward the two-story farmhouse that was in need of a good coat of paint. Before they stepped onto the porch, the door flew open.

"Where have you been, young man?" a thin woman with a pinched mouth and threadbare dress demanded. Her eyes warily took in Daman's presence then oddly enough, she chose to ignore him as she berated her son.

"You disappeared with all kinds of chores left undone, Ricky Rayburn. Your pa'll have your hide for this." Her withering glare caused Ricky to shrink back into Daman.

He took a step closer to the woman. "Allow me to introduce myself, Mrs. Rayburn. My name is Daman Rutledge. Ricky has been with me at—"

"We don't cotton to strangers, mister."

Daman turned and saw a stout man with a hoe in his hand rounding the corner of the house.

"I don't care who you are or where you're from. Get off my property." He turned an angry stare upon his son. "And you, boy, go up to your room. You and me and the switch will be having a long conversation."

Ricky looked at Daman, his eyes pleading. Daman's heart twisted tightly in his chest. Suddenly, it didn't seem that long ago when he himself had been as young and helpless as Ricky.

"Go on, Ricky. I'll speak to your parents about our business."

Ricky fled, rushing up the steps past his mother and into the temporary safety of the house without a backward glance.

Daman looked back at Mr. Rayburn, his mouth set tightly in disapproval as he glared at his uninvited guest.

"We got no business with no foreigner. Move on. Or else."

The threat hung in the air as Rayburn's eyes narrowed into slits. Daman knew the words he would now summon were the most important of his life. He crafted words for a living but these could actually mean life for Serena.

"My name is Daman Rutledge. Serena Sullivan is my wife."

Mrs. Rayburn gasped. Her husband remained watchful but silent.

"Your son saw Charles Rayburn attack Serena. He also witnessed how his uncle fell from the window by accident. You hold Serena's life in your hands, Mr. Rayburn.

"I know what you did before, sending the boy away. I know why, too. Families hold secrets at times, to keep the world at bay. My family did the same. In England—as here in America—a family and its reputation means everything."

He paused, hoping his words would strike a nerve as he watched the farmer's grip tighten on his hoe until the man's knuckles were stark white against the wood.

"From the outside, the world saw my titled family as the epitome of all that was proper and good. On the inside, we festered with wounds that could never heal."

Daman's legs began to tremble as he unraveled for the Rayburns what would never be spoken aloud by any Rutledge. He balled his hands into fists, willing himself to stand tall as he shared his story.

His gaze met Rayburn's. "My father was an earl but he was also a drunk. A vindictive, nasty drunk. In fact, he fell down a flight of stairs to his death in a drunken stupor. We covered it up, naturally. Couldn't let Polite Society know how he really died.

"But my family hid an even darker secret, Mr. Rayburn. My father repeatedly abused my older sister, Cynthia. Forced her to pleasure him over and over and over again—until her only way to escape meant ending her life."

Daman raked his hands through his hair as he flashed back to the events that molded his life.

"My mother died in childbirth so Cynthia raised me from the cradle. She was my entire world. Can you imagine how helpless I felt as a small boy to learn of such wicked horrors and not be able to do anything to save her?"

He moved to stand directly in front of Rayburn. His gaze burning into the one person who stood between Serena and freedom.

"I found my sister's broken body. She had been so desperate, she had thrown herself from the roof of our manor house. She died in my arms, Mr. Rayburn. And yet my family's precious reputation was all that mattered. Men were paid off. The secrets remained. My father's reputation was spotless at his death."

Daman fell silent, allowing his words to sink in before he continued.

"I could not save my sister. But your boy can save my wife. Will there be gossip? Inevitably. Will you and yours be judged by your brother's actions? Possibly.

"Yet if you step forward, you will give your son the greatest lesson in life—that truth is the most important thing in the world. If you do what is right, Ricky will love and honor you as a child should. If you have him lie by omitting what he knows, you will sacrifice even more than a good woman's life. You will strip

Ricky of his innocence and any respect he will ever have for you."

Daman swallowed hard. "You can do more than save Serena, Mr. Rayburn. You can save your family and make it whole. The choice is yours."

BUD PARKER STOOD and strutted across the half-filled saloon as if he owned the world. Come to think of it, he did. He chuckled to himself, knowing all was right in his world. The widow had given him a good romp, he had had three slices of her fresh apple pie, and The Witch would sway in the hot wind tomorrow as she dangled from the end of a rope.

Life didn't get any better.

Now, after knocking back a few drinks, he thought he'd check on his two prisoners before heading home for the night. He had already decided they would forego an evening meal. The Witch probably wouldn't have swallowed a bite anyway. She hadn't the last time, so why bother?

As far as the Brit went, Parker had never taken to strangers, especially those involved with the likes of criminals. Let him go hungry tonight and good riddance, to boot.

Parker pushed through the bar's doors and stepped out into the heart of his little spot on the Kansas prairie.

And froze in his tracks.

His office porch, directly across from the saloon, swelled with people. Known and unknown alike. His gut lurched.

Calling up a jovial smile, he marched as well as a man using a cane could across the street as if he owned the town. By God, he did. No one would take it from him. He would ram the cane down anyone's throat that tried.

"What's a flock of folks hanging out at the likes of—"

"Cut the bull, Sheriff."

One of the strangers, hair black as night, stepped forward and stared hard at him. Something about his gaze seemed so familiar.

Parker gasped aloud. Damn. The Witch's amber eyes glared back at him in this man's face. Rage seethed just under the surface and Parker knew this man could snap at any second.

"We need to move inside, Sheriff Parker."

Another man addressed him, tall and lanky, in a finely tailored wool suit. He had stepped from the shadows and Parker recognized him instantly as a circuit judge that rode the route a few years back. He'd heard the judge had retired and gone to work for the governor.

He was in deep. And the hostile group didn't look like they'd be tossing him any shovels.

He looked over at the Rayburn family and saw his only allies had deserted him. He glanced pleadingly at James Rayburn but the farmer averted his eyes, suddenly finding the dirt in front of his feet a might too interesting.

"Too crowded inside for this many," he chortled, trying to ease the tension that blanketed the group.

"Then we'll do our business out here." Again, those amber eyes burned into him, making his soul go cold.

Parker nodded, seeing he had no choice.

"I'm Judge Marshall," the tall man said. He pointed to the two men next to him. "This here is

Phineas Jolson, an attorney out of Abilene, and Bill Chance."

Chance's eyes narrowed as he studied Parker. "I'm Serena Sullivan's twin brother," he said softly, his words full of menace.

"And you know the Rayburns," Judge Marshall continued.

All three Rayburns continued to study their feet.

"It's over, Sheriff Parker."

This came from Jolson, the lawyer, "I have a sworn affidavit from all three Rayburn family members that says you knew Miss Serena Sullivan was not responsible for one Charles Rayburn's death. Yet you withheld that evidence from the court. Even recommended young Ricky be sent out of town for the duration of her trial so he couldn't testify as to what he saw."

Parker's face grew flush. "Why, I couldn't give credence to Ricky's tall tales. He's only a boy. He didn't know what he saw. He's too young to understand—"

"Not according to my opinion," interjected Marshall. "I've talked to Ricky, and I'm satisfied he not only is aware of the situation but also comprehended what he saw and can testify accordingly to the truth of the matter."

Jolson added, "Ricky Rayburn's evidence is new information, previously withheld by you, Sheriff Parker. It warrants not only a new trial but also charges to be brought against you. How dare you play God with a woman's life!"

Parker wiped his perspiring palms against his hips. "She was found guilty. That whore needs to pay for poor Charles being impaled."

Chance took a threatening step forward. "She was only found guilty thanks to you maneuvering the truth. It should be you that hangs. You let down the people of this town. You took the law into your own hands."

Panic caused Parker to tremble noticeably. He couldn't control his shaking.

He was ruined. He'd go to prison. And if he survived the beatings that the inmates doled out to a former lawmen, he had nothing left once released.

All of it was The Witch's fault.

With a speed and strength he had never known he possessed, he pushed past those crowded around him. Judge Marshall fell back into Phineas Jolson, knocking both men to the ground. Chance, off-balance, was easily thrust aside with a thrust of the cane to his belly. Parker threw open the door to his office. He hurried inside and slammed the door behind him.

Turning the lock quickly, he backed away from the door, his cane falling to the ground. He drew his six-shooter slowly, only one thing on his mind.

He would kill Serena Sullivan. Then turned the gun on himself.

32

D aman paced four steps and turned, repeating the pattern over and over until Serena found herself dizzy.

"They should have been here by now," he proclaimed angrily. "Bill should be back with that bloody lawyer. What can be taking them so long?"

Serena glanced at her husband in the next cell. "Maybe you should have waited with the Rayburns outside. You're like a caged tiger."

"I feel like one!" Daman snapped. Immediately, a contrite look crossed his handsome features. "I'm sorry, love." He closed the short distance between them and reached for her hands. "I just thought we'd know something by now. I thought Bill and the Rayburns would have confronted Parker."

He brushed a stray lock of hair from her face and tenderly cupped her cheeks. Serena closed her eyes, living in this moment of time, unwilling to think about what might come in two minutes or two hours.

Daman pressed a kiss to her brow and pulled away. Reluctantly, she opened her eyes and faced reality.

"So, the Rayburns were to wait for Bill here?" she asked, twisting her gold locket.

"Yes. If Bill brought back the promised attorney, the Rayburns were to tell him what they knew. I doubt they have time to give written depositions but surely hearing what they have to say would be enough to confront that bastard Parker when he returns."

"Maybe that's what's taking so long. They might be having trouble locating him. If he—"

Serena stopped and listened. A door slammed in the distance.

"He's back."

Her heart skipped a beat in anticipation. A silent prayer went out that Bill had found someone to help her win a new trial. Daman had already done his part by convincing James Rayburn to let Ricky testify on her behalf.

Serena allowed hope to blossom as she looked at Daman. This man had changed everything when he interrupted her hanging. She'd loved well and found her long-lost twin.

Now, she waited to see if justice would prevail.

The door to the small cellblock opened and her breath caught in her throat. Only Bud Parker stepped in, half-drunk, a wild look of despair in his eyes.

He leveled his gun at her.

"Say your goodbyes," he snarled. "You ain't gonna have time to swing from a rope now. Your brother's causing too much trouble for that."

The lawmen glanced at Daman. "You have to be involved in this, though how you could sweet-talk the Rayburns into talking bad about me from behind bars is beyond me."

Daman saw from the corner of his eye that Serena

was trying to pull the pistol he'd given her for protection without Parker noticing. He knew he had to draw the sheriff's attention and keep it.

"We Brits are a glib lot, Sheriff. And you might find it fascinating that I'm a playwright. I wordsmith for a living. If anyone could convince the Rayburns to do the right thing in order to save an innocent life, then I suppose that would be yours truly."

"Shut your mouth, boy, or I'll shoot you in the gut first and make her watch you die." Parker started to glance in Serena's direction.

Daman lunched at the bars to distract him and buy Serena more time. Parker swung back toward him and fired.

The noise was deafening. Hot fire scalded Daman's shoulder. He reached up and touched it as the lawmen fell to the ground.

Daman pulled his hand away, sticky with blood. He saw blood pooling under Parker's body and was confused. How had his blood gotten on the sheriff? He heard Serena screaming his name.

Then pain engulfed him. He surrendered to the darkness that rushed up to greet him.

HE AWOKE TO SUNLIGHT. Daman squinted as it flickered across his face. He started to raise a hand to shield his eyes but groaned at the flash of pain.

"It's about time," a voice said from across the room. A dark angel floated to him and blocked the bothersome light. She bent and kissed him.

And that's when he knew he lived heaven on earth. With his good arm, Daman cupped the back of

Serena's nape to keep her close. The kiss heated up and he heard the soft moan that escaped from her.

His wife pulled away and beamed at him. "Welcome back to the land of the living, Mr. Rutledge."

Daman frowned. "How long have I been away?"

Serena chuckled. "Long enough to have slept through this morning's brief trial." She brushed his hair off his brow. "Judge Marshall presided. Phineas Jolson served as my counsel. And Ricky made a wonderful witness for the defense."

He smiled up lazily at her. "I'll presume the new verdict was not guilty?"

"Yes." A shadow crossed her brow. "There was a second proceeding." Serena took his hand as she sat next to him on the bed.

"Parker shot you, Daman. I saw what he was about to do and so I fired. I think it happened at the same time but I can't be sure."

Serena visibly relaxed. "Judge Marshall ruled in that matter, too." Her voice dropped to a whisper. "We are free, Daman. Free. No more looking over our shoulders."

He caressed the palm of her hand with his thumb. "I don't know. I rather like fleeing the law with an outlaw muse." He pressed a hot kiss to the center of her palm and grinned mischievously.

"Maybe we should try it on an annual basis. You know, I might even get a play out of this little adventure."

Daman pulled her on top of him, ignoring the throbbing in his shoulder.

"So, are you up for it, Mrs. Rutledge?"

Her eyes danced as she looked down at him.

"Only with you, Mr. Rutledge. I'd follow you to the ends of the earth."

Serena's mouth closed over his.

And Daman found they were transported to paradise.

ALSO BY ALEXA ASTON

ABOUT THE AUTHOR

A native Texan and former history teacher, award-winning and internationally bestselling author Alexa Aston lives with her husband in a Dallas suburb, where she eats her fair share of dark chocolate and plots out stories while she walks every morning. She enjoys travel, sports, and binge-watching—and never misses an episode of *Survivor*.

Alexa brings her characters to life in steamy historicals, contemporary romances, and romantic suspense novels that resonate with passion, intensity, and heart.

KEEP UP WITH ALEXA
Visit her website
Newsletter Sign-Up

MORE WAYS TO CONNECT WITH ALEXA

Lightning Source UK Ltd.
Milton Keynes UK
UKHW040631091221
395374UK00001B/43